MURDER IN ELY

A THIRD-CULTURE KID MYSTERY

MURDER IN ELY

D-L NELSON

FIVE STAR
A part of Gale, Cengage Learning

GALE
CENGAGE Learning·

Farmington Hills, Mich • San Francisco • New York • Waterville, Maine
Meriden, Conn • Mason, Ohio • Chicago

GALE
CENGAGE Learning®

LIBRARY OF CONGRESS CATALOGING-IN-PUBLICATION DATA

Nelson, D. L., 1942–
    Murder in Ely : a third-culture kid mystery / D–L Nelson. —
First edition.
      pages ; cm
      ISBN 978-1-4328-3043-4 (hardcover) — ISBN 1-4328-3043-0
(hardcover) — ISBN 978-1-4328-3035-9 (ebook) — ISBN 1-4328-
3035-x (ebook)
     I. Title.
PS3614.E4455M875 2015
813'.6—dc23   2014041554

First Edition. First Printing: April 2015
Find us on Facebook– https://www.facebook.com/FiveStarCengage
Visit our website– http://www.gale.cengage.com/fivestar/
Contact Five Star™ Publishing at FiveStar@cengage.com

Printed in the United States of America
1 2 3 4 5 6 7 19 18 17 16 15

To Rick, for wanting a cup of coffee at Starbucks.

ACKNOWLEDGMENTS

To Julia of the twenty pages: thank you for the eagle eye and the words "let's go to lunch."

To Pauline and Peter Stonehouse: thank you for being great neighbors and introducing me to Ely.

To Rossi: for being the role model for Mercury. I look forward to playing with you.

To my friend and former Chaucer professor, John McLaughlin: thanks for the tons of books. Even if this wasn't your period, each book contained a small sentence or a fact that I could pull out about the Anglo-Saxon period.

To Mike Petty and all those that meet regularly at the Ely Library who love the history of the Fens: thank you for your welcome and help in narrowing down what historical figure I would use in the novel. There was so much richness in the area that it was difficult.

The DVD *Saint Etheldreda* by Mary's Dowry Productions gave a great overview of Etheldreda's life.

CHAPTER 1

"Go, go, go," the crowd screamed. Three men ran by each carrying a twenty-pound sack of potatoes on their shoulder. They were followed by another two, then one, then five and after that, the remainder of the field in dribs and drabs.

Shopkeepers stood outside their High Street stores to cheer on the teams that were representing them in the Ely Potato Race for charity.

Annie Young-Perret was in front of the butcher's looking down the street for her husband, who was part of her friend Roderick MacKenzie's team. Rod had been planning to run, but a hit-and-run bicycle had creamed him full-on last week. Only his quick reaction by rolling away from the wheels had saved him from an oncoming car, but it had left him with a broken foot.

"I can't see any of my team." Rod swayed on his crutches as he stood next to Annie. Despite his broken foot and the pleas of his wife, Janet, who flanked his other side, he had insisted on watching the race at curbside.

"Look. No one." Rod stood on one foot and pointed his right crutch down the street. "No T-shirt with *MacKenzie Web Answers* in sight. Did they stop at a bloody pub?"

Janet and Annie exchanged glances recognizing how Rod was often short of patience unless it involved code or keyboards. With his glasses and gangly body, he could have been a poster boy for nerddom.

The couple had been friends with Annie since Rod and Annie had shared an assignment at a Zurich bank and an apartment near where they worked a few years back, although it was Annie and Janet who were the close friends. Their conversations covered everything and anything that might catch their interest. With Rod, if it wasn't technology-related, there wasn't much he had to say.

Annie and her new husband, Roger Perret, were in Ely because Annie, much to her surprise, had found a publisher for the biography she'd written, *Hilke Fülmer: A Swim to Safety*. Granted it was a historical publisher specializing in esoteric subjects. Even more of a surprise to her was that the story about the woman who'd wanted to be an Olympic swimmer but had ended up in a Nazi concentration camp and then was put on a ship that was bombed by the RAF had had a modest success.

Because her publisher had arranged for a reading in an Ely bookstore, she had told Janet and Rod that she would be in Ely, where the couple was now living near the famous cathedral. Annie had looked forward to the reading, seeing her old friend and meeting with her publisher, who'd said that he wanted to talk to her about another project. With a chance to explore another place and curiosity as to what her publisher might have in mind, it took Annie only a nanosecond to say yes.

Annie, noting how tired her new husband was, had urged him to come with her. Roger had pleaded that he was too busy to get away from his job as police chief in Argelès-sur-mer, France.

She insisted, pointing out that early autumn was quiet after the summer tourists had gone back to Paris, London, Amsterdam, Frankfurt, Copenhagen or wherever else they'd come from to descend on the beach town during the summer.

Too tired to fight further, he had caved.

Because he had capitulated on that, she had given in when

Roger offered to substitute for Rod in the race where contestants ran relay exchanging twenty-pound sacks of potatoes hoisted on their shoulders in place of batons. She'd thought he would just tire himself more. Roger reminded her it was only a quarter of a mile.

The race had started at the Market Place. The other runners had already shifted their load, and Rod's staff member, the second in the relay, was the only one left waiting for his potato sack.

A niggle of worry hit Annie.

"Where's my team? I'll fire all their sorry asses," Rod said.

"Grumpy," Janet mouthed behind Rod's back.

Annie pointed to Rod's foot.

"No excuse. He's always short of patience, more so lately even before his injury," Janet mouthed.

Rod headed toward the start line. He still hadn't mastered the crutches and almost fell when he placed one crutch on an uneven part of the sidewalk.

"Go sit in the coffee shop. We'll go check," Janet said in the tone that Rod usually acquiesced to because she used it so seldom. They were a couple that Annie couldn't understand: chalk and cheese, cat and dog, black and white, computer nerd and artist, but somehow they worked.

Lord knows, as a couple she and Roger were just as different, not only because he was older, but because he was wrapped up in his work. He loved staying in one place. She, as a part-time translator/tech writer, traveled all over Europe. She used work as an excuse to follow her real passion, historical research, which he didn't care diddly-squat about. When she started talking about some event in the distant past his eyes would glaze over. What he did care about was having her at home as much as possible.

Still, she'd given into his pleas to marry for one reason—she loved him. The rest is just detail she'd say to anyone rude enough to ask.

Ducking through one of the small medieval alleys lined with tiny shops, Janet and Annie reached the spot along the route near the starting point to see a pile of filled potato sacks on the sidewalk. A group formed a circle around someone lying in the street. Five were race runners, two of whom wore bright red T-shirts with a large potato on the backs. Annie knew the front bore Rod's company's logo. The rest were race spectators or regular afternoon shoppers.

As they got closer Annie saw Roger on the ground. His long-ish curly pepper-and-salt-colored hair stuck to his face, which was gray and as wet as if he just had a glass of water thrown on it. A man with a cable-knit sweater held his hands on Roger's chest and pumped in short, quick spurts.

Annie pushed her way through the gathering crowd. "Let me in, let me in. I'm his wife." The crowd shifted to make room for her.

She knelt next to him.

Roger rolled his eyes toward her, barely focusing.

She thought he whispered, *"Ça fait mal, très mal, ma poitrine,"* but she couldn't be sure.

"I'm a doctor. My surgery is right behind you," the middle-aged man in the cable-knit sweater said. "We've already called the first responders. An ambulance is on the way."

No sooner had he spoken when a white ambulance with alternating yellow and green rectangles on the bottom arrived. A man and a woman jumped out of the driver and passenger seats, opened up the back and brought out a stretcher along with an oxygen tank. They fitted Roger with the mask as the doctor kept pumping his chest. "Get him in the ambulance, I'll ride with you."

"Thanks Doc Willson," the woman said.

"Where are you taking him?" Annie held onto Roger's hand as the first responders moved toward the open doors of the back of the ambulance, pushing the gurney.

"Addenbrookes," the woman said.

"Let me go with you," Annie said.

"You'll get in their way. I'll drive you," Janet said.

Annie and Janet rushed by the cathedral, across the lawn and under the arch to where Janet and Rod lived across from the almost five-hundred-year-old King's School. The distance walking to where they'd planned to watch the race seemed a lot shorter even with Rod on crutches than the return trip.

The MacKenzie home was a light brick, two-story house with a few rows of black and white tiles separating the front door from the iron fence at the beginning of the sidewalk. Translucent flowers, victims of an early frost, were in the miniscule front garden. A few autumn leaves lay where yesterday's wind had blown them.

Janet's key stuck but she jiggled it until it caught. The door opened into a hallway with a staircase leading to the next floor. At the left of the front door was a pegboard with hooks for keys—all empty.

"I must have left my car keys in my bag in my room." Janet took the stairs two at a time and thundered back down in seconds. "I'll just leave a note for Rod." She picked up a piece of chalk and wrote on the blackboard nestled between the paintings that filled almost all the wall space, not just in the entry but in the entire house. Many had been done by Janet, but a variety of artists' works were represented.

"We'll phone him, but he doesn't always keep his mobile on," Janet said over her shoulder as she headed to the car. She pushed the automatic unlock button on her key chain.

Annie never paid any attention to the car makes. All she knew was that Janet's was yellow and small. Three such cars were parked in front of the King's School.

As Janet started to pull out of her parking place, two senior students in their blue plaid skirts and blazers stepped in front of the car. She slammed on her brakes. "Shit."

One of the girls stuck her tongue out as Janet maneuvered the car onto the road.

For Annie it seemed like hours had gone by from the moment the ambulance had pulled away: when she looked at her watch, less than twenty minutes had passed.

"We'll get there," Janet said after they had quit Ely and were riding along a road with flat Fens on both sides. A cow watched them and then went back to munching grass. "Look in my purse for my phone and call Rod."

He didn't answer his mobile but picked up the house landline. "I'll find a ride and meet you at the hospital," he said.

So many times Annie had heard the expression, "Time stood still." Time was standing still now, yet the car wasn't as the Fens disappeared and were replaced by an upper-scale housing area.

"Almost there. Don't worry. The hospital is one of the NHS's best," Janet said.

Annie saw the signs long before she saw the hospital, not a single building but a complex of buildings.

"I'll let you off at A&E. That's where they'll have taken him." She slammed on the brakes in front of a door with a red sign sticking over the sidewalk reading "Accident and Emergency."

Janet took Annie's hand and repeated. "I'll park and catch up with you."

Annie burst through the doors into a narrow hallway. A nurse in a green uniform at a desk blocked any further entrance into the building. To her right was a glass-enclosed waiting room with half the seats filled. One woman had a bruised face. A small boy was holding his arm and crying as a woman, probably his mother, rocked him back and forth. It didn't seem to comfort him.

Three people were in line in front of Annie; she wanted to push them aside, but she waited, shifting from foot to foot until she reached the desk. Although she wanted to scream, she spoke slowly and with a moderated tone. "My husband was probably just brought in by ambulance from Ely. I think he has had a heart attack."

"If you take a seat, we'll find out."

"His name is Roger Perret," Annie said. The nurse wrote it on a piece of paper. "I want to be with him."

"Take a seat."

Annie did as she was told. Within an unknown quantity of long minutes Janet was beside her. A few patients were called. The nurse continued to direct people. Annie hadn't seen her pick up a phone. This isn't like me, she thought. I usually take control of a situation.

Janet went to ask but came back fast, sat next to Annie and shrugged.

The clock on one wall didn't move. Only after Annie turned around and saw another clock did she realize that the first clock had stopped.

The next time she looked at the desk Rod was standing there. "I got a ride with a neighbor."

Annie jumped at his voice. The first thing that came into her mind spilled out her mouth. "I can't find out anything about Roger."

He hobbled to the nurses' station, pushing in front of two men and a woman waiting in line. "Tell me where in the hospital my friend's husband is."

The nurse glanced up from the paper she was shoving into a file before handing it to the first man in line. "I'll find out as soon as I can. Please wait your turn."

Rod took off his glasses and hovered over the nurse. Even a

nerd at six-foot-four could look imposing. "That is the wrong answer. I want you to find out now."

"When I clear this line." The nurse pointed at the people behind Rod, who were frowning, but her voice quavered.

Rod took his phone and dialed. "Chet, Rod Mackenzie here . . . Remember me . . . Fine . . . I've a problem. I'm in A&E. I've a friend . . . brought in on emergency from Ely. We can't find out where he is." He listened for a moment before handing the phone to the nurse.

"Yes sir . . . Yes sir . . . Yes sir." She hung up and dialed another number. "Did you bring in a possible heart attack victim from Ely? About . . .," she looked at Rod. "When?"

"No more than an hour and a half ago."

"No more than an hour and a half ago."

"Roger Perret . . . yes, I'll hold . . . really? Hold on a minute." She put the phone to her chest. "No one by that name."

"He didn't have any identification. Ask if they have a person in a red T-shirt saying *MacKenzie Web Answers* on it: a man in his late forties, dark curly salt-and-pepper hair. Wavy. Needs a cut."

The nurse repeated the description, then hung up. She turned to Annie. "He's with the doctors now." She took out a map and marked the path that they needed to follow to find where Roger was.

As they walked down the corridor as fast as they could without knocking over patients or having Rod fall off his crutches, Janet asked her husband, "How did you do that?"

"A major problem with the hospital's computer system four months ago—I fixed it in five hours. They didn't have to go through regular channels. The head of the hospital thanked me and said that if I ever needed a favor, he'd do what he could."

When they reached the next nurses' station, Rod asked for information of the middle-aged woman in the blue uniform sitting at the desk.

"We don't have a name, but the man the receptionist described said something in French before he fell unconscious."

At the word "unconscious," Annie would have sagged to the floor if Janet hadn't grabbed her. "He's French. He does speak English."

"With heart attacks, people often revert to their mother tongue, especially if they don't use the second language much," the nurse said. "I'll get one of the doctors to give you additional information as soon as I can."

As if by order a female doctor with a stethoscope draped around her neck appeared. As soon as they established who Annie, Rod and Janet were, the doctor said, "Come with me." She led them to a small room where Annie found herself telling them all she knew about Roger's medical history. "No, he doesn't have, or at least didn't have, a history of heart problems . . . the only medication? Kenzen for blood pressure . . . nothing for cholesterol . . . he's a police chief . . . yes he's often stressed . . . he's been really tired lately . . . he was putting in long hours . . ."

Annie couldn't provide any of the information that they requested on Roger's parents' medical histories. They had died before she'd met him: he had never said what had caused their deaths.

"Can you tell me how he is?" Annie asked.

"We're waiting for the results."

Back to the well-named waiting room: more waiting and more waiting and more waiting. Janet went for three cups of tea. Finally the doctor came out. "We've taken him up to surgery. Three of his four arteries are blocked."

CHAPTER 2

"More tea?" When Annie nodded, Janet filled her thick blue ceramic mug from a matching teapot. "Any more word from the hospital?"

The wooden table in the MacKenzie home where breakfast was spread was of an undetermined age, but probably had seen many families' meals served for at least a couple of hundred years before Janet had rescued it from an old barn. None of the furniture in the MacKenzie household was anything but antique or junk. Janet had refinished and/or reupholstered all of it, giving it beauty as well as creating an atmosphere that could have been featured in a multitude of home-decorating magazines anywhere in the world.

The first time Annie had visited, Janet had told her how and where she'd found many of the pieces, insisting everything she owned must have a memory or at least be useful. Although anyone might think the topic boring, her description of climbing over a tractor to liberate a rocking chair, spilling a fast-drying varnish and trying to get it wiped up before it damaged something made Janet an artist not just with paints, but with words.

"When I called, they said I could see him any time after lunch. He's resting comfortably . . . all that typical hospital blah blah," Annie said.

"I'm surprised they did a bypass." Janet reached for another piece of toast and lathered it with apple butter made with fruit gathered from an orchard on the Fens. "I thought they just did stents, but what do I know? I've only walked by medical schools."

"I guess he was too blocked. Yesterday, they told me it was a wonder he hadn't collapsed before," Rod MacKenzie said. These were the first words he'd spoken since he'd entered the room and sat down to eat.

Both women turned to look at Rod.

"What? You blame me for having him run?"

Annie got up to put her arms around him. "You may have saved his life by bringing on the heart attack when it did. Supposing it happened as we were flying home?"

Rod just nodded. Neither Annie nor Janet expected much more from him in the way of conversation. If there were ever a meat-and-potatoes type of conversationalist, it was Rod. Janet had confessed to Annie she liked it that way. It left her time to paint and do her own thing.

"So what's up this morning?" Janet asked.

"I'm heading to the boat to check on Simon," Rod said.

"Simon?" Annie asked.

"Simon Bartlett. We're working on a project."

Annie didn't expect any more of an explanation.

"You know Simon. He was in Zurich when we were there," Janet said.

Annie tried to think of whom they meant. There had been so many programmers and computer people in and out while she'd been working with a Zurich computer consulting firm at different locations that five years later most faces and names were muddled together.

What she did remember more was the frustration. No sooner would she finish a manual on one process, and translate it into German, French and Dutch from the English, than the programmers would change the whole thing, requiring rewrites and new translations. The one-month assignment had turned into nine months. At least it had happened during the time that she and Roger were broken up over her many assignments away from home base.

She made a face. "Doesn't ring a bell. Maybe if I could see him . . ."

"Big red-headed guy, freckles. Rode his bike to work all the time."

She ran through her memories of different people she'd met. "Yes, I do remember him. I met his wife. Her name was . . ."

"Sharon," Janet said. "When I drop Rod, you can go in and say hello to Simon. And then I'll drive you to the hospital. By the time we get there it'll be time to see Roger."

The Ouse was only a few blocks down the hill from where Janet and Rod lived. Small shops lined the road leading to the banks. The river itself was not that wide, although there was space for riverboats to dock on each side while still allowing other medium-sized pleasure crafts to sail through with no scraping of sides.

Many of the boats looked as if they could be lived on quite comfortably. A few still were used for the eel fishing that had given the place its name and had been its main industry from Anglo-Saxon days. The bright blues, reds and greens along with the polished wood and fiberglass surfaces of the boats made the river a colorful place.

Along the banks trees tried on their fall costumes of bright yellow. On one bank, where ducks rested, Janet was able to pull over so Rod would not have to manage his crutches on uneven soil.

"It's the *We Will Do It.*" Janet pointed to the blue boat, which looked as if it had just been painted the previous week. Unlike some of the other boats there were no flowerpots but there were two deck chairs and a table.

"His bike isn't here." Rod almost stumbled on the uneven ground.

Annie steadied him.

"Might be inside," Rod said. "Kids were fooling with it yesterday. Simon! Simon?"

The women helped Rod swing onto the deck. Using one crutch, he knocked on the door leading below deck, but there was no answer.

He tried the door. It was unlocked.

"Can you make it down the stairs?" Janet asked.

"Did the other day." Neither woman commented, knowing how much Rod hated being helped physically.

Annie and Janet maneuvered him down into the boat. To the left were a fully equipped kitchen and a small living area with a television and chair on one side and on the other a bank of computer equipment.

"Simon?" Janet called.

Rod adjusted his crutches. "Can't imagine he'd not lock up if he went out."

Annie guessed there were several thousand pounds' worth of computer equipment, all top quality and all of it relatively new, tempting to any smart robber.

The riverboat had a corridor with four doors leading to the stern.

"Toilet and bedrooms," Rod said. He opened the first one. Clothes were flung all over. The bed was unmade. Annie noted how grimy the sheets were. Typical bachelor and computer nerd, she thought.

Janet opened the bathroom door and screamed.

Annie and Rod turned to see Simon sitting on the toilet, his pants down. His throat had been slit. His T-shirt was covered in blood. With his staring eyes, there was no question he was dead.

CHAPTER 3

Annie felt she was in an English detective show, only the detectives were not a suave lord, a little old lady with a purse or a man, with a French accent and mustache. The men, who introduced themselves as Detective Sergeant Welch and Detective Inspector Lake, looked as if they could walk into any BBC or ITV crime series. They had sent her and Janet off the boat while they talked with Rod on deck while waiting for the medical team.

Annie did not want to be in the MacKenzie's car with Janet waiting to be questioned. She wanted to get to the hospital to be with her husband. No matter that when she phoned the hospital, the duty nurse said he was doing well. "How long do you think?" she asked her friend.

Annie was not used to the wheel being on the right side of the car. She wanted to take the mirror in the middle of the windscreen, as Janet called the windshield, and turn it toward herself.

"I imagine they'll want all kinds of information from Rod, what with him being Simon's partner and all." Janet kept tapping the steering wheel.

"Then us?"

Janet moved the seat back so she had more room to stretch her legs. A few bicyclers passed by with every rider wearing the same green jersey. "Probably, but I'm not sure what we can add at this point."

"What about Simon's wife?" Annie had finally remembered the couple from Zurich. What she did recall now was that the couple hadn't been all that happy. Sharon, yes that was her name, resented Simon's long hours whilst she spent time in a country where she did not speak the language and had no desire to learn it.

As a contractor Simon moved from place to place and often country to country. His wife hated being left behind in England but didn't like having to adjust to new places either. It came back to Annie that she had shared one meal with the Bartletts: her memory included the fact that the tension and snipping had left her so uncomfortable that she had refused any future invitations.

Sharon had made a couple of attempts for them to do girl things together, but that didn't go anywhere, although Annie thought she might have liked Sharon under different circumstances. Annie put in as long hours as Simon did and had no time to develop friendships during assignments.

"Sharon left Simon a couple of years ago. She found someone who she said was steady: read had a safe job with the local council and could guarantee he'd be home each night for tea and wouldn't lock himself away with the computer when he *was* home." Janet leaned her head back against the seat. "Her new love's greatest quality, she told me, was that he wasn't obsessive."

Annie didn't need any more explanation. She'd worked with too many computer consultants who could have gone on working on their projects a week after the world ended without realizing that any catastrophe had happened.

An unmarked van pulled up and six people in white suits got out. The tallest man removed a gurney and also a stretcher. The woman had a camera hung around her neck. The second man carried a case that Annie guessed contained the standard analytic equipment for medical examiners. The rest just followed.

Poor Simon. Still, despite her sympathy for him she wanted to head for the hospital, not sit in Janet's car watching Welch string yellow tape marking the crime scene.

A half hour, an hour, an hour and twenty-three minutes passed. On the boat, a stretcher with a body bag was carried to a waiting ambulance followed by Rod hobbling across the deck. The two policemen helped him navigate with his crutches over the edge of the boat and onto the uneven ground until the three men reached the car.

"You're next," Detective Inspector Lake said to Annie. "Show me exactly what you did before discovering the body."

Annie looked at her watch.

"Do you have someplace more important to be?" His tone was sarcastic.

"My husband was operated on yesterday—heart surgery, and I wanted to get to the hospital but I know this is important."

"You could call him," Detective Sergeant Welch said.

Annie had doubts that Roger would like to hear that she had found a body and was being questioned by police. The fact that she had interfered in other murders was a contentious point between them. His "stay out of trouble" pleas often went ignored along with his requests that she stay home more. "I don't want to upset him."

"I can call and say we've a bit of a problem with the car," Janet offered. "Not a total lie if the police won't allow us to drive off in it. I just won't mention what it is."

Annie nodded and followed the policemen. Step by step she described to them how they'd gone on board and looked for Simon. "We thought it strange how he had left all that computer equipment unlocked."

Annie and the inspector climbed onto the deck. A breeze had

come up, making the air even cooler but inside the boat, it was warm. There was no odor of rotting flesh, which made Annie think that the murder was recent. "It must have just happened," she said. "There's no bad smell. Just coppery blood." She resisted putting her fingers in it to see if it were still wet.

"Are you trying to be a detective?" Lake almost growled the question.

"No, just observing."

The blue sky of the morning was giving away to gray.

"We can sit down now that the crew has finished collecting evidence here. But touch as little as possible," Welch said.

Annie was grateful. She felt shaky. Between Roger and Simon, it was too much to handle. What was to have been a fun few days had turned into a disaster—no: make that two disasters.

Overhead they heard the footsteps of the two men remaining behind to dust for prints and the woman taking photos. Annie knew what they were doing because their voices drifted through the stairwell leading from the living area to the deck.

Inside, Annie sat on the couch, which was no longer covered with the papers that had been there when they'd come down to see Simon. Likewise the computers were gone. Annie assumed that the police had taken them when she wasn't looking. However, she found it strange that the murderer left the computers. Obviously not robbery, she thought, but her instincts told her Lake would not want to hear any conjectures from her.

"How long did you know Simon Bartlett?" Lake asked.

"We worked together some years ago in Zurich."

"Were you close friends?"

"Not really. I'd almost forgotten who he was. But since I was visiting Rod and Janet, I thought it would be nice to say hello as Rod was coming down here anyway."

"What were you doing in Zurich?"

"I was doing tech writing and translations into English,

French and Dutch from the German for ZBPI. Simon was one of the programmers there at the time, as was Rod."

"ZBPI?" Lake, who was taking the notes, bit his pencil.

"Zurich Bank for Private Investment."

"You speak four languages? Whew," Detective Sergeant Welch. "Why?"

"My parents kept moving from country to country when I was young. I didn't have much choice. They'd throw me into a new school system and I'd have to pick up the language if I wanted to survive." She didn't add that her parents helped her with private tutors with each country change.

"And Simon?"

"Only English. The Swiss banks often hire foreign contractors to do their analysis and their programming. I've found in each country stereotypes have a basis and people from each country have different ways of tackling a problem."

"And how do the English compare to . . ." Welch started to ask, but Lake's facial expression stopped him finishing his sentence.

Annie couldn't wait any longer. "I'll be happy to come to the station and answer any questions you would like later, but I really want to go see my husband. Would that be all right?"

The policemen exchanged looks.

"If I had something I could add, I would, but my knowledge of Simon since I worked with him wasn't even an occasional e-mail sharing a joke."

Lake took his card from his wallet. "You're staying with the MacKenzies. Let us know if you leave and where you'll be. At this point, I don't think you can be of much help."

Annie wanted to say she had already indicated that and she hadn't noticed any bloody person carrying a knife when they'd pulled up near the boat, but she knew this was no time to be a smart mouth. "Thank you."

"Will you send in Mrs. MacKenzie, please," Lake said as Annie headed toward the car.

"She's driving me to the hospital."

"No license?" Lake asked. "You can't do it yourself?"

"Not used to being on the other side of the road. I don't want to give the police any more work because I crash into someone or something."

"We have a job to do," Lake said. "You're a big girl."

Annie thought how it would be really, really easy to dislike that detective as she walked to the car. Janet rolled down her window. She had a magazine on her lap open to a Sudoku puzzle. Only two boxes were filled. "I couldn't concentrate, but I'm incapable of sitting in a car without at least pretending to be doing something."

"They want you next."

Janet opened the door and got out. "You take the car. Program the GPS to the hospital so you won't have any trouble."

Annie doubted that. "How will you and Rod get home?" Annie imagined him limping up the hill on crutches.

Janet pointed to the building across the Ouse. A flock of ducks was on the grassy bank before the road. "He can make it across the bridge where we can find a taxi."

With misgivings Annie slipped into the driver's seat, then adjusted it to her leg length. She didn't like driving at the best of times, refusing to own a car and preferring to walk or rely on public transportation. Driving on the left-hand side—well, she just hoped that she wouldn't end up needing a hospital bed herself or causing anyone else to need one either.

CHAPTER 4

Martin Bruber slathered his face with the hot lather he'd whipped up. Electric razors were not for him. He took pride that he rarely cut himself with his single blade. At the last stroke he rinsed his face, patted it dry with the fluffy towel, which he folded once before hanging it with the edges matching.

Back in his bedroom his wife had placed his white shirt on his silent butler. Before he put it on, he double-checked that there were no wrinkles, even though he knew that her ironing skills were top-notch.

"I don't think Picard responded fast enough when Dr. Crusher was kidnapped." The voice of his twenty-two-year old son drifted in to him from the kitchen. "Of course, Patrick Stewart played his part perfectly as always."

Martin sighed.

"When Kirk and Spock searched for the Soul of Skoor . . ."

"Dear, finish your roll, your ride will be here, soon," he heard his wife say.

Martin thought the series very clever in all its incarnations, but he would have been content to watch it once, not hundreds and hundreds of times. He did not know how his wife stood their mentally challenged son's endless talk about each minute detail.

Johann knew everything: producers, plots, stage sets, and he compared them endlessly. Too bad there wasn't a quiz show on the Swiss German television channels where the contestant was an expert in a single subject. Johann would win hands down. Make some money to cover his very expensive school, the same school that was sending the car to take him to classes, giving Martin's wife a few hours respite.

Not that he begrudged doing the best by his son and not that he was badly paid. Heading security at the Zurich Bank for Private Investment, or ZBPI, was a lucrative post. Granted he spent a major fortune on antacid pills as worry after worry about missing some detail that would lead to a catastrophe plagued him.

"Get your coat on," his wife said to their son.

Martin heard a chair scrape against the tile kitchen floor, where he knew his wife would be putting his breakfast on a tray for him to eat in his office once Johann had left. If his son was a disappointment, his wife was not. He glanced at his watch.

If anything went wrong today he wouldn't be fired, but he would be offered some guard duty at some bank out in the countryside, which would make him quit.

Sometimes that didn't seem such a bad alternative. He imagined opening a little store in the mountains where only a broken jar would raise his blood pressure instead of the thousands of details that had to be checked and rechecked. Sometimes, never knowing what tiny thing he might have overlooked would bring disaster down on the bank and then on him and his family, brought on nightmares.

"Can we watch the first *Star Trek* movie tonight?" Martin could see Johann slipping his arms into the coat his wife was holding for him by the front door of the apartment. Johann was calling to Martin.

"I won't be home tonight and tomorrow night, and then I'll probably be late after that." Martin walked over to his son and rubbed his hair as the boy lowered his head to Martin's chest, a morning ritual whenever Martin was home. "Bet your mother would enjoy it."

His wife rolled her eyes. Innumerable sweaters had been knit-ted as she watched the same episodes for the umpty-umpth time. She followed the boy down the stairs to the waiting car, then came back. "I'll have your breakfast ready in a few min-utes."

He wished he had time for a chat in the breakfast nook of the kitchen. The apartment was small, yet big enough for their needs. As long as Johann could watch the television he stayed in the living room. The third bedroom had been turned into Mar-tin's office. Unlike the rest of the flat, which was furnished with antiques that he and his wife had found one by one, it was all flat-pack furniture, although with a dark wood finish that made the clean lines look a bit less modern.

He entered his office and turned on his laptop. The date came up along with the itinerary, which he began to review.

11:00: Three black limousines will be at the private jet runway of Zurich Airport. All three will have two armed bodyguards each. Three gray Volvos, also with two body-guards each, will be at the strip, one for each limo.

Total number of personnel: fifteen. The drivers in the cars with the dignitaries are trained in several types of hand-to-hand combat. All are crack shots with almost any gun one can name, although they only travel with Glock 19s—good for backup as well as easily concealed.

The limousines will be equipped with coffee, croissants, champagne, *The Financial Times, The Wall Street Journal* and *The International New York Times,* which used to be called *The International Herald Tribune.*

11:30: Arrival of Jerome Masterson, CEO of Harrison, Harrison, Jackson (HHJ) Investment Bank, New York. Travel by private plane.

11:35: Arrival of Nigel Carter, CEO of Landon Investment Bank, London. Travel by private plane.

11:46: Arrival of Peter Wang, CEO of Singapore Banking, Singapore. Travel by private plane.

The ZBPI CEO, Christophe Auer, was already at the destination. Auer was Martin's boss. Until Martin had heard of Auer's safe arrival about an hour earlier by text message, he had been uneasy.

Although he knew that he had done everything possible that there was to do, he still felt a niggle that something unexpected might happen. No matter how careful he was, no matter how many details he checked and rechecked, missing something would be disastrous.

Despite his dreams of escape to an easier work life, if he ever left, he wanted to leave a blotless career behind. That record justified his salary.

Money was not the only reason. Martin realized that he was a proud man, probably too proud if one was to believe his wife. Sometimes she used the term "anal" but "anal" was why he held the post he did.

Whenever Martin thought of money, his mind jumped to the fees at his son's private school, although the school occupied more of a day-care position now that the boy was out of his teens.

Johann had come as far as he could come. He could read, write, do math, but his chances of ever working were minimal. Probably Martin's greatest worry was not to be able to afford the life insurance policies that would insure the boy a home when something happened to him and his wife.

Did he regret the decision to keep the boy with them when they discovered he would never be the son for whom Martin had planned? Not really, although he would watch with envy fathers teaching their sons to ride a bike, throwing a ball back and forth or just walking through a shopping center talking.

Life was what it was: Martin could think of many worse ones. And right now he shouldn't be thinking of his personal life at all, but be concentrating on his work for the next few days.

Martin had driven the route in the Bernese Oberland to the village of Bergendorf yesterday. This village was entirely owned by ZBPI, although it looked like any ordinary Swiss mountain village with its wooden chalets, geranium-filled window boxes and belled cows standing almost to order in the pasture above the houses.

It was anything but an ordinary Swiss village: every house was occupied by ZBPI employees who acted as if they were normal farmers, waitresses, hotel personnel or shopkeepers.

The schoolteachers where the employees' children went were real teachers but also in the employ of ZBPI. They were paid much better than the already extremely well-paid schoolteachers in the Swiss public school system.

ZBPI used it for their most important bank customers. The wealthy would fly in from all over the globe to be whisked away to Bergendorf where their financial alternatives would be laid out on one of the antique desks, outfitted with the latest model laptops and tablets.

Sometimes the guests would want to hike or ski, depending on the season, but usually they were much too busy or thought they were too important to linger in frivolous pursuits that did not impact the bottom lines of their businesses or personal accounts.

For those that wanted female companionship, ZBPI employees provided that too. Those women were required to speak several languages and know about art, music, literature, sports and the history of the country of their clients. No ordinary streetwalker or even high-priced call girl was good enough. Martin had six ladies on call this time, although based on

32

experience during past meetings s̶
would probably not be needed.

As for the women themselves, ̶
food. Two were mothers and their ch̶
the village. Gisela, for example, had told
it was for her to be a single working mom
ment then when she'd been a secretary. Son̶
several weeks without ever having to do anythi̶
the girls said they were more like well-trained geish̶

In Bergendorf he had met with the event coordi̶
had first briefed the entire three-hundred-person villa̶
smaller groups of employees who would have direct c̶
with the four CEOs.

Magali Baumer, one of Martin's assistants, was a whiz a h̶
job. She knew what each of the executives liked to drink, eat̶
and read so that the rooms were properly and individually
provisioned. Chefs were ready with menus of all the invitees'
favorites as well as Swiss specialties. Martin and Magali often
marveled that their special guests would take the fondue, *raclette*
and *viande seché,* although most often it was during a cold winter
night. In summer lobster, steak, caviar, and barbecues were the
preferred dishes, except for Masterson, who was a strict vegetar-
ian.

Unlike in regular hotels, guests could take the logo-less
designer bathrobes with them.

Christianne Bruber stood in the office doorway with a
wooden tray bearing a coffee pot, bringing Martin back to the
moment. A small dish, divided into two parts, held two types of
jam, both red. His wife had cut three pats of perfectly squared
butter. She put the tray down on his desk and kissed him on the
forehead. "What should I pack for you? Or are you all set?"

Bruber kept a wardrobe at the small apartment in the
mountains that was for his use alone, including business suits

age. He kept duplicates there so he could leave at
t and arrive at the village needing nothing but his

CHAPTER 5

If Annie were Catholic, she would have crossed herself when she shut off the car in the hospital's car park as an act of thanksgiving that she hadn't been killed nor had she killed someone unlucky enough to cross her path. Once she'd headed into the roundabout the wrong way, and twice she made turns on the wrong side of the road.

She wasn't sure where Roger was in the many-building complex. Yesterday had been too much of a blur. She'd left the hospital right after she'd been told he'd come through surgery well after being allowed to peek at him in recovery. A nurse, with gray hair and wearing a mask, said she that would watch over him for the next few hours before his transfer to his room.

Janet and Rod had taken over propelling her to their car. Annie had paid no attention to where she had been or where she was going.

After asking many people who looked like they worked at the hospital, she did reach Roger's room. She felt like a mouse that had earned his morsel of cheese for successfully negotiating a maze. Putting her hand on the door, she steeled herself for what she would find.

Roger was the only patient in the four-bed ward. She pushed open the door to see her husband sitting up with three pillows behind his back.

Annie suddenly understood what people meant when they said "going weak at the knees." Except for the hospital gown and the medical bed, he looked as if he could be watching television in their own bed.

"Bonjour chérie. Est-ce que je t'ai fait peur?"

"Did you give me a scare? My hair should be white."

He started to cry. She had never seen him cry. A nurse walked in at that moment and said, "It's natural to be teary after a bypass, Mr. Perret." She carried a funny looking device with a tube attached to a mouthpiece. "You need to blow into this."

Roger sniffed. Annie reached for a tissue in a box next to his bed.

"Like this." The nurse demonstrated, only without letting her lips touch the mouthpiece.

Roger did and winced. He put the instrument on the hospital nightstand to the right of his bed. The nurse handed it back to him. "Not a choice."

When she left, Roger said, "I suspect she would be good at one of those torture camps."

Annie knew from past experience that Roger was a terrible patient. Even when he had a simple cold, he acted as if he had come down with double pneumonia and that his recovery was in doubt. This would not just be the "in sickness and in health" part of her vows but the worst of the worse part. She pulled up a chair.

"I haven't called Gaëlle, yet. I wanted to wait until I saw you."

"Does she really have to know?"

Annie guessed that Roger didn't want to either worry his daughter or have her think of him as anything but eternal.

"Yes, because if we don't, she'll be furious."

"I suppose that you could do it now."

How unlike Roger it was to give up so easily. Annie took out her cell and dialed the 0033 for France and the girl's mobile number. She wasn't sure that Gaëlle would even have her phone on. According to her watch, the teenager should be between classes. Gaëlle answered and Annie heard the girl squeal her name.

"Have you done the reading yet . . . did you meet with your publisher . . . is Papa relaxing . . . I have three tens on tests I took . . . Guillaume is here next to me . . ."

In one of those flashes of intuition that she sometimes had, Annie knew the best thing to do without any doubt whatsoever and said, "Let me say hi to Guillaume."

There was the sound of the phone dropping and a clatter of background noise.

Roger was no fan of Guillaume. Annie had persuaded her husband that Guillaume was not only all right but, in fact, preferable to many of the boys that Gaëlle could have been dating. Roger had to admit he didn't hang around with a bad crowd, but he thought his daughter was too young and would start multi-conversations with "she should . . ." at which point in the conversation Annie would respond . . . "blah, blah, blah, blah."

Guillaume had used part of their large garden over the summer to grow vegetables and took his produce to sell at the Saturday *marché* in the village. He and Gaëlle had made jelly from the surplus plums and kaki fruit that grew in their orchard, which they also sold at the *marché*. When school was in session, both kids maintained good grades. Their teachers reported no disciplinary problems.

Roger would complain that they were always together, and when they weren't they either talked on the phone or texted each other. "What can they say to each other?" he would ask over and over.

"Weren't you ever young and in love?" Annie would say each time.

"I can't remember," he'd answer.

What Annie would never tell Roger was how she had gone to her studio to work one time, only to discover the two teenagers naked on her *clic clac.* Her first remark had been stupid—"What are you doing?"—when anyone versed in the facts of life would know exactly what they were doing.

Her next comment had been, "I'm going around the block and when I get back, I want both of you dressed, the *clic clac* put back as a couch instead of a bed and a pot of tea brewing in my antique teapot."

She had known that Gaëlle would realize that meant a serious conversation was about to happen. The white pot with the gold trim and hand-painted violets was only used for their important talks.

She had given the teenagers an extra five minutes before going back into her studio. The climb to the fourth floor had never seemed quite so long as she tried to think how to handle the situation.

Although Annie's studio was very small, there was room for a table and chairs near one of the two windows looking out on the red-tiled roof of her neighbors. The houses on the street were built in the sixteen hundreds and so close that a large SUV would not be able to maneuver through the space without knocking off the side-view mirrors.

Her cathedral ceiling sloped downward to the two windows so low that Guillaume could not stand up under it. He'd positioned himself on the far end of the table.

The kids' expressions might almost have made her laugh had she not envisioned babies crying in the night or Gaëlle giving up school to mother them.

"We used a condom." Guillaume had showed her the empty package. "I don't want anything to happen to Gaëlle. I love her." He'd reached for her hand.

"Are you going to tell Papa?" Gaëlle had asked.

Annie's first instinct had been to say, "No, you are." Instead, she'd taken a deep breath.

Roger would go ballistic. No matter what they said about French men being open about sex, he was a strict father protective of his daughter, whom he'd raised on his own since his wife had been killed by a criminal just of out of the jail where Roger had put him.

Gaëlle had been ten. Over the last few years he'd spluttered and raged about her multicolored hair, her wanting the freedoms of ordinary girls her age.

Sometimes Annie felt like the tennis ball at a Federer/Nadal match. Other times, the better times, she only felt like the referee.

"I love him, Annie. You said my first time should be with someone I love, not someone who forced me or claimed to love me just so we could have sex."

Annie thought of the song *"Déchiré"* with lyrics about being torn in two. "How long have you been . . . ?"

"About three months."

She couldn't imagine them stopping and maybe they shouldn't. "I won't say anything to your father, but—and it is a big but—in fact there are two big buts—you have to promise me you'll always use protection and you won't do it in my apartment. Roger will kill me if he thought I knew and didn't say anything, and he'd kill me twice if I gave you permission to use my studio."

Both kids had nodded furiously.

"And I'm going to suggest you think about the pill, Gaëlle."

Guillaume studied his hands. "I'd rather she didn't mess up her body. I don't like wearing condoms," he turned bright red, "but it is better than Gaëlle taking medicine."

Again Annie had smothered what she wanted to say. She knew he was into natural everything: he was true to himself.

Young love would not be stopped.

Annie's thoughts came back to the present and to the news she had to tell Gaëlle. The phone made strange noises as she waited for Guillaume to pick up.

"Hi Annie," he said. "Sorry. Gaëlle dropped the phone."

"Listen, Guillaume. I'm about to tell Gaëlle that her father has had first a heart attack and secondly heart surgery. She's going to need you to help her keep calm."

"I understand."

When Gaëlle came back on, she told her what had happened starting with, "Your father is recovering . . ."

"Why didn't you call sooner?" Gaëlle's words dripped anger.

"I had to wait to know what was happening."

"You should have told me." Still angry.

"Probably. If you want to fly over . . ." She ignored Roger shaking his head.

"I do." The answer came as fast as Annie had expected.

She gave Gaëlle her own credit card information and asked her to e-mail her when she'd be landing at Luton Airport.

When she'd hung up, Roger said. "She shouldn't miss school."

"She needs to see you. School can wait." She kissed him on the top of his head. His gray-streaked black hair was a bit greasy and curled around the back of his neck. She loved that there was no sign of baldness despite that he was heading toward fifty. Dear God, let him reach fifty, sixty, seventy.

"You concentrate on getting better. It's my job to worry about everything else." Taking the device the nurse had given him she pushed it at him. "Now blow."

CHAPTER 6

Janet and Annie sat at the MacKenzie dining room table, a bright red teapot and a plate of bakery-bought chocolate biscuits between them.

The dog, Freddie Mercury, known as Mercury or Merc, stood on the couch by the bay window cocking his head as students from the King's School streamed by. Every now and then he would let out a tentative woof as if expressing an opinion more than a warning. He was a beige fluff ball that showed some poodle DNA.

"Mercury does that every day at this time," Janet said. "If I'm in the studio and he's on the floor, he gets up and heads to the window. Maybe he dreams of being a border crossing guard or something."

"Or maybe he thinks he's singing, considering his name." Annie giggled and realized that this was the first time since Roger's collapse that she'd laughed if only for a second. "You really got more than you bargained for when you invited Roger and me to stay during my reading and meeting up with my publisher."

"That's what friends are for."

"But we'll be here longer and with Gaëlle and Guillaume coming . . ."

Janet's hand shot out and covered Annie's. "I wouldn't have it any other way. More tea?"

"I love the way you change a topic."

"You didn't plan to get involved in a murder." Janet poured

41

the tea. "Now what's the program for tomorrow?"

"The kids are landing at Luton around 12:30. They can take a bus to Cambridge and then catch . . ."

"They can find us standing at arrivals and forget the bus thingamajiggy. And I bet Gaëlle will want to go directly to the hospital."

Before Annie could say the words, "are you sure?" Janet said, "The new painting is going horribly, and it will be a favor to me to have a full day without the smell of oil paint in my nose."

"Liar," Annie said. "You use acrylics more than oils."

"Yes."

The dog jumped off the sofa and ran to the front door, visible from where both women were sitting. His tail beat out a welcome. Instead of his usual greeting to the dog, Rod stormed into the dining room as fast as anyone could storm on crutches.

"God damn the police!"

Janet jumped up to help Rod off with his jacket, positioning the chair nearest the buffet so he could sit and still keep his crutches within easy reach.

The dog, who had run to pick up his favorite toy—a small teddy bear chewed into something barely recognizable—sat in front of Rod, his head cocked, as if puzzled by his master's behavior. When Rod didn't throw the toy, as was the normal routine, the dog sighed and jumped back on the couch, the toy between his legs, waiting in case his owner realized what he should be doing instead of ignoring him.

Janet reached for another mug and poured Rod a cuppa, but he pushed it away. "Idiots, idiots, idiots."

Annie started to get up to leave but Janet, who was standing behind Rod, shook her head. "Who are idiots?"

"The police. They took all the computers from the boat, but you know that. Today, I asked if I could have them back . . . or at least when I could have them back. Have you any idea of how much important work there is on them? Any idea at all?" He slapped his hand on the table hard enough to make the teapot top rattle.

"I'm sure the police aren't going to give away any of your company secrets, or your clients," Annie said.

"I wish that was all. They had to have done something stupid to them. They said all the computers were empty."

"Empty?" Annie asked.

"Empty?" Janet asked.

"Empty! Empty! Empty! God damn! Empty! Not a word. Not a formula. Not an e-mail. Not even cookies for a YouTube. I mean empty."

Annie never remembered Rod being so vehement or so wordy. The word "taciturn" had been invented for him as she'd once told him. Rod hadn't minded. "I am what I am," he'd replied.

"Backup discs? Cloud?" Janet asked.

"We don't put anything out there in cyberspace."

"Why not?" Annie asked.

"You never know who's listening in," he said.

"Another copy off-site?" Annie asked.

Rod's body seemed to relax for three or four seconds, then stiffened. "Simon always said he kept backups."

"Well then . . . ?" Janet poured herself more tea.

"Didn't tell me where. God fucking damn it!" Rod had never sworn to Annie's knowledge. Taciturn he might be, but he was also very polite. He'd always pulled out her chair if they ate at the cafeteria in the bank in Zurich where they had been working. Of the many nerds Annie knew, Rod had been one of her favorites.

"Nothing was found on Simon's computers. *Nada! Nicht! Rien!* That young policeman told me while I was at the station. The old one wouldn't say anything. The young one waited until the older one had left the room."

Annie hadn't realized that Rod had gone to the station. "But can't they go into the hard drive?" Annie knew that it was almost impossible to erase everything from a computer.

"Cleaned."

Annie and Janet exchanged looks.

Rod turned around so he could see his wife and then looked at Annie. "Aren't you listening?"

"Listening, but it's hard to believe," Janet said.

"So I'm a liar?"

Janet took her place back at the table. "I know you're upset . . ."

"God damn right I'm upset. Months of work . . ." he waved his hands . . . "gone . . . gone . . . gone! And at the worse possible time."

"The someone who broke in had to know what they were doing. Then this couldn't be a casual robbery," Annie said, "especially if they cleaned the computers."

"Got it in one. And it gets worse. The police took all my office computers. There was no sign of anyone being at my office." Rod reached for his crutches and one clattered to the wide floorboards. Janet picked it up.

"Oh fuck," he said after a few other curses.

Neither woman spoke.

"Are you a suspect?" Janet voiced what Annie was thinking.

Rod tried to pace as much as anyone could pace in limited space with crutches. "Maybe. They're too dumb to think I could have killed him like this?" He pointed to his foot.

People on crutches could be killers, but Annie wasn't going to say that. She couldn't imagine Rod killing anyone, much less his partner. Also there were no crutch marks in the blood on the floor.

"I've no alibi. I was working alone here before the race." He turned to Janet. "You and Annie were out."

"Do the police think the murder has something to do with what he was working on?"

"You don't understand." Rod left the room and slammed the door, almost hitting the dog in the face.

Janet and Annie sat there without saying anything for a few minutes. Annie broke the silence. "None of this makes any sense."

CHAPTER 7

Gaëlle's and Guillaume's plane was delayed a half hour.

"Noodles." Annie headed for the Luton Airport food court where oriental dishes and other fast foods were for sale.

For the first time since Roger's collapse, she was hungry. The only reason she'd eaten at all was that Janet kept putting food in front of her. Usually Annie remembered almost everything she'd eaten, but she couldn't recall one meal that she'd consumed, or rather picked at, during the last couple of days.

Janet nodded as she lifted the noodles into her mouth with cheap wooden chopsticks. "Another good thing about coming to the airport is to be away from Rod. He's a bear, although I *do* understand why."

An elderly couple settled themselves at the next table. The wife had made sure the husband was comfortable before she went and bought their food, dropping a kiss on the top of his head as she passed. Annie wondered if she would feel so tender to Roger in their later years—or even if they would have later years. Of all the things she'd worried about that might happen to hurt her marriage, a heart attack wasn't on any of her lists.

"Rod was right to take his laptop and tablets out of the house and put them in the car temporarily," Janet said.

"And he probably gave good advice when he told me to take mine with me during the airport run."

Annie was not thrilled at having to tote her own laptop around with her, but better than having it confiscated, although she could get everything out of her cloud account if necessary. To be without her laptop was a bit like being without her right and left arms. Emails, assignments, chatting with friends, research projects she was doing for herself or for clients were as much a part of her daily routine as taking a shower. She also admitted to playing games daily, something Roger did not understand. For him the computer was a necessary evil at work. He certainly wasn't going to use it in his free time.

"This really isn't making you calm for your reading tomorrow."

Annie hadn't practiced at all. Although winging it wasn't her style, it would have to be tomorrow. With Gaëlle coming she would need to give the girl her attention. How frightened the girl must be over the potential loss of her father, she could only imagine.

By the time they finished and returned their trays, the kids' plane had landed. "I'm not sure I would recognize Gaëlle. I only saw her at your wedding." Janet gathered up the trays and carried them to a rack before heading to the area in front of arrivals.

Annie was nearly knocked off her feet by Gaëlle, who was about three inches taller. A boy, dressed in scruffy jeans and a sweatshirt wearing a backpack and carrying Gaëlle's backpack, stood behind her, looking around.

"You must be Guillaume." Janet took the extra backpack from him. "Are you all right with English?"

"*Un peu.* A little."

"How is Papa?" Gaëlle stepped back, giving Annie a chance to kiss Guillaume on both cheeks.

"I'm so glad you came with her, Guillaume." Annie was sure Roger would be less thrilled, although his only real objection to his daughter's boyfriend was that he was his daughter's

47

boyfriend. "Let's get to the hospital. And if you can encourage him to blow into his device strengthening his lungs, well that would be great."

When Roger saw his daughter, he teared up again. He was still the only patient in the room. "They tell me everyone is emotional after . . ."

Annie noticed that Roger never used the words "heart attack," "surgery," or anything that might explain why he was in the hospital. His dislike of not admitting weakness was something that annoyed her more now than normally. It annoyed her more that she felt she shouldn't say anything about the annoyance.

"You have to stop scaring me, Papa, although it is great to have an excuse to come to England. Maybe I can check out Cambridge University while I'm here."

Roger looked over his daughter's shoulder at Annie, but spoke to his daughter. "What is this, plan 3985J for your future?"

Since Annie had become involved with Gaëlle there wasn't a career she hadn't considered, most of which were dreams. Annie had made Roger stop being negative to the ideas, encouraging Gaëlle to research them herself. Reality woke most of the dreams. The one constant was that Gaëlle wanted to go to university albeit she had chosen many different ones in many different countries.

"*Non*, 4322L. I like to keep my options open." Gaëlle reached over and pulled the device that Roger hated to use from the table next to the bed, which also had a reading lamp, tissues, a water pitcher and glass and a cup with a teabag draped on the saucer. "What's this?"

"Just a thing."

Gaëlle fiddled with the tube. "Looks a bit like a water pipe without tobacco."

"It's something I need to do to keep my lungs happy."

"Show me."

Roger did and while he was blowing, Gaëlle turned around and winked at Annie.

CHAPTER 8

Martin Bruber was due to meet with Herr Fuchs, the head of the Zurich airport border police. He looked forward to seeing his old army buddy. That they both had ended up in some form of security didn't surprise him. Like much in Swiss politics, especially Swiss German politics or Swiss German business, organizational ranks usually mirrored army ranks.

Fuchs showed Bruber into his office and automatically poured a demitasse of espresso that could have melted the spoon. "So who is coming in today?"

Bruber reached into his beige-leather, trapezoid-shaped briefcase, more like an old fashioned valise, because he kept spare rounds of ammunition for the gun that hid at his waist.

Sometimes he thought of himself as a cowboy that could pull his gun at a moment's notice and shoot the rattlesnake spooking his horse. He was not usually given to fantasy or imagination, but the cowboy theme went back to his childhood when his father would take him to the *kino* to see American westerns. Not for the first time he wondered if his father had become as sick of westerns as he was of space programs.

"By the latest count, which I just checked an hour ago, I've nine people, three big shots, each with their personal assistants. And bodyguards. Here are copies of their passports, which I know you'll destroy when I tell you they've left the country."

Fuchs thumbed through them. "Big names here. If a bomb drops on whatever hotel they're in, that could cut a big hole in the world's financial system."

Bruber smiled.

Fuchs stood up and put the information in his safe. "How's your son?"

"The same."

"I signed him up for a Trekkie magazine for his birthday," Fuchs said.

"He'll be pleased. And your kids?" He knew he would get a simple "fine." Fuchs was not about to rub in how well his own son was doing at law school or how his daughter with her top grades would be heading for medical school in the fall. He appreciated that in his friend.

"We need to get together for a dinner. I'll have Mina call Christianne," Fuchs said.

The sky was a brilliant blue with one white cloud wisp shaped like a comma. The hills were turning brown and yellow. The first frost had hit the city the week before and it had already snowed in the mountains.

Bruber drove his Volvo to the private landing strip maintained by ZBPI. There were two black S550 Mercedes limos parked to one side. They were more understated than some stretch limos, but that was one less than he expected. However there were three Volvos. He wasn't sure why the changes—he'd have to ask his secretary. She was always able to adjust to last-minute glitches and, at this point, never bothered to check with him. Why hadn't she told him?

He took out his phone, only to discover the battery was dead. He cursed himself. The phone had probably come on when he brushed up against it. He felt a wave of wanting out of this kind of work. Enough was enough, except it wasn't enough. Never had he felt so trapped in his life and he knew he would do nothing, absolutely nothing, about it.

The drivers/bodyguards were in a group talking. The drivers wore crisp black uniforms while the bodyguards were in what anyone would think was casual clothes, except they wore identical black pants and logo-less sweaters. Over the sweaters were black jackets, which Bruber knew hid their Glocks.

One of the drivers was smoking—against orders. Bruber didn't want him to have the smell of cigarette smoke on his clothes, even if he would be in the front seat with a closed window between him and the VIPs.

Bruber walked over to the group and took the cigarette away from the smoker, who said nothing. "Where is the third limo?"

"Masterson got in early, so they took off for the village already."

"And his bodyguard?" Martin pointed to the three Volvos.

Rolf, the oldest of the chauffeurs and the one Martin had worked with longest, put his hand on Martin's shoulder. "It was a mess. His plane landed an hour before its arrival was due, and of course you hadn't had time to clear the plane with the border guards. Not only that he brought with him his own bodyguard, a Burt Johnson, and of course he wasn't on your list. Looks like a real creepy character right out of a tough guy, kill-'em-up movie."

"Any problems?" Martin was afraid to ask.

"Not after Masterson called the president."

"Of the bank?"

"Switzerland."

Martin sighed. No matter how he planned a schedule, the CEOs did what they damned well pleased. At the same time, he didn't want the cars to convoy. It would look too suspicious. He looked up into the sky. It looked like Wang's plane was about to land.

This was going to be a very long, very worrisome few days.

CHAPTER 9

Annie had not expected a big crowd at her book reading of *Hilke Fülmer: Swimming for Her Life*. When she'd sussed out the bookstore, it was small but exactly the type of store where she would love to get lost for an afternoon as she delved into book after book. With her own crowd of Janet, Gaëlle and Guillaume, she thought there wouldn't be too much room for many others.

She'd told Guillaume he might be uncomfortable with the English, but he'd said he wouldn't miss it.

Rod begged off to buy new computers for his business. "Thank God, they don't know about the off-site backups," he'd said. He'd left them there instead of calling attention to their existence. "Unfortunately, some of the material is out of date by a few days." Rod never made any bones about his not trusting cloud storage. "Hackers are everywhere. I don't care how carefully I encrypt it all, someone might break through." At one time Annie might have thought him paranoid, but with the revelations of government spying, she no longer did, not that Rod would be doing anything of interest to a government.

Even a day was too long to leave his staff idle, and the police had given no indication of how long they would keep his equipment. Although Janet had grumbled that her husband should be more supportive of their attempts to catch Simon's murderer, Annie had told him that she understood.

The first person to drift in seemed surprised that there was an event going on despite the sign outside and the newspaper adverts announcing the reading. She wore a bright red coat and carried a package of what she said were sausages bought at the butcher across the street, and although she said that she would love to stay, she was afraid the meat would go bad.

Eileen, the shop owner, was a woman in her fifties. She offered to put them in the refrigerator in the staff room, more a staff closet, and with the speed that Ms Redcoat handed the bag to Eileen, Annie assumed that she really wanted to listen.

"I love meeting writers. I can't imagine how you do it," Ms Redcoat said.

Annie didn't answer as she would have liked: "I'm not a writer. This book is a fluke." Instead she thanked the woman for staying. "I hope you won't be disappointed."

An elderly couple tottered in as Eileen came out of the staff room. She introduced them to Annie as local history buffs.

"My father was an RAF pilot. When I heard there was a part about an RAF pilot, I wanted to come. I was just that too young to serve. My father was almost too old," the man said as his wife helped him to a chair.

Annie made a mental note to read the bit about the pilot who bombed the German ship the Cap Arcona, which was carrying concentration camp prisoners, especially for him. In writing the book she'd been lucky enough to trace down the pilot's daughter, although he had died many years before.

She decided to explain why she'd written the book: how a woman she'd worked with at a museum had handed Annie the memoir of the German woman who had swum to shore after the ship she was on had been bombed by the RAF during World War II. Annie had previously shared her hope to write a biography one day to that co-worker, who remembered Annie's desire and had dug the journal out of the museum's archive and made a copy for Annie.

Before the appointed time for the reading, eleven people,

mostly retired if the gray heads were any indication, drifted in. Annie assumed that younger people were at work during the day.

Eileen had arranged chairs strategically. Gaëlle, Guillaume and Janet were perched on the narrow staircase going to the tiny mezzanine, which held two more bookcases with room for no more than two customers to browse. The store was no place for anyone with claustrophobia, but for those who wanted warm and friendly, it was a treasure.

"Break a leg," Gaëlle mouthed from her stair as Eileen introduced Annie.

Annie knew that the three seconds of panic she felt would disappear as soon as she began. It always had in her few attempts at acting in local drama clubs or making presentations before clients. By looking into her audience's eyes she could tell when she was holding or losing their attention. She decided to sit on, not behind, the table because she didn't want to put a barrier between herself and her listeners. She alternated that position when reading with walking around as much as she talked. It was just a presentation trick: if she walked and read at the same time, her chance of tripping increased.

The bell over the door tinkled. A young man entered or at least he was young compared to the others in the bookstore. He did have a few crow's feet around his eyes on his otherwise perfect complexion. Dark blue jeans emphasized his slimness. He wore a dark blue striped shirt and a blue suit jacket that was neither wrinkled nor well-pressed.

Annie paused for a second. His head was a mass of curls worn shoulder length and he had a face that looked as if it could only smile. He shut the door and stood there listening.

Annie stuttered, then regained her verbal footing. When she brought her reading to a close the applause was polite.

Eileen stood next to Annie. "Thank you. We've her books for

sale. Annie will be happy to sign them, won't you Annie?"

"Gladly."

"I know it's early but one would make a great Christmas gift. And we've arranged for you all to have a tea and sweet at the tearoom next door. Just pick up your voucher at the cash register before you leave," Eileen said.

"I hope you don't mind if I write in the margins," a woman said as she put a copy on the table.

Annie remembered her friend Mireille, who had gone missing after killing her professor/lover. "I've a friend and when we exchanged books, we always made margin notes. We loved seeing what the other thought was important, interesting or even not well-written. Of course, there's nothing not well-written here." She winked and the woman winked back. Annie wished she knew what had happened to Mireille and hoped that wherever she was, she was all right.

A man with a cane approached the table, the book clutched in his hand. "Please?"

Bizarre, she thought. I'm usually the one asking for the signature in a book from an author, not writing mine. The whole day was more like appearing in a movie than living part of her real life.

Annie was aware of the curly-haired man staying in his chair as she signed each book and answered people's questions.

"No, I don't plan another book."

"I'm enjoying my stay in Ely."

"The cathedral is incredible. I want to make sure I take the complete tour before I leave."

"I used a computer. I can't read my handwriting, which is why I printed what you wanted written on your copy."

In the middle she glanced up to where Gaëlle was peeking through the spokes on the staircase. The girl gave her a thumbs up.

The late-arriving man with the wonderful curls was almost slouching in a chair in the last row. The smile was still there.

After Eileen had rung up the sales, not just of Annie's book, but others that the audience had found before leaving, she went over to the man. "Can I help you?"

"I'm here to speak with Ms Young."

Annie, who was gathering her things, handed them to Gaëlle and went over to him.

He put out his hand. "I'm Quentin Taylor, your publisher."

"I'm gobsmacked, as you Brits say." And she was. She'd talked to Quentin on the telephone. They'd exchanged tons of e-mails both over contract negotiations and corrections to the manuscript. It was Quentin who had helped her locate the daughter of the RAF pilot, whom she'd written about. The woman had been invaluable in rounding out the personality of the man who'd dropped the bombs.

All the time, Annie had this vision of Quentin as an older man, a much older man, almost a Charles Dickens type working at a desk wearing a green eyeshade with the only modern thing in his cramped office space being a computer. She had no idea why she'd formed that image.

"Let's go to lunch," he said. "We've a lot to talk about."

"Don't worry about us," Janet said. "I'll take the kids home and feed them good English food that will put the French cuisine to shame."

When Quentin walked across the store, he almost glided. He picked up her backpack and as if by magic it floated over his shoulder. He helped her on with her coat and followed her to the door, which he opened before she could even think about reaching for the latch.

CHAPTER 10

Annie and Quentin made a quick stop at the tearoom where she snaked her way through the early lunch crowd. She found about half the audience reading at the back. "I just wanted to thank you for coming and being such good listeners."

"Aren't you sweet," the oldest-looking woman at the reading said. Long ago Annie realized that people didn't necessarily look their age.

They tried to talk her into joining them. She sat down for about five minutes before saying she had to go.

"You're good at PR," Quentin told her as they walked up and down High Street trying to find a restaurant. One with a curry special looked great but it was full and noisy. A few doors down they found a pub where the first floor was crowded with those wanting a pint, but the second floor dining room was almost empty. Quentin glanced at his watch. "This should work."

"Jacket potato with cheddar and coleslaw," Annie ordered. "I don't feel I'm truly in England until I've had a jacket potato."

Quentin ordered the same.

"Funny how food and countries seem to go together, croissants and France, wurst and Germany, pasta and Italy," he said.

The waitress, who had a long blond ponytail and was probably just out of her teens, brought their food so fast Annie guessed it had been prepared in advance and just needed to be slapped onto the plate.

"I'm paying for lunch as your publisher." Quentin waved his

fork as he talked. "Mainly, because I have a cheapskate proposition for you: matches the cheapskate meal."

Annie saw his eyes twinkle.

"If you think I'm good at PR, I think you're good at setting expectations."

His laugh was more of a soft roll. "I'm serious. My father bankrolls the publishing house, mainly to keep me out of trouble and to feel as if his paying for the King's School and Cambridge University at least had some merit, no matter how miniscule."

"You're a local boy?"

"Only in education. My family is from Edinburgh and my father is a typical Scot who did well, very, very well. He didn't need to go to America like Andrew Carnegie to make his fortune but set up a series of corner shops based on market research."

Annie cocked her head.

"He noticed what people bought by watching them come out of the shops. Then he watched what stayed on shelves. Got himself a job at one little shop. Asked customers what they would like that the shop didn't carry. Built the business of that establishment and when the owner died with no heirs he took over. He now owns fifty-two all over Scotland."

Annie wondered if his father was disappointed in his son. "And you didn't want to go into the business?"

"I always had my head in a book. And I'm sporty. I run. Done most of the local marathons and a few others: Paris, Dublin, Geneva. Reading and running, that's my game. Ask me again, and I'll tell you the same." Another twinkle and a shake of his curls.

Annie noticed that the three young mothers and the two gray-haired ladies were trying not to stare at Quentin. The word "charisma" had to have been invented for him.

The waitress stopped to ask Quentin if everything was all right. Annie suspected that if she'd said that she was about to die of food poisoning, the waitress wouldn't have heard her.

Quentin signaled with a smile that it was. As soon as the waitress left, he continued. "He, my father that is, had just about given up on me. I'd been bumming around the world, picking up computer gigs here and there, when I came to Ely to visit an old school friend. He lived next door to a hole-in-the-wall publisher who was going out of business. I convinced my father to buy it at the price a hole-in-the-wall publisher should be paid and my father exacted a piece of my soul, which he claimed he would release after five years."

"Which was?"

"I had to turn a profit."

"How long ago?"

"Seven years. We are almost breaking even."

"He hasn't pulled the plug."

"He threatens to, but every now and then I publish a book that wouldn't be published otherwise and he gives my soul an extension. Your book was one of those. Also, my father loves anything to do with World War II."

"Is that why you published it?" Annie remembered how surprised she was that after eighteen rejections she received an e-mail offer from Quentin. She doubted she'd have sent the book out for a nineteenth rejection, although she remembered reading some cartoonist saying something about never giving up because the umpty-umpth submission might be it and if a person gave up at umpty-umpth minus one, they would have missed their opportunity.

"About twenty percent. I really loved Hilke's story. And I loved that we could include photos." More eye twinkling. "I publish about five titles a year in paperback, like yours. I put them on Kindle. I've enough library standing orders that I don't *always* lose money, but yours made some . . . much to my father's surprise. And mine."

Annie opened her mouth but didn't get a chance to say anything before he continued.

"But not much. I only publish things I find interesting, mostly historical stuff and people aren't just all that interested."

"But mine made money."

"Enough to pay your pitiful advance . . . and . . ."

Annie felt as if there should have been a drumroll before he continued.

". . . and I've a check for another £1,750.32 for you today."

"So because I'm a successful author you are treating me to this sumptuous meal?"

His smile increased from normal to beaming. "Yes . . . I've enough of my father's genes to try and figure out why your book won a bit more interest than the others I've printed, so I asked several readers."

"And . . . ?"

"It was about real people and you wrote it a bit like it was a novel. They wanted to know what happened to Hilke. They cared when an RAF pilot died leaving his wife and son, because, even if it hadn't happened in their families, it had happened in families that they knew. Also, it wasn't filled with academic drivel and fifty-five-word sentences crammed with boring facts."

Annie wasn't sure how to respond. Turning Hilke Fülmer's journal into the book had been a labor of love. She had woken up in the mornings during the period she was involved in the writing of it and almost cursed anything that kept her from sitting down at the computer.

She didn't have the original journal, which was in a faded black cover. Hilke's daughter hadn't wanted the original out of the museum's hands, which was understandable enough. Written on quadrangle-lined paper in a spidery hand in German Annie had typed it word for word to get the feel, to make it easier to read, and to find certain things with her search key.

Bless word processing. Although the journal was written in German, Annie had produced the manuscript in German and English. The German version didn't get even a nibble from any German publishers.

Hilke seemed so lifelike to Annie that she'd wanted to sit and have a cup of tea with her and ask her to delve into details. But women long dead aren't up for cuppas and sharing details of their lives.

Annie had talked at least a dozen times with the woman's daughter, now a widow living in the north of Germany, only to discover that her mother had never shared anything she'd gone through in World War II. The daughter had only learned about her mother's past after her death when she'd found the journal in a safety deposit box. Still the German woman was able to share some of her mother's mannerisms with Annie, which she'd sprinkled throughout the story.

Fate had turned Annie into an accidental author.

"How long are you staying in Ely?" Quentin broke through Annie's mental drifting.

"We were planning on leaving tomorrow after the meeting you and I had originally scheduled, but my husband has had emergency heart surgery so I don't know."

Quentin's hand shot out to cover Annie's. "Is there anything I can do?"

Annie shook her head. "His outlook is good."

Quentin's smile grew bigger. "I'm here to help if needed, but while you're here this is even better for what I'm about to offer you."

"And that is . . ."

"Another history book, which would be set in Ely and written in novel format."

"Another?"

"It's about St. Etheldreda who lived from 636 to 679 and set up an abbey here. She was married but refused to sleep with her husbands."

"I don't suppose she left a journal like Hilke?"

"Don't I wish. We've limited source material, including some sparse references in Bede's writing. You do know who he is, don't you?"

Of course Annie knew about Bede, who'd lived in the seventh and eighth centuries. Granted his goal had been more about his point of view in his writings about the local politics of his time than trying to earn what eventually became his unofficial title: The Father of English History.

At the University of Geneva she'd worked with his wording as well as his handwriting when she was learning how to decipher old manuscripts, probably one of her hardest courses ever, and one that she had been grateful for many times over.

"That'll give you your start. There are other bits and bobs, mostly from the church promoting the religious perspective, but you'll need to do more digging to get the feel of the era. I want Etheldreda to be a real woman to those that read our book."

The project sounded fascinating. "It's a little hard to make a commitment at the moment because of Roger, that's my husband. In fact, this afternoon my stepdaughter and I need to spend time at the hospital after we finish here."

"I can drive you and we can talk on route. I don't mind hanging around while you're with him, if it won't bother you."

Annie guessed if he only published a few titles a year, Quentin wasn't overworked.

He signaled for the bill. "Where are you staying?"

"Across the street from the school. Barton Street."

"You're just down the street from my office. I'll walk you home and you can pick up the kid and we'll head for the hospital. Which one, by the way?"

"Addenbrookes."

"It's a great hospital."

"Okay, but don't think I've accepted your offer yet because I'm accepting a ride to the hospital." Annie wanted to say yes, yes, yes but with Roger's condition so much was uncertain that she didn't want to take on something that she wouldn't be able to deliver.

"I consider it the first step in building a friendship and hopefully a partnership. I'll grab a submission from my office to read while you're visiting your husband."

The walk from the restaurant to the MacKenzie house was short as they cut by the cathedral. Annie could almost picture the workmen in their medieval clothing putting the stones in place. As for the grassy field across from the cathedral, there were still horses grazing as they might have been centuries ago.

As they neared the King's School, Annie noticed trucks with different TV stations' logos written on their side: BBC, Sky and ITV. Two men and one woman with television cameras slung over their shoulders were leaning against the truck. Another man was smoking next to one of the vans and ignoring three others who were in a circle and off to one side. Two other men and one woman, all of whom were well-dressed and well-coiffed, stood in front of the MacKenzie house.

Mercury could be seen through the window on the sofa in the bay window he used as a perch and if the cluster of humanity outside moved too much he would let out a perfunctory bark.

"Holy shit!" Annie said.

"Maybe it has something to do with that boat murder?"

Annie frowned when Quentin said that.

"You know," he added, "some computer guy was killed on his boat on the river. The morning TV shows covered it and it was in the papers too."

"That's where I'm staying."

"You knew him?" he asked.

"Long story. I need to get in or at least get the kids out."

"Is there a back door?"

"Only if I go into someone else's house and climb over their fence into Janet's back garden."

He handed her his phone. "Call them."

The answering machine came on. "Janet, if you're there pick up. It's Annie and I'm outside. What do you want me to do?"

There was a click and Janet came on the line. "I can see you from the upstairs window. They have trouble seeing me through the sheer curtain. The guy from the reading, how come he's with you?"

Annie told her that Quentin was her publisher and had offered to take her to see Roger. "Is Gaëlle with you?"

"I'll put her on."

"This is exciting," Gaëlle said. "We're guessing because Simon was Rod's partner and he doesn't have any relatives, they are trying to get information from Rod."

"Where is he?"

"At one of his employee's houses. The press was at his office too. Here's Janet again."

"I'll call my neighbor and send Gaëlle and Guillaume out through our touching courtyards to meet you. Her front door is around the corner."

"Are you sure she's home?"

"I saw her come home. I need to apologize to her for this mess. Hope you can come back in the same way if that crowd is still out there."

Quentin led Annie to the break in the stone wall surrounding the King's School where they waited until Gaëlle and Guillaume strolled up to them. "We're trying to act cool," Gaëlle said.

"Just don't tell your father about this when we see him," Annie said.

"Be grateful he probably won't be watching English news," Gaëlle said.

Annie was.

CHAPTER 11

The hospital had the same buzz, the same smells, as the day before. Annie, Gaëlle, Guillaume, and Quentin headed toward Roger's room. Annie chided herself for expecting anything different. The difference between French, Swiss and English hospitals might be age or wall color, but other than that there was a similarity that made it almost impossible to identify which country one was in, save for hearing the language.

Only the women were going to visit Roger. Quentin offered to buy Guillaume something to eat. As the man and boy headed toward the cafeteria, he pointed to a bench and told Annie she could find them there later. She and Gaëlle should take their time.

Guillaume took Gaëlle's hand and whispered softly enough that had Annie not had excellent hearing, she'd have missed, "I'll be here if you need me."

Roger was not alone this time. The other three beds were occupied: one by a man of indeterminate age reading *The Guardian*. He looked up from his newspaper and frowned. A second man was snoring, while the third seemed unconscious with oxygen clips in his nose and a drip going into his left arm.

Annie and Gaëlle kissed Roger's cheeks at the same time.

"When do you think I can go home?" he asked before they could say anything.

"Home to Rod's and Janet's? Or home to Argelès?" Annie

pulled up a chair as Roger patted the bed and Gaëlle hoped up on it.

"Both. I want to get out of here. I want to get back to work. *Tout de suite.*"

Before Annie could answer, two doctors walked in, a man and a woman, both young. Only once had she assumed that a woman with a stethoscope around her neck was a nurse and not a doctor, but in the United Kingdom she noticed that many nurses wore blue. Just like many doctors were called "Mr" without the period, not "Dr," also without the period.

"How's the patient today?" the man with the nametag saying David Hardy and thinning strawberry blond hair, asked.

"I want to go home."

"Not too much longer," Mr Hardy said. "You'll need aftercare. Do I have your permission to talk about your condition to your wife?"

"If it will get me out of here faster," Roger said. It was almost a growl.

"Go," said Gaëlle. "I'll stay here and amuse the grump."

David Hardy's office was bigger than a breadbox but smaller than a broom closet. It held a square table and two chairs. His diplomas and certificates were on the wall to the right of the miniscule window.

"How is my husband?" Annie still found the word "husband" strange. She'd expected to be single all her life out of choice, but as Gaëlle would say, using American slang she'd picked up visiting Annie's parents' second home in the States, "Shit happens."

Did she regret the decision?

No. It had made her life easier, especially when she had to be away on a tech writing assignment. Roger handled things like telling her about her mail and making sure the bills were paid. On the other hand, she found herself taking more translation assignments where she could stay home.

She'd even invested in a translation certificate course as well as buying translation software, although her greatest advantage was having been through Dutch-, German- and French-speaking schools so she read and wrote all those languages as if they were her mother tongue.

Companies that wanted to localize their product in several countries found that she saved them money. She earned more for a multilanguage translation but the company paid less than they would for individual translators—and she got to stay home. Her enjoyment of staying home more made her look in the mirror and wonder whom she'd become.

"Your husband is recovering, but he will need a long convalescence. He has other heart problems, probably stemming from his rheumatic fever as a child."

Annie hadn't known he'd had rheumatic fever. Roger hated discussing his health. Hated even admitting when he was tired although his eyes might be closing like some three-year-old trying to convince his parents he really, really could stay up to see this or that television program.

David Hardy went into a long discussion with medical terms that Annie didn't understand.

"Did you tell my husband this?"

"Yes. He didn't like hearing it. I said it in French as well, and he didn't like it any better in French. We also told him that we would help him with the paperwork to support a claim of disability, although I suppose he'll need some kind of official translation."

"Disability?"

"He can work, but not in a high-stress job, or a job that would require sudden physical exertion."

Annie hadn't realized she'd been sitting forward in her chair until she sat back as if slapped. Roger loved being a policeman.

Despite a law degree, all he wanted to do from the time he was a little boy, he'd told her, was to be a *flic*. And this doctor was talking about something so close to retirement as to frighten even her. Roger would have *another* heart attack when the implications of it all became apparent to him, she thought.

"I'm going to suggest you spend at least the next couple of months here so we can monitor him." He held up his hand. "I know that the French health system has been rated best in the world by the World Health Organization but despite all the bad publicity about the NHS here, we do keep the majority of our patients alive."

Annie was amazed that Roger hadn't checked himself out of the hospital before the doctor finished explaining the situation to him.

"What do you want from me?"

CHAPTER 12

Martin kicked the thick duvet off his bed at the ZBPI retreat hotel. He walked to the window and opened the shutters. The Alps were in their full glory with the sun rising over the peaks. At this time of year, the leaves were a brilliant yellow, although this high up, it was possible to have snow at any moment. It had snowed another five hundred meters higher.

He wasn't here for the scenery. Yesterday had gone off almost without a hitch except for that goddamned Masterson. Martin felt that the man redefined arrogance. Still in his flannel pajamas that looked more like sweats, Martin walked over to his computer.

This was his room even when he wasn't here. He kept clothes for every occasion, from outdoor garb needed to lead a search party for a missing bigwig in the mountains to full smoking attire for formal occasions. He hated tuxes, but if that were part of the job, then so be it.

Today he knew that dark blue pants and a dark blue turtleneck sweater would be the uniform of the day. All his staff would be wearing the same, identifying them as security and also go-to people if anyone needed information. No logos, no badges: clothing coding information was part of the packet given to each of the bankers' personal assistants.

His room was equipped with a bank of multiple TV screens where he watched France 24, DW, CNN, BBC, RT, Bloomberg, MSNBC, CCTV and Al Jazeera without sound. It looked like a display in a store specializing in undersized plasma screens. He watched an Asian country with destroyed buildings, a reporter talking into a microphone outside the White House, the weather and publicity. He tried to read the news feeds running underneath, his eyes jumping back and forth. Nothing appeared about a bankers' meeting in Switzerland.

He could shower in relief.

When Martin entered the dining room, a man, the only other person in the room other than the wait staff, stood. He was a good six-foot-three. His frame blocked Martin's view of the ten, white linen tablecloths and the breakfast buffet running the length of the room. Like many Swiss men, Martin was not tall, a mere five-foot-eight. This man towered over him. His chest made a wall.

"Who are you?" The man's voice was gentle, a contrast to his manner and bulk.

"I should ask you the same thing."

"Burt Johnson."

"Martin Bruber, head of security." He stuck out his hand.

Johnson hesitated a moment before thrusting out his own.

Bruber remembered his mother telling his sister that the man she was dating, and whom his mother had disliked, had bear-paw hands, hoping that would discourage her daughter, whose previous boyfriend was a pianist with delicate hands. His sister had loved the pianist's hands, not their owner. His mother's hopes that the hands would discourage his sister were in vain. She loved and married the owner of the bear paws. The marriage had been successful. Hand size and niceness were not correlated, Martin knew.

Burt Johnson's hands made Martin's brother-in-law's hands look delicate.

The big man returned the handshake. "Nice to meet ya."

Breakfast for Martin wasn't just to fill his empty stomach, although the spread of cheeses, meats, breads, eggs, *rösti*, juices, hot chocolate, tea and coffee did serve that mission. He was there to observe.

The four bankers entered the dining room within minutes of each other. They were dressed ski-lodge casual and no one looking at them would have any concept that between them, their organizations controlled a large percentage of the financial market, including the shadow market, which was rapidly outpacing the formal one.

Over the years, Martin had been growing more and more uncomfortable with what he read was happening: scandals, fines, too big to fail, too big to jail. Not that he could do anything about it. He would pick up bits and pieces of conversations, but his education did not lend itself to finance and much of what they said made little sense to him.

At one time he had been proud to do work for ZBPI, but over the past few years, his conscience pricked him. When it did, he counted the two main and interrelated reasons for his staying: his excellent salary, and the cost of his son's special educational costs. The Swiss school he had found for Johann served problem children from some of the wealthiest in the world. Over and over he had to keep reminding himself ad nauseam of why he was still in the job that he was rapidly growing to hate.

Martin took out his phone and texted his secretary. "Find out all you can about Burt Johnson." He gave the few details that he had.

Chapter 13

Janet let Rod off in front of the crematorium and chapel where Simon's service was being held. An open hearse was in front. As far as anyone could tell Simon had no living relatives and had made no plans for his death. "At thirty-nine why should he?" Janet had stated, never expecting an answer as she parked the car in the almost empty parking lot behind the building.

To leave Ely, everyone had used the neighbor's house to get in and out without facing the news teams, which were still camped outside the MacKenzie house. Several other news crews were stationed at the curb.

The two women, unable to find a back entrance, walked to the front of the building and entered, keeping their heads down. At one point, Janet put her hand in front of one of the television cameras.

"The Bartlett service," Janet said to the man at the door.

"Third door to the left." Inside, the smell of flowers sweetened the air to the point that Annie felt nauseous.

The room was almost empty. Detectives Lake and Welch and two men that Janet whispered she'd remembered as owning boats near where Simon's boat docked were also seated at the back. "Those people work with Rod and Simon." Janet pointed to a row as they walked down the center aisle.

"Rod's secretary arranged it all." Janet seated herself next to Rod, who had come ahead of the women. "They," she pointed to the detectives, "asked us unofficially not to cremate the body.

We signed the papers to do it anyway, although I'm not sure we have the authority."

"Will they follow up after the cremation?" Annie asked

Rod leaned toward his wife. "Who knows?" He looked at his watch.

Simon's body was in a simple, closed coffin in the front of the chapel. A small wreath of different flowers was near the top, where Annie assumed Simon's head would be resting. She shuddered.

The service was rather a strange one. A vicar said a few words, although it was clear from his talk of everlasting life and being cut down too young from such a rich life, that he probably hadn't met Simon and that Rod's secretary had given him few hints.

The twenty-third Psalm was read. A recording of an organ played what Annie guessed was "Nearer My God to Thee," but she couldn't be sure.

"That was not particularly satisfying," Janet said as they filed out past rows of chairs.

Rod told his staff to get back to work.

A woman called Annie's name, then Janet's. It took Annie a minute to recognize Simon's ex-wife. Since she'd last seen her in Zurich, she'd lost weight and highlighted her hair, which instead of being in the pixie that Annie remembered now fell to her shoulders. She was dressed in a navy blue suit with blue opaque stockings and blue medium heels.

"Sharon?" Janet and Annie said together. They decided to go for coffee.

They sat on easy chairs around a table with the morning's *The Guardian* turned to the financial pages. Sharon returned with a tray of three coffees. After Janet moved the newspaper to make room for the tray, the man at the next table picked it up.

Annie thought he looked familiar before remembering he'd

been at Simon's service. She debated asking him to join them, but decided against it.

"It's been a long time," Sharon said. "I guess that's a little trite."

Annie wasn't sure what to say. "What have you been doing? I guess that's a little trite too."

"Maybe funerals lead to trite," Sharon said. "When we came back to Ely, I got a job in a bank, which infuriated Simon. Working for 'banksters' is immoral, he would say. I'd rather have you sleep around." She blushed. "So, I did."

Annie wondered how one should respond to such bluntness. Does one ask if Sharon's lovers were good in bed?

"Anyway I got remarried and am living happily ever after. At least my new husband notices me. After Zurich Simon went almost nuts between his hatred of banks and working on that special project with Rod."

Janet frowned. "Project?"

"Maybe Rod wasn't as fanatic. Simon put in nineteen hours a day at least. Bought the boat to work on. I would go *days* without seeing him. Finally I left. He never knew about my lovers."

"I'm sorry," was all Annie could manage to come up with.

"Don't be. We weren't meant for each other. But I'm sorry he's dead. Now tell me about you two."

CHAPTER 14

Annie woke to Roger's snoring. Only when she automatically tried to get him to turn over did she become aware that it wasn't Roger. Her husband was still in the hospital. Mercury had snuck up on the bed and his head was on the pillow next to Annie. He gave her big good morning licks across her face. A second look at the dog and Annie realized that the animal had placed himself under the duvet just like a human.

Light was peeking through the crack in the drapes. No sounds came from the kitchen downstairs. Nor did she hear water running from her hosts' bathroom.

She had so much to do today.

First, she needed to find a place to stay while she worked on the new book now that she'd agreed to do it. She was a firm proponent of the idea that fish and guests stink after three days, and that didn't begin to cover having guests with heart surgery and teenagers.

Second, she needed to get the paperwork started for Roger's disability, skipping over the part of convincing him that he couldn't pop out of bed, take a plane and get back to work.

Then Gaëlle and Guillaume needed to be sent back to Argelès as soon as Gaëlle was reassured about her father. However, Roger didn't want his daughter left alone. Annie made a bet with herself that her parents would be happy to go down and stay with the teenager: Gaëlle adored Annie's parents and vice versa, so that should go smoothly. Phoning the Youngs was also on her to-do list.

Her parents were another worry. With all the pressure the United States was putting on banks worldwide, the Swiss banks were closing American accounts. Her father had complained that although his bank said they would keep the account open for now, he'd been turned down for a car loan. "There is no bank that will give me a loan, much less let me invest in anything," he'd said a week before when they were chatting on the phone.

A week ago—how could your whole life turn around in a week? Silly question. It just did.

Somewhere among her worries, she fell back asleep only to be wakened later with a tap on the door. Janet appeared with a tray on which she had a teapot, two mugs and toast. "Merc, get off the bed." Before the words were out of her mouth, the dog had slithered off and was out the door with his tail between his legs.

"Breakfast in bed?" Annie asked.

"I just thought with all you've been through, you needed a little babying."

"The kids?"

"Still asleep." Janet settled the tray over Annie's legs and placed herself on the left corner of the bed. "What do you need done today? I'm all yours."

Annie felt herself tearing up.

Janet's hand reached out and took Annie's. "Friends are the ones who are there for the problems."

"As if you don't have your own."

"Rod has them with the business." He had gone back to work immediately after the funeral. "He didn't come home last night, but he has been known to work all night more times than it is possible to count. He has so much data to restore, and the rest of the new computers to set up that I really don't expect to see much of him until things settle down."

Annie poured herself a mug of tea. Nice and strong. Green. Just like she loved it. She told Janet her list of things to do.

"You can cross looking for a flat off your list, right now. There's plenty of room for you and Roger here."

Annie gave all the imposition arguments she could muster.

Janet brushed each of them away. "Besides, Rod is in his own world. It will be nice to have someone to talk to who doesn't specialize in grunts and groans."

Annie wasn't sure how it would be for Janet to have a recovering Roger around. "Tell you what, we can try it, but if it gets too much, let me know and we'll find a short-term rental somewhere."

"Now you're being sensible." Janet spread honey from a honeycomb onto her toast.

CHAPTER 15

When Annie arrived in Roger's room, he was talking to a pretty blond in her mid-forties. "She's a DJ," he said.

Annie had taken Gaëlle and Guillaume to the station to catch the train to London to play tourist. Although Gaëlle had wanted to spend time with her father, Annie had persuaded her that she needed to cajole Roger into being a proper patient recovering from heart surgery. If she failed then Gaëlle would be the reinforcement, and if that failed, they would double-team him.

Annie was not looking forward to the conversation with Roger and was almost relieved to find someone there to delay it.

The woman stuck out her hand, which Annie shook. "We have a music program here for recovering patients. They tell me what music they like and we beam it into them."

"No French singers, but a nice choice of American and English pop, jazz and classical," Roger said. "But I still want to go home. Home to Argelès."

The woman ignored him. "I've got your requests. Seven tonight?"

Roger nodded. The DJ left.

Annie figured she better get straight into it all before she lost her will to do so: disability; staying in Ely during his recovery; her parents, who had said they would be more than willing to watch over Gaëlle when she'd talked to them right before coming to the hospital. The teenagers had tickets to Geneva for the day after tomorrow and then the four of them—Gaëlle, Guillaume, and Susan and David Young—would do the seven-hour drive south. "My parents send their love and my mother says to tell you to behave."

"How does Gaëlle feel about this?"

"At first Gaëlle balked at leaving you, but she wanted to show her grandparents' house by the lake to Guillaume," Annie said. "I reminded her they both needed to be back in school."

She didn't mention her worry that her parents might not be able to stay there if they couldn't find a solution to their banking problems. Like most American ex-pats they were finding their accounts being closed thanks to the American law called FATCA, which required that the banks report all their American clients' accounts. The banks rather than spend millions to implement or pay the high fines to the United States for "disobedience" they found it easier to throw the customers out. Her parents had already been denied a car loan and another bank was closing their main account.

She thought of her parents' neighbors. Lisa was American, Jacques was Swiss. When a bank tried to close their accounts, Lisa signed everything over to Jacques, who immediately left her for a younger, prettier woman, leaving Lisa stranded. It wasn't an option for her only American parents. Not that she could picture her father ever leaving her mother for another woman.

Okay, Annie thought. I've enough on my plate. I can't let my parents' problems much less their neighbors' intrude on what I need to do.

She tuned into Roger's tirade. "Don't like that boy."

"That boy has been a rock to your daughter throughout this. He adores her."

"Puppy love."

"And a wonderful thing it is too. However, maybe this puppy love will become dog love and they'll live happily ever after, so you better get used to it."

Roger not only looked tired, he fell asleep. Annie pulled out a book about St. Etheldreda she'd bought in the tourist office and started to read. She knew she was in for a lot more grumpiness from her husband.

Chapter 16

During important meetings, Martin always checked that the dining room of the Golden Aigle was laid out for breakfast even though Magali, the event coordinator, would have done it as well. He'd met his goal to be there at 6:30, an hour before anyone else was expected, which was why the presence of Burt Johnson had taken him by surprise. He didn't like surprises; he liked Johnson even less.

Martin walked by Johnson and opened each of the two glazed windows covered with the typically Swiss lacy curtains and half closed the shutters so that when the sun came up, anyone trying to shoot in would have to be an incredible marksman. They reminded him of the slat windows in the castles of the Middle Ages, which let the castle inhabitants shoot out, but it would take a miracle for an arrow to enter. Even if it did, it would have been next to impossible to hit a human target, unless that person was pressed against the opening.

The room itself was wood paneled and featured carvings of bears, deer and trees in bucolic scenes on the friezes under the ceiling, all in bas-relief. Tablecloths were not the stereotypical red checked but white linen.

The food on the table would have fed the Swiss army, should it happen to drop by, with every kind of cold meat, cheese, breads and eggs that the chef could locate. Six kinds of juice, eight cereals and an assortment of fruit from every continent would guarantee that the world's most powerful financial players could find something that would please their palate.

Martin tried not to think of the millions of people throughout the world that did not have enough to eat. He couldn't bundle the leftovers and mail them to wherever the hungry were. In fact, the leftovers would not be wasted. One of the benefits of working at the hotel was that employees got whatever leftover food there was, although dried out scrambled eggs would probably go to village pets instead of humans.

As Martin walked to the table with the coffee pot, he felt Burt Johnson watching him. The smell of coffee hovered in the room, mixing with that of bacon and fresh baked bread. He poured himself a cup.

As he returned to his place, the word "pristine" jumped into the Swiss man's head in reference to Johnson. Martin knew that the Swiss laundry and dry cleaning services in the village were the best in the country, but he wondered how the American bodyguard had been able to get his clothes looking as if they had never been worn and weren't being worn currently.

The man's crew cut had to have been recently done with every hair standing on end to exactly the same height. The man's appearance made Martin's own hair stand on end figuratively. He didn't know why, but he just didn't trust the man. He did trust his instincts.

Martin put his cup on the table and watched as Johnson took some muesli, yogurt, and a cup of coffee and came over to where Martin sat.

"You've checked everything?" Johnson asked.

"Of course." He looked at the VIPs eating at the table on the other side of the room. He could have told Johnson how the hotel itself was guarded. The concierge, desk clerk and porters had all had defense training. So had the maids and waitresses. Some sixth sense stopped him. Martin did not want to reveal the depth of the security to this man for whom he'd taken such a dislike.

"Everything is under control." Martin excused himself to fill his breakfast plate. Long ago, he had learned to eat when he could, because daily requirements could shift without notice and he might not get a chance later.

Today the schedule was that the bank CEOs would meet in a conference room during the morning, then have lunch in the early afternoon. Everyone but the Asian planned a couple of runs down the north slope of the mountain, the only one with snow, albeit man-made for them, before their late afternoon meetings. Martin had called for reinforcements not only to check out the slope but also to be stationed along the route. Tomorrow would be another meeting day.

Peter Wang, CEO of Singapore Banking, didn't ski. He limped: one less CEO to worry about. Even if an ordinary accident happened, the village had a fully functional hospital able to handle any emergency. A medically equipped helicopter was always on call to fly anyone to the main hospital in Zurich if necessary.

Martin glanced up at the televisions against one wall, to see if any one of the stations was reporting the whereabouts of the CEOs. The last thing they needed was for the press to discover that they were hunkering down together.

"By the way," Johnson said. "You should keep better care of your dossiers on our four friends."

Martin pretended he hadn't heard. Johnson didn't repeat the remark.

CHAPTER 17

"Rod isn't at the office." Janet greeted Annie as she walked in through the back door after cutting through the neighbor's house. The news crews were still outside, but none of them seemed to have figured out how anyone inside the house was getting in and out or even if they were coming and going.

Annie was upset from her visit with Roger, which hadn't gone at all smoothly. He almost whined about having to stay in Ely. She understood that he wanted his normal life back and that he had not yet accepted that he would never have it back. He wasn't even willing to consider the changes that his heart attack had caused. How she could help him was not something she'd figured out yet.

It had been after dinner when Annie had parked the car. She was relieved to have been able to return Janet's car still in the condition in which she'd found it. Slowly, she was growing accustomed to driving on the other side of the road. However, when she got out of the car each time, she felt the tension in her muscles let go a little. At least today she had taken all the turns the correct way and entered the roundabouts on the left rather than the right almost automatically.

As she took off her coat and hung it in the closet under the stairs, she asked, "Could he be at a client's?"

"If he is, he didn't tell any of his staff and he doesn't answer his mobile."

The two women went into the lounge where Gaëlle and Guillaume were watching a DVD in English with French subtitles. Annie didn't recognize it but there were teenagers dancing and one couple seemed in love. Another was having a fight.

Gaëlle jumped up and hugged Annie. "How's Papa?"

"Grouchy. But he seems to be considering thinking about accepting that we will be here for a while. Disability doesn't make him at all happy. I didn't bring up early retirement." She spoke in English.

"Smart." Gaëlle translated for Guillaume who added, *"Bonne idée."*

"How was London?"

The teenagers told them about the Tower of London, riding on the tube, and seeing Buckingham Palace. "The queen didn't invite us in," Guillaume said.

"Silly, she wasn't there."

"How do you know?"

"Her flag wasn't flying." Gaëlle turned to Annie. "I still wish we could stay longer."

"You need to get back to school: Guillaume's parents want him back."

CHAPTER 18

Frazzled.

That was the only word to describe how Annie felt as she watched Gaëlle and Guillaume go through the gate for the Geneva-bound plane. Her stepdaughter, none too happy about leaving, had balked over breakfast, which had led to one of the few fights they'd ever had. Even knowing that Annie's parents were to meet the young couple in Geneva and drive them to Argelès had not placated Gaëlle.

Normally, she adored being with Annie's parents. "I want to stay with my father," she'd said, asking what would happen if he had another attack. Only when Annie assured her that she would call immediately if there was the slightest deterioration in Roger's health, did she agree to leave, but her pout would have done an angry two-year-old proud.

At the last minute, she had hugged Annie American-style rather than give her the French cheek kisses. Annie felt grateful that Gaëlle found it difficult to stay angry. They had not had enough experience being on the outs with each other for her to be good at conflict or conflict resolution. Usually Gaëlle used Annie to explain teenage girls to her father. When Annie agreed with Roger, it often made Gaëlle rethink her position.

Roger was due to return to the MacKenzie house the next day, although Annie continued with her doubts about imposing on Janet.

Rod had not appeared in the last two days, so unlike him.

Janet kept expressing her worry and at the same time repeatedly reassuring Annie that their presence would help keep her sane.

As for the project on St. Etheldreda, Annie had signed the contract, but had not even begun to think about where she would start. The one book, which was supposed to be helpful, made the woman a cardboard character. Although she'd let her imagination run, she wasn't sure of what she was doing, a feeling she detested.

She knew she had a short deadline. Fear that she wouldn't be able to finish the project at all niggled at her. Once she had more information, she could start writing, and change things later if she discovered more. This would be a juggling act from start to finish.

Rather than go to the hospital directly from the airport, Annie stopped at a tearoom in a tiny village whose name she didn't even know. It was small with only four tables and lace curtains on the windows. Taking the tea and a piece of chocolate cake to an empty table, she sat and slowly consumed the goodies. It was the least hectic moment she'd spent in the last few days.

She and Janet had looked for Rod, driving up and down streets hoping to spy his car. Since it was automatic he could have driven it with his one foot in a cast. Nothing.

"If he was trying to get away to work, he'd have said something to me," Janet repeated over and over and over.

Annie agreed, knowing under normal circumstances Rod would be fanatically trying to get his office back to normal. She was tempted to raise the idea of a mistress, but Rod just didn't seem the type, whatever that type was. Janet knew that too, but it might have provided a less drastic source of worry than her unspoken fear that Rod might have been killed as Simon had been. Annie didn't even want to consider what the police might think, should they discover Rod's disappearance, assuming he was alive.

When she finished the tea, she picked up a newspaper and pretended to read it article by article, but if she had had to take a quiz on content, she would not have answered a single question correctly.

"Are you sure the kids got off all right?" Roger asked as she sat by his bed. There was one other visitor for the old man next to him, probably the man's daughter, since he didn't look like a man who would have arm candy. Also, the woman spoke of her children as his grandchildren, showing him a drawing that one had done.

One of the other patients slept. The last had earphones and was listening to something.

"Unless they came back out of the gate after I left, yes."

"You'll be here first thing tomorrow?" Roger asked.

"For the tenth time yes."

"I still don't see why I can't go home to Argelès."

"And for the tenth time, it is so they can do follow-up here."

"You are getting really good at math for someone who is number-phobic," he said.

She leaned over to kiss him. On her to-do list once he was home was to sit him down with the paperwork for his disability: the PDF forms had been e-mailed from France and she'd filled out what she could, but she still needed his input and—more importantly—his signature.

What concerned her on her long list of worries was how he would handle retirement. He was not a man who could sit around and do nothing. Nor did he play golf or tennis with any real enthusiasm. A once-a-year horseback ride did not constitute an interest that would become a pastime.

He did read, but that was usually a few pages a night before he fell asleep with the book on his chest. As for hobbies, that word existed for him only in the dictionary. Until he found something to occupy him, life would be difficult, for her as much as for him.

Had she not married him, had she stayed single as she had wanted, would she still be there for him?

Probably.

More than probably, but instead of feeling trapped she would be doing it out of choice. She knew that this differentiation was at best dumb, but a long time ago, she had learned that recognizing her emotions was better than pretending that she was feeling what others thought she should. None of this would she share with Roger—at least not until this was all behind them.

And that was another thing that bothered her. When she had a worry or something was bothering her she could talk it out with him, even if he always tried to find a solution rather than just listen to her bitch, which was what she would have preferred. When he was the problem, she couldn't use him as a sounding board.

"I'll be here with bells on by 10:30 at the latest. I just don't want to face morning drive time," she said.

"You're more comfortable driving on the left?"

"Not comfortable, but I suspect you won't have another heart attack riding with me."

CHAPTER 19

"I'll only close my eyes for a minute," Roger said as Annie pulled the flowered afghan over him. The late afternoon autumn light streamed through the window, making the room comfortably warm, but not too hot. Mercury looked as if he were about to jump up on the bed, but instead laid down next to Roger's side on the floor with a long sigh when Annie shook her head.

Within seconds Roger was asleep. Annie left the room, leaving the door open just enough to allow the dog to leave if he so wished rather than have him scratch to be let out, thus disturbing her husband.

Although she was grateful that Roger was out of the hospital, his demands to go back to France wore on her. He was like a child not understanding why he couldn't have his way, but then again, he was used to being the one giving orders, not taking them. *I must try and be more understanding,* she reminded herself.

Downstairs Janet was working on a new portrait commission in her atelier. Annie debated disturbing her, but since her friend was working against a new deadline combined with her worry about her husband, who had not come home for three days and wasn't answering his telephone or his e-mails, she decided that it was better to have a pot of tea ready when Janet emerged.

Annie also could use the time to research East Anglia in the 630s on the Internet, although she preferred to be stomping around the area even if it bore no resemblance today to what it might have been then.

The deadline her publisher had given her made her feel pushed. A later deadline wouldn't have been possible. Quentin wanted the book for a historical symposium being held in Cambridge in the spring, which meant that Annie had less than three months to complete the project. By Christmas, if not before, it must be in Quentin's hands.

Work had always had a way of taking her mind off any problems that she might be having, but with a recuperating, exceedingly grumpy husband physically close, her usual formula was impossible.

As she poured the hot water over the leaves in the teapot, the front doorbell rang. Mercury pounded down the stairs barking to ward off the invaders—Lake and Welch. Annie hoped that the dog wouldn't wake Roger: not so much that her husband needed to rest, but his demands and unhappiness were more than she wanted to deal with at the moment.

Janet came out of her atelier with a brush in her hand, which she dropped. "It's Rod. Is he dead?"

"No, he's not dead," Lake said, "that we are aware of, that is. But we would like to know if you know where he is."

Stupid, Annie thought. Considering Janet's reaction to them, she obviously didn't know. Maybe they thought she was a great actress.

She wasn't sure whether to invite them in or not but Janet ushered them into the lounge. The fireplace was full of cinders from the last fire that no one had had the energy to clean out. The room was cold. A wind had come up earlier in the day: the couple only heated the rooms they were in. The lounge was the least used room of any in the house. Janet, like Annie, maintained the kitchen was the heart of the house and the bedroom the soul.

Annie tried to remember the British police ranks. She knew

Welch was under Lake who she thought was a detective sergeant from the local Criminal Investigation Department. She wished she had paid more attention when she watched all the British murder mysteries on BBC World or ITV.

The men settled themselves on the red leather sofa, but did not lean back. Instead, they rested their elbows on their knees.

Mercury stood at the door and watched them, a guard ball of beige fluff poised for action to protect his hearth. When Janet told him to go lie down, he looked almost happy to be relieved from duty and trotted back to his regular position on the couch in front of the dining room window.

Welch took out his notepad.

"You seemed to think your husband might be dead," Lake said. "Why?"

"He hasn't been home in three days. He's not answering his cell."

"Is this unusual?"

"He has gone away before on business. Sometimes at the last minute and doesn't tell me verbally. I'll find a note. Or he'll have his secretary call and tell me where he'll be, including phone numbers," Janet said.

"And you didn't report it?" Welch asked, earning a frown from Lake.

"Would you have started looking, that quickly?" Janet asked.

"Because of the murder, yes, we would have," Lake said.

Annie wondered what the detectives were thinking, but wasn't about to ask.

"His office said they had no idea where he was. We put out a trace for his car. Strangely, we found it—at Gatwick Airport," Lake said.

"Gatwick? Rod wasn't planning to go anywhere. Excuse me. Let me check on something for you." Janet went upstairs. From the footsteps Annie guessed she was in the bedroom that had been converted in Rod's electronics-filled cave. He had perfected a growl for those who dared to enter.

Annie offered the two detectives a cup of tea. Welch accepted; Lake first declined, then accepted. At least preparing a tea tray for the tea already brewed kept her out of the room, which meant she did not have to talk to the two men.

When she picked up the tea tray and walked by the stairs, Janet was descending. "I checked on Roger and he was sound asleep. How he could sleep through Merc barking, I don't know."

Annie figured the trip from the hospital to the house had more than exhausted him, another worry in itself.

The detectives stood when the women entered the lounge.

"I found his passport." Janet handed it to Lake, who thumbed through the pages.

"Several visas." Lake's expression looked as if he'd discovered a terrorist.

"He was a contractor up until three years ago. He took assignments in Japan, New York, and one in Saudi Arabia."

"I thought he worked in computers," Welch said.

"Many computer people prefer short-term contracts. I do myself," Annie said. "You don't get caught up in company politics and the scene is changing so we don't get bored. Not to mention that the money is great." She hoped that the mention of money wouldn't annoy them if they thought that their own salary levels might be lower.

"Can you think of any reason your husband would be running away?" Lake asked.

"If you are implying he was having an affair or if he had anything to do with Simon's death, you're totally mistaken. My husband lived and breathed computers and not much else."

"How long have you been married?" Lake blew on the cup of tea that Annie had poured.

"Ten years. He rented a room when I had an attic atelier in London. We met when he was just out of college and working in the IT department of a London bank, although I'm not sure which one. He's worked in so many banks over the years." Janet accepted the mug Annie offered, but cupped it in her hands.

"You knew each other before?" Lake asked.

"No. He answered an advert I'd put in the paper. I was trying to make my living as an artist. I needed someone to help with the rent. He wanted a place close to work."

"And you fell in love?" Welch asked.

Annie noticed for the first time that Welch wore a wedding ring and Lake did not. She wondered if the younger detective was a romantic.

"More or less."

Annie knew that Janet and Rod had begun sleeping together and fell into marriage after several years together, more for convenience than passion or deep love. Each let the other concentrate on their work, so the arrangement suited them. Janet had enjoyed the lack of pressure Rod's salary brought, meaning she could accept commissions or not. No waitressing any more to have enough money for rent and paints.

Rod found it nice to have someone who cared for his basic needs and who didn't care if he worked all night long. Neither felt taken advantage of by the other. Better than many marriages, Annie thought, even if she knew it would never be enough for herself.

Janet's painting was beginning to pay off as she earned more and more for her portraits, and if portrait painting wasn't her first love, it still satisfied her artistic endeavors. She insisted on making the paintings tell something about the person; thus a subject might be curled up on a couch with a book, or fly fishing or even swinging a golf club. The distinction gave her the leeway to feel she was exercising her talent, not selling out for money.

"And as for an affair? His mistress is his computer," Janet said.

The policemen exchanged looks as if to say, sure, sure, sure . . . the old *I'm working late* excuse.

"I agree with Janet. Getting his attention on anything that doesn't involve a keyboard or algorithm is not that easy," Annie said.

"Is the car still at the airport?" Janet asked.

"We've impounded it. For evidence," Welch said.

After the police left, Janet said, "That was his English passport. His Swiss one is gone."

CHAPTER 20

Martin Bruber watched as Christophe Auer spoke to everyone in the dining room, including the security guards. He was dressed in brown cords and an Irish knit sweater that accented the graying hair, which he wore slightly touching his collar.

At the buffet table, he thanked the woman who was adding scrambled eggs to the serving dish, using her family name along with *Frau*. The CEO of the Swiss bank was not like the other CEOs at the meeting, who would only speak to their equals. If they were to address an underling it was to demand something with the words please or *bitte* never crossing their lips.

Auer never demanded. He always added a please, as if someone would or could refuse him. Bruber had said "no" once. Auer had looked shocked. When Bruber explained the safety issue, Auer had thanked him. However, Martin knew at a gut level to say "no" without a reason would not go down well.

"Everything all right?" Auer asked Martin as he passed by with his tray. He had chosen a small amount of eggs, a *brötchen* and two strips of bacon. There was a bowl of fresh fruit, a glass of fresh-squeezed orange juice and a cup of coffee. Martin had never seen Auer overeat or overdrink.

"Yes, but as always we are checking and rechecking."

"This isn't Davos. No press has any idea yet?"

Martin didn't need to be reminded that the press was the last thing any of these men wanted. The thought of notifying them had entered his mind, but for the press to learn of this village

. . . well, his imagination was not able to calculate the consequences. "My secretary has already looked at the morning papers and I've watched the news channels. There's not a word about the whereabouts of anyone here."

Auer patted Martin on the shoulder. "I knew I could count on you."

That was the other trait that Martin found interesting in Auer but that he didn't see in the other CEOs. He praised when praise was due. He praised in public. However, let an employee do something wrong, the criticism was swift but in private. The words, "Herr Bruber, can you please come in here," followed by a door shutting behind them could be frightening.

Martin returned to his own room as soon as he had finished his breakfast and the CEOs started their meeting in the conference room next to the dining room. Last night Martin had done a personal sweep of the meeting place to make sure that the only recording device was his.

The old trick of leaving a hair on a door to see if anyone unknown had entered a room was too well known for Martin to try. In its place he photographed his own room completely to see if anything was out of place. One of the things he loved about the modern technology was the ease of using his phone for these photos. So much better than the Polaroids of the old days.

His room, as a staff member, was plainer than that of the guests, but it still had a five-star quality. His wall decorations were not original art works that would make Sotheby's weep with joy, but original art by lesser-known yet very accomplished artists. The bed had a thick feather duvet and pillows, but not a canopy. The room was about half the size of his flat in Zurich, which was spacious enough for three people to live in without feeling crowded.

Martin compared each part of his room to the photos on his telephone.

Someone had been in there. His hairbrush was about half an inch to the left of where it had been. His underwear was slightly askew. If Johnson—and who else could it possibly be?—had searched his room, he was good. Very, very good.

He went to the safe and removed his laptop. Using a secure line he called the vice president of information technology at ZBPI and asked him to check to see if anyone had hacked into his computer. "When were you on it last?" the man asked.

"This morning and last night." Martin listed the times approximately.

While he waited, he reviewed the profiles of the four CEOs given to him by his assistant, one of the most thorough people he'd ever met. In Zurich Martin also had copies of any article ever written about any of the four CEOs along with translations if they were in any language except English, French or German. Although he knew the information by heart, he still believed in double-checking.

Martin was proud of his memory, and wondered if his son's ability to recite almost everything known about *Star Trek* was partially because of one of his genes.

While he waited for the vice president to call back, he mentally reviewed the dossiers.

Jerome Marshal Masterson
   Title/Bank: CEO, Harrison, Harrison, Jackson Investment Bank (HHJ listing on stock exchange)
   Born: September 9, 1969 Westchester, NY
   Parents: Margaret Marshall Harrison, socialite, wife, Edward Daniel Masterson, banker
   Education: Philips Academy Andover (asked to leave for unknown offense—still working on it) finished his diploma

at Hyde School in Bath, Maine. Yale, Harvard Business School.

Marital status: Married to Caroline (Caro) Jackson June 9, 1994

Children: Andrew Marshall, born July 4, 1995. Currently a senior at Phillips Academy Andover

Languages: English mother tongue: no other languages

Profile: Masterson was a problem child, spoiled by his mother. Janice Manowicz, his fifth nanny, said as a little boy he threw tantrums constantly to get his own way and it worked. The other nannies (see attached list) had quit because he was so hard to deal with.

Likewise in school, he was a difficult child with a short attention span. This was before ADD was considered a treatable condition, although he was never diagnosed as having ADD, and his attention span today is perfect.

His parents did not have any other children because of his mother's "delicate" health. Read drying out several times. List of places she was a patient attached. The summer before he transferred to Hyde, there was a car accident with a friend. Both teenagers had been drinking. The friend, Peter Haskell, was killed. I suspect that this was a watershed moment for the young Masterson. From then on he did everything right: grades, sports, etc. through Harvard Business School.

He was taken on at HHJ after his marriage to the daughter of James Harrison III, who had taken over from his own father as CEO while his father was still chairman of the HHJ board. Their marriage was much like royal marriages of the Middle Ages bringing kingdoms together.

His father and father-in-law had him work in all departments but there was no question that he would end up as CEO.

He took to the rather conservative bank and came up with new products and built HHJ into a too big to fail, too big to jail bank. He also knows which politicians and regulators to buy, although nothing can be proved.

Martin found himself distinctly disliking Masterson, which he chalked up to his Swiss German belief that showiness was somehow indecent.

Nigel Carter

Title/Bank: Nigel Carter, CEO Landon Investment Bank
Born: October 9, 1966 Bath, UK
Parents: Helen Wright Carter (homemaker) and Jonathan Carter (successful stockbroker, very)
Education: Eton, Oxford, where he earned a first-class degree in philosophy, politics and economics, and London School of Economics for a masters
Marital status: Married to Jemima Stockbridge (1989–2009), then Eileen Carey (2009–present). Carey is 20 years his junior and his former secretary.
Children: Jonathan born 1991, Frederick born 1992, Sybil born 1999. Children became estranged from him after or because of his divorce.
Languages: English mother tongue, fluent French, Malay, Cantonese with basic Tamil
Profile: Always an achiever with top grades. Hates to lose at anything. Excellent tennis player but his staff deliberately lose to him rather than face his anger. Got his original job at Landon through his father's connections, but quickly proved himself. Worked in New York, Singapore and Syd-

ney as he was making his way up the ladder. A true workaholic, although since his second marriage, his hours have been cut back to something closer to normal. Demands 100% loyalty from staff, but will allow people to contradict him if they have the facts to back up whatever they tell him.

Martin thought the word "smarmy" was invented for Carter. He had a way of asking ever so politely but in such a manner that said "you will do it or else." Martin still hadn't figured out exactly how he did it. Often his requests were peppered with, "If it is not too much trouble," or "when you have time," with both parties knowing that having time meant at that moment and even if it were trouble.

Carter was never seen with a politician, but it was said that he knew them all and that he was the money behind the power structure of much of the English government. It was said, they said, unnamed sources said . . . Martin didn't have much use for the rumor mill, but at the same time, he knew that rumors are more often fact-based than not.

Too many times he'd heard things in meetings only to have them turn up on one of the business channels or in the media— not always immediately, but within weeks or months. He had no doubt that if these four men could harness energy, climate change would be solved and that it wasn't because they decreed it shouldn't be.

Peter Wang

Title/Bank: CEO Singapore Banking and Investment Corporation and a series of subsidiaries

Born: October 15, 1966, Hong Kong

Parents: Father An Wang, owner of the Wang hotel chain, Wang shipping, Wang Energy, Wang Electronics

Mother Lelia Sorenson, Swedish daughter of leading electronics manufacturer, maker of typewriters, calculators. Company was bought out by An Wang in 1970 and became Wang Electrics.

Education: Privately educated at home until he went to Eton, Wharton, then the London School of Economics

Marital status: Widower. Married Jing Quan when he was twenty. She died in a car crash a year later.

Children: None

Languages: English, Swedish and Cantonese mother tongues, fluent French, Italian, German

Profile: Wang in many ways is a loner and has no known personal life outside of work. He refused to go into business with his father although he serves on the board of all his father's corporations, all of which are based in Hong Kong. Peter Wang went to work at Singapore Banking and Investment Corporation as a teller after graduating from business school. The bank was private and mismanaged; Wang persuaded his father to buy the faltering bank and then built it into the second largest bank in Asia. Wang is known for making the smart deal and like most of Singapore, which is considered one of the least corrupt countries in the world, is known for his straight dealing. The bank did not get caught up in the subprime, derivative or hedge fund scandals of the past few years.

Wang was in a motorcycle accident. As a result he limps badly. He hates using his cane, although he does because he thinks falling is worse and hates anyone mentioning his disability.

Martin found Wang the hardest to get to know, not that his security position would mean that he would ever "know" any of the CEOs. Once when he had a sneezing fit, Wang had produced a handkerchief while the other three looked annoyed at the interruption, even his own chief.

Christophe Auer

Title/Bank: CEO Zurich Bank for Private Investment

Born: November 11, 1970 Zurich, Switzerland

Parents: Ulrich Auer and Marianne Farber

Education: Le Rosey in Rolle and Gstaad, Switzerland (School of Kings), Harvard University: began Harvard Business school and changed to Stanford Business School and finally got his MBA from Columbia. He did postgraduate work at the London School of Economics. (He claimed he wanted to test out different environments and his grades were always in the top one percent.)

Marital status: Married to Johanna Albrecht, PhD, from the Norwegian School of Economics September 14, 2001, an economist whom he met at the Davos World Economic Forum in 1999. She has a specialty in family economics and ethics and teaches at the University of Zurich.

Children: None

Languages: Swiss German, German, English, French, Italian—all fluent

Profile: Auer never raises his voice. He keeps his staff, bringing them up through the ranks (matching the Swiss army ranks as well). The bank is a family bank that has been in business since 1795. His father had almost destroyed it, and the son rebuilt its reputation. At no time was the bank involved in any of the tax evasion scandals with the United States that brought down the Wegelin Bank, and caused several Swiss banks to pay huge fines to the United States government as well. It has offices in

London, Singapore, Tokyo and Frankfurt. Other than work, his only other interest is skiing, which he does every weekend at his chalet in St. Moritz during the season. He refuses to use the company town for his time off. His wife sometimes goes with him. She is not an avid skier.

Knowing the profiles of the men his security staff was assigned to protect was just the preliminary part of Martin's job. The information was sent to an off-site computer in the basement of one of the chalets in the village. Only he and his assistant knew about that computer, which bore special encryption.

Martin found each of these men disgusting, and when he couldn't control his thoughts, found himself disgusted for working for them. It didn't bother him that they had more money than he did. Envy of their wealth was not in his makeup.

The dossiers were not paper copies, but on his computer. What was Johnson up to with his remark about keeping better control of them? Could he have had time to break into the safe? Had he hacked into Martin's computer? If he did . . . then when?

The man had thrown down a gauntlet and Martin chastised himself for not picking it up. His instant decision to say nothing until he knew more about his opponent, for he already thought of him as an opponent, was chiseled into his brain as effectively as any jackhammer.

He walked over to the window and looked out on the village. A delivery truck drove by, probably headed for the local grocery store. Unlike every other Swiss village it was neither a Migros nor a Coop but was owned and operated by ZBPI. Its vendors were carefully screened. Prices were kept lower than the major stores for all residents.

The phone rang and it was the vice president of information technology. "Your computer was scanned, hacked."

"And?"

"I suggest you change all your passwords."

When Martin hung up, the last thing he wanted to do was spend time changing his passwords, but one couldn't be too careful.

CHAPTER 21

Annie made breakfast for everyone. Roger had come downstairs for the first time since he'd arrived yesterday. He'd slept through the police visit and dinner. That he hadn't reacted as he normally would have when there was a murder was just one more item on her to-worry-about list.

"Think about taking a walk later," Annie said. "The doctor recommends it."

"What if I get too tired to walk back?" he asked.

"I'll carry you," she said, imagining his almost six-foot body on her five-foot-six frame.

Janet had already gone into her studio, although the sun still wasn't up. Annie wondered if she was using work as a worry preventative. If she were, Annie hoped it was working for her.

Her temptation was to make bacon and eggs, but the idea of re-stuffing Roger's newly cleared arteries just didn't seem right, so she settled for porridge and tea. Janet joined them when the food was served.

The three of them sat around the table, each lost in his or her own thoughts.

It was Roger who broke the silence. "Janet, is there anything we can do about Rod?"

Annie wanted to say, "You need to take it easy," but she didn't. Her husband had given a typical pre–heart attack response. Thank goodness, she thought.

"I was debating going over to the office today, to see if any of the staff has any idea about where he might have gone and why," Janet said. "I was trying to think up questions while I was painting."

"Multitasking women," Roger mumbled into his porridge.

Rod's office was two stories. The bottom floor held the desks of the three computer programmers and Maud, the receptionist/secretary. The top floor was a training room for those who knew nothing about computers and wanted to learn or those who wanted to learn a new software program.

The firm contracted teachers for the classes on as-needed basis. None of the programmers had the patience to break down the instructions into the simplicity a neophyte needed.

One salesman used one of the two offices at the back, but he was usually out on the road trying to convince companies that they should send their staff to Rod's office. If the company wanted the trainer at their site, Rod would send one of the contract teachers.

"Have you heard anything?" Maud jumped up to greet Janet, Roger and Annie.

Janet shook her head. "We were hoping to talk to everyone."

"The police have done that." Tom, the youngest of the three programmers, said. "They think he's run away."

"They don't know Rod like I do," Janet said.

Annie wondered if Janet really did know her husband. Did anyone ever see inside another human completely for that matter?

"Is anyone in the training room upstairs?" Janet asked. "If not we can use that."

Upstairs, they rearranged the chairs that had been behind the table of computers around a small circular table.

Maud appeared with coffee and toffee biscuits. She kept the office supplied with the baked goods that she loved to make, but didn't want to keep at home to add any more chubbiness to her already generous frame.

"Let's talk to you first," Roger said.

Maud settled herself in one of the chairs and handed the basket with the biscuits around, taking three for herself. "Anything I can do, I will. I'm worried and you, Janet . . ." Her hand covered Janet's.

Annie noticed the flicker in Janet's eyes that implied she would prefer not being touched. She suspected her friend was trying to hold herself together, and too much concern would break down the emotional barriers Janet had erected to protect herself.

Roger asked all the normal questions that any policeman would.

"Are there financial problems with the company?"

"Are there any clients who might be angry at Rod?"

"What was Simon working on?"

Maud shrugged her shoulders and said, "What Simon was doing was so hush-hush we sometimes forgot he was part of the company. If I hadn't paid him each month, I wouldn't have guessed he was working for us."

"Was Rod working on the same project?"

"I've no idea. I do know he wouldn't let anyone come behind him when he was writing code, and when he finished, he downloaded whatever he'd been doing onto two USB keys. He would lock one of them in the company safe."

Roger glanced at Annie with an "aha" look. "And the other?"

"He would put in his pocket. His shirt pocket." Maud frowned. "And then he'd pat it twice."

Roger leaned forward. "Did the police take the material in the safe?"

"They didn't know a safe was there." She stood up and went to a cabinet that held manuals. She pulled out all the manuals, and then maneuvered it to one side to reveal a safe.

"Good God," Janet said. "This is unreal."

"However, only Rod has the combination."

CHAPTER 22

Annie padded down the hall in a bathrobe borrowed from Janet. The door to the bedroom at the top of the stairs was open and she could hear Roger's soft snores.

Not only had Janet made the Young-Perret contingent feel at home, she had offered a second bedroom, when it became apparent after the heart attack that neither Annie nor Roger slept well together.

Last night Annie hadn't slept well in the separate bedroom either. Worry about her parents' banking problems, Roger, Simon's murder, Rod's disappearance, and her looming deadline on the biography of St. Etheldreda on which she'd done diddly-squat left her dozing off only to startle her awake several times. Each time it had taken longer to fall back asleep.

She decided to use the ground-floor toilet. Too many years of living in Swiss apartments with the *no-flushing-after-ten-at-night* dictate had left her self-conscious about the noise when she was visiting elsewhere, even when there was no rule. Besides, Janet's upstairs toilet seemed to have a microphone and amplifier installed in the water tank.

The window at the other end of the hall let in no light, but there was no reason it should. The sun was not due to arrive for at least three more hours. Rain hitting the glass told her its arrival would not be seen.

Downstairs she found Janet sitting at the table.

"I made myself a cup of cocoa, and there's some left for you."

Annie had a flashback of herself and Janet sitting in a Zurich coffee shop next to a fountain discussing whether the best way to describe the drink was *hot chocolate* or *cocoa*. Of course, they had ordered *heisse Schokolade* along with a tart made with kiwis and strawberries. Janet talked about how comforting it had been on winter nights when her mother would say she'd make them all cocoa before bedtime. They would sit on the floor around the gas fire and her mother would tell Janet and her siblings a story.

"Couldn't sleep either?" Annie brought a mug of cocoa to the table.

"I'm thinking if Rod is alive then when I see him again, I'll ream him out like he has never been reamed before."

"For putting you through this?"

Janet nodded. "We don't have a traditional marriage . . . I don't mean that we do strange sexual things in groups, although our sex life is okay."

Annie didn't want to hear about Janet and Rod's sex life but if Janet needed to talk about it so be it. She was wondering if she'd ever have one again . . . would Roger be capable? She then felt guilty that she wasn't more grateful he was alive with or without sex.

"I'm wound up in my painting, and you know what Rod is like . . . a computer is an extension of his body. If I need to talk about anything, well, that's what my girlfriends are for."

Annie understood. There were things that intrigued her, but when she brought them up with Roger, his eyes would glaze over. So she didn't and without resentment. She would share them with her mother and the friends who shared that interest.

To expect Roger to be all things to her or her to him was not reasonable. She'd read somewhere that women have a physical reason for being more talkative than men, but she'd forgotten what it was. However, she believed it.

"But if I need something, Rod is there for me. When I had that lump in my breast and I was going for the biopsy, he insisted on going. When I went to get the results, he was there holding my hand. He never holds my hand. Thank God, it was nothing."

Annie understood that too. She remembered how Rod had taken over the night at the hospital getting her the information she needed. The cliché, actions count not words, was too clichéd to say.

"Do you think by any chance that the bike that hit Rod had any connection to Simon's murder?" Janet asked.

Annie had been wondering the same thing in her tossing and turning during the night. "Maybe."

"At least the press is gone. Thank goodness for the missing child in Cambridge." Janet's face registered horror. "I didn't mean that like it sounded. I meant . . ."

". . . that it got the press off your doorstep."

Janet ran her hands through her hair. "Thank God, you're here. Being alone in the house would be awful. I know I've friends, but they all have their own lives and family, and although they'd be here during the day, at least the ones that don't work, what about the nights? I can't make a phone call at three in the morning and say 'I'm feeling badly.' With you here I know I can go into your room, and you'll listen."

"But you didn't. You came down here."

"Knowing and doing are two different things. Want some toast with the cocoa?"

Annie stood in the kitchen, holding her mug and watching Janet slice bread and put it in the toaster. "Is there anything we can be doing? Is there a place Rod goes to get away from it all?

An old friend's house that might be off the radar? A cottage by a lake?"

Janet turned around with the knife in her hand. "I've been racking my brains, and no. Rod doesn't have friends like you and I do. He doesn't have a bolt-hole, I think that's the expression Americans use. If only I could go through his computers . . ."

Annie knew her friend's ability with computers was limited to e-mail and maybe an easy web search. "The police have been through them. Another topic . . . what is going to happen with the business?"

"I was going to ask you a huge favor. I know you're trying to deal with the book and everything, but I've no business experience. Would you go with me to the office so we can see what is happening? I know we've been there once . . ."

"But we were asking about Rod, not the business." Annie did not want to take any more time from the book she wasn't researching and wasn't writing because too much in life was swamping her but she added, "Of course, I will. As soon as it opens."

CHAPTER 23

Despite the boss not being around all three programmers were at their desks, bent over their computers, when Janet and Annie entered Rod's office. The clock said 8:32. The women closed their umbrellas and dropped them in the stand to the left of the door.

Maud was just hanging up her raincoat. She handed Annie and Janet coat hangers. "I'll get the coffee going. I've brought in chocolate biscuits."

"Is the training room being used today?" Annie asked.

Maud shook her head.

"Then let's use it for a staff meeting."

No one seemed to question her authority. Annie had them move their chairs from behind the banks of tables with computers so she could see their faces. Outside the rain battered the windows.

"Janet has asked me not to check up on the company so much as to try and understand it so if decisions have to be made, she can do it. We haven't heard from Rod and frankly . . ." she put her hand on Janet's shoulder . . . "we don't know if he is alive. We hope so. We can't do anything about that but we can make sure that the company keeps running and everyone still has jobs."

"So what do you need from us? From me?" Maud asked.

"We'd like to talk to all of you one by one, see what projects you're working on, what business you are trying to get in, what

116

bills need to be paid, what invoices need to be collected, that sort of thing."

"No problem," said the oldest of the programmers. "I've been with Rod since he started and I know I speak for the others when I say we will do everything we can to help."

The programmer named William was fifty-one. For the next three hours he and the others gave Annie and Janet insight into the status of every project for every client, the rates they would be charged and who was working on what. Rod had a well-run shop going for him.

They had three contracts to train clients on new software that their companies were installing. The salesman, Malcolm, was sure he would be bringing in at least two more before the end of the month but William explained how Malcolm was often off on his timing. "The contracts come in, but usually later than he predicts, probably because the clients fart around."

At lunchtime, Annie and Janet thanked them and headed into the storm. The rain pelted down. "Let's go to a restaurant that goes back to the eighteen hundreds. I know you love history," Janet said. "And it's my treat."

The restaurant was almost empty and the women guessed that the weather had kept everyone away. While waiting to order Annie called Roger, who grumped that he *supposed* that he could fix something for himself.

When their lamb stews arrived along with their salads, Annie said, "At least you know that you'll have an income."

"But I can't run the company," Janet said.

"No, but you can hire a manager or promote William. Have an accountant check the books. I'll tell you what questions to ask for as long as you need me to."

"You were brilliant this morning," Janet said.

"Only because I've been in and out of that world for most of my adult life. Put me on a painting course, the word 'brilliant' is removed from the dictionary."

"I wish I could find that stick thing he always carried, but it is probably with him."

"Stick thing?"

"Maud talked about them. It was a thing that went into the computer. He had two of them. He would mutter he wasn't going to be caught up in any clouds."

"They're USB drives, or keys. Different places have different names for them, like in America they're called 'thumb drives,' " said Annie. "As soon as we finish eating we're going home and look for them."

"But you need to work on your . . ."

"After the search."

"Before. I'll go home, make sure Roger has everything, do a bit of my own work and tonight we'll start hunting."

"But . . ."

"No, you need to start finding out stuff about Ethel whatever her name was."

CHAPTER 24

Martin Bruber's instinct screamed something wasn't right with Johnson, which had nothing to do with the fact that Johnson had so subtly taunted him about searching his room that he could have assumed it was his imagination.

After putting on his ski jacket and boots, he left the Golden Aigle. An unpredicted light snow drifted down, not enough to interfere with the afternoon skiing, but enough to lay a cover on the slopes where the man-made snow had been spread.

It was still early for snow even up on the mountain. In Zurich, Geneva and Lausanne the leaves were still turning color and the pickers with their large baskets on their backs were harvesting the last of the grapes. It would be great if climate change acted in favor of the ski lodges this year. If many of the higher stations could open six weeks ahead of schedule, it would be good for the local economy, he thought.

The weather probably would enhance skiing for his CEOs, for Martin thought of them as his whenever he was in charge of their security, a bit like teachers who called the students in their classroom "my kids."

The skiing did not enhance his assignment. There were too many places along the trail where a sniper could hide. No matter how many men he assigned, it was impossible to cover the entire run. More than once at one of these meetings, a CEO had gone off *piste*.

Idiots, he thought. They think they are invincible.

Martin wished he could have time to do a couple of runs. As a boy, growing up in the Bernese Oberland, he was on the slopes every winter day after school let out. His dreams of being an Olympic skier were destroyed with a bad fall that had twisted his leg, not so badly that he couldn't ski, run or play tennis, but enough so that high-level competition was out of the question.

He missed the simplicity of his childhood just as he missed the mountains and forests whenever he was down in the city. Despite all his years in Zurich, he was still a mountain boy at heart.

Günther was sweeping off the sidewalks on the left-hand side of the street across from the supermarket where the villagers bought their groceries. A pregnant woman, wife of one of the electricians, waddled out. Her three-year-old son tagged along behind her rubbing his eyes. Martin remembered her name was Antoinette. Even though it was early in the day, she looked pale and worn.

"How would your son like a ride on my shoulders?" he asked the boy.

"Herr Bruber, that would be wonderful." When she smiled she looked only slightly less tired.

Martin hoisted the boy up and told him to pretend that he was riding a reindeer.

"Can't you be an elephant? *Mutti* read me a book about an elephant king."

"I can be an elephant." Martin had never been able to have a conversation like that with Johann. He had been five before he talked.

It is what it is, he thought. The mother and son lived between the grocery store and where Martin was heading. When the woman started to slip on a piece of black ice, he grabbed her before she tumbled.

"Please be careful," he said as she entered the gated garden leading to her chalet, and he put the small boy down. "Your elephant needs to check out the rest of the jungle."

The child laughed.

Martin continued to the small chalet at the end of the village almost out of sight in the forest. It was the smallest building in the compound, four rooms: living room, bath, kitchen and safe room, which wasn't like the safe room built into houses where people could run if there was an intruder. Nor did it have the bomb shelter that had been required for every Swiss building.

This was a room that he had designed and had insisted be built into this building, the least conspicuous one. He had had special wiring installed and a single line to his office, which he called.

Anne-Joëlle Savary, his personal secretary, although she hated being referred to as a secretary, picked up on the first ring. He didn't need to have a webcam to know that there would be a huge mug of coffee next to her. No dainty demitasse for this woman, who was large in every way and in everything she did. Without her, he would have been lost.

The reason she hated being called a secretary, he knew, was that she had been thoroughly trained by the Swiss security forces. Her abilities to discover the undiscoverable were some of the best he had ever seen. Secretary was the title decided upon because Martin had learned long ago that people often talked in front of secretaries as if they weren't there. So many people underrated secretaries in other ways, not knowing how powerful some could be, and Anne-Joëlle was one of the powerful ones.

"Johnson?" he asked her.

"I don't think that's his real name."

"Why?" He regretted asking as soon as he said it. She never discussed her information searches.

"Can you get me some fingerprints? DNA would be even better."

"I'll try." The bank operated its own labs for fingerprinting, DNA testing and many other investigative procedures, surpassing many police departments. All Martin had to do was tell Herr Auer what he needed, and he was given the okay to order it.

"There's another thing," she said.

"What?"

"I'm not sure. The anger against the banks is picking up again."

Martin sighed. The anger against banks had been ongoing since the crash of 2008. "Do you have anything concrete?" He could imagine her shaking her head as she always did when she said no. "Look into it as much as you can. I'll help when I get back to Zurich after this meeting."

When he disconnected, he sat there for a few minutes. He needed to do another sweep of the conference room to make sure there were no listening devices other than his own. That the CEOs changed from the conference room in the hotel to the conference room in the chalet was another security feature. If it said hotel on the agenda, then the meeting would switch to the conference room.

He called Claude, one of his technicians. Claude appeared as a kid to Martin, even though he was pushing thirty. He had those innocent eyes of a teen and just enough pimples to enhance the youthful image. Martin knew that given a few more years, Claude would be one of the best security men in the business. His instincts combined with his technical knowledge made Martin feel old and out of date. It was Claude who brought new equipment and ideas to Martin.

When Claude arrived in jeans and his Irish knit sweater, they unlocked the door to the wood-paneled conference room. The beams in the ceiling had been carved with images of leaves.

Unlike ninety-nine percent of conference rooms in the world, this one had no huge table. The first thing anyone saw entering the room was a massive fireplace, which had logs and pinecones ready to be ignited before the CEOs were due.

Red Persian rugs with complicated designs covered the broad plank wooden floors.

A small kitchen area had a refrigerator stocked with every-thing they might want to nibble or drink. Meals could be brought down from the Golden Aigle, but seldom were.

Television screens and audiovisual equipment were hidden behind wooden panels, but were seldom used. Auer said this was because most of the men, and it was always men because of the masculine environment, liked the old-time feel.

The cabin looked authentic and old, but in reality had been built only five years before. Auer felt that for some clients and as well as for his fellow CEOs the atmosphere was more relaxed.

Six red leather chairs were flanked by small tables, each with a laptop embedded in the wood. Martin hated those laptops, the only touch of modernity visible when anyone entered. Too easy to hack into, and although he had tried to persuade his boss to remove them, Herr Auer had ruled that they were going to stay. Twice Martin had come back with reasons to at least dismantle them: twice Herr Auer had refused. Martin was still debating a third go-around on the subject.

Martin didn't like that this cabin was being used at all. The way it was located at the edge of the forest, people could move up and attack it, but Auer liked it because it was more informal, which made many clients feel more at home.

Martin respected that with Auer he could raise an issue more than once as long as he presented additional facts of which he was sure. If he had any doubts, those too could be presented. Auer was a reasonable boss compared to some Martin had had in the past, which was why he did not want to make a mistake.

Claude used his latest toy, as he called the equipment that

would reveal a camera or microphone.

"I've got one." Claude's voice registered glee. "A camera."

"That's mine," Martin said.

"Holy shit," Claude said, then frowned. "Were you testing me?"

Martin shook his head. "I wanted to see if anyone came into the room. It was a double check in case the sweep missed something. When you have time can you check what's on it?"

His cell phone rang. A glance showed it was his home number. His wife almost never telephoned him at work.

"What's up?"

"The school called. Johann has disappeared."

Martin understood the meaning of the phrase "his heart sank." His son was not capable of being out on his own. He would get on trams without a ticket and not think to look for cars when crossing the street. He did know where he lived because they had played a game where the apartment was the Starship Enterprise and Johann was the satellite ship going to dock. Johann had led his parents directly to the flat every time they played the game, but he didn't know the actual street name or number. "How long ago?"

"About an hour. I'm heading to the school now."

Martin weighed his alternatives. "I'm coming home. If you find him call me."

Auer would not be happy. However, he had a Down syndrome cousin, which helped him understand, at least somewhat, when there was a crisis with Johann.

Martin left the cabin and went to the bottom of the slope to wait for Auer to finish his ski run.

"A problem?" the CEO asked. His cheeks were bright red from the cold. Unlike the other CEOs his ski clothing did not look new but well used, which it was. Martin had overheard Auer joking with the other CEOs, who teased him about his ski suit. He claimed that he preferred spending every spare minute on the slopes during the winter season rather than taking time looking for new duds.

Bruber also knew that Auer was not one to chase the latest anything. He bought top quality and wore it out. His car, which he kept in top condition, was nine years old.

Martin explained about Johann.

"Go."

As Martin turned to go, Auer asked, "Who'll be in charge?"

"Claude Müller."

"Good man, let me know about your son."

On the way down the mountain, he pulled over to call his wife to tell her he was coming. He pictured her sitting in the headmaster's office listening to their excuses.

His phone indicated another call was coming through.

"Hold on, love, I'll be back with you in a minute."

Claude was on the other line. "Where are you?"

"Heading home."

"Home?"

"Family emergency."

"There's an emergency here. The tape showed someone coming into the conference room." Claude was breathless.

"Can we see who?"

"He's got on a ski mask I think . . . he's deep in shadow. And he never put on any lights. If the shutters had been closed there wouldn't have been enough light to even see that much."

Martin thought about the corridor lights, which were operated by a switch that people pushed: they lasted for three minutes before going off automatically. He'd asked that the lights be changed to those that were body heat sensitive, but Auer had vetoed it as being unnecessary saying "You think of ninety-nine things out of a hundred. I'll risk that hundredth." Had those lights been installed, the door could not have been opened without triggering the light and the camera might have made it easier to identify the man.

"I'm coming back."

He switched the phone back to talk to his wife. "There's an emergency here. I have to go back to the village." He hung up before he could hear her reply, but he imagined she would be furious. He was furious with himself too because he knew he hated his choices.

Chapter 25

For the first time since his release from the hospital, Roger showed some positive enthusiasm as he, Janet and Annie started a house search for Rod's computer keys. The idea that Rod might have them with him didn't deter them.

By agreement they started in Rod's home office, which resembled an electronics store. Two mismatched chairs, one of which was on casters, were on one side of a desk; on the other side was just an ordinary folding chair, one that could be found in any church hall.

The walls were forest green. Several of Janet's paintings, of shops, kids in school uniforms, two musicians on a bandstand and scenics, covered about eighty percent of the free wall space opposite the shelves. The remaining space had a whiteboard with algorithms that made no sense to any of them. At least Annie guessed they were logarithms.

Heavy forest green drapes came to the floor. Venetian blinds of the same color were shut. Janet opened the blinds just enough to let in dribs and drabs of light.

One of Rod's laptops was on the desk. Janet admitted she didn't know how many computers, laptops, tablets or smartphones her husband owned and even if she did, she wasn't sure where he would have kept them.

"I'm surprised the police didn't ask for all his equipment," Roger said. "But then they may have not understood how many gadgets he did have."

Annie noticed a flicker cross his face, which she read as sadness. Having gone from being one of the best murder detectives in Paris to running the Gendarmerie in a small French tourist village had been hard enough. Raising his daughter had helped him justify the change, but every now and then when they were talking in bed, he'd admit how much he missed the challenge of the hunt, as he called it.

"I found a tablet under the mattress when I changed the sheets this morning. I guess when they took the office computers, he hid other equipment here in case they came for them."

"A good police search would have looked here *and* under a mattress," Roger said.

"Did he use them all?" Roger asked. "Do they all have the same information on them, do you know?"

Janet shrugged. "I kinda knew he wasn't always using the same one, because the covers had different colors and designs. My favorite had pretty purple swirls. It's in the clothes basket in our bathroom. Should I get it?"

"Yes," Roger and Annie said at the same time.

While she was gone Annie said to Roger, "He was insane about backing up. At ZBPI, he used to drive everyone nuts. I swear if you hit one key, he wanted three backups. Simon was the same."

Janet returned and put the laptop on the desk in front of Annie, who turned it on. It made the usual startup noises. Annie hit a couple of keys and then threw herself back in the chair. "Damn!—password protected. Why should I be surprised?"

"Think you can crack it?" Janet asked.

"I'm a tech writer, not a hacker." Annie closed the cover. "We need a hacker." She sat back in the chair.

"What about Marc?" Roger asked.

"Marc?"

"You know the kid who used to live on the same floor when

128

you lived near the airport: the one whose father was killed?" His tone was that of someone talking to a kindergarten kid.

Annie hated it when he used that patronizing voice. Had he been healthy, she would have challenged him.

"What's he up to?" Roger went back to a normal tone.

Annie thought about it. She hadn't seen Marc in over a year. "He's moved to Lausanne to study at the EPFL. I never thought of him as a hacker."

"When I talked to him at our wedding, he said he was majoring in computer science. Might be worth giving him a call to see if he'd like a weekend in the UK," Roger said.

Annie wasn't certain his number was on her phone, but she went into the bedroom to retrieve her pocketbook with the phone. She called it her dumb phone. Despite her dexterity with computers, she had a hatred for phones, landlines or mobiles. "They interrupt me," she claimed. She kept her dumb phone off, putting it on only if she was meeting someone who might need to talk to her or if Roger asked her to for some reason. Only four people had the number: Roger, Gaëlle and her father and mother. Anyone else she gave it to had to promise to erase it as soon as they didn't need it for whatever meet-up they had scheduled. Annie didn't go so far as to check if they did, although she wanted to.

On the other hand she used all the other social media, having "friends" and "business contacts" galore on this or that social media site. She would talk for hours on Skype to a friend, but let that same friend use the telephone and Annie hung up fast. "I don't care if it makes sense or not," she said. "Sometimes I want to be totally incommunicado, especially if I'm on a train or bus."

However, she was beginning to realize that a mobile phone could be used for her banking and a whole lot more things. Maybe she'd upgrade but she knew she still wouldn't give anyone her phone number.

She thumbed through her contact list. To Roger and Gaëlle she'd admitted it wasn't fair that she had friends' phone numbers but wouldn't give out hers. "Consistency sucks."

She did have Marc's number. She pushed the buttons, muttered when the call didn't go through, then redialed, remembering this time to use the forty-one country code.

Marc picked up. "Annie, I thought you'd forgotten me," he said.

She pictured him as a little boy when he used to hang out in her flat and again as a teenager who grew so fast he couldn't quite keep up with his body and shouldn't have been allowed near anything breakable.

He'd sought refuge with her parents when his mother had been accused of killing his father. They'd helped him reestablish a relationship with his mother in the aftermath, although the woman was sadly lacking in any maternal instinct.

Their history meant that time lapses between their seeing each other didn't matter.

"I'd never forget you." Annie then explained what she needed.

"I'm not sure I'm good enough to break into a computer of someone you describe as a computer genius. Why isn't he available?"

"He's missing. We are hoping what is on his computer will help us find him."

Silence.

"Are you still there?"

"Yes, I'm thinking of someone I know, but I'm a bit afraid of giving you the name. You never know who might be listening to us."

Annie didn't like the sound of that. She hoped Marc wasn't getting in with a bad group of hackers. "Could you ask him if he'd be willing to come over and look at the computer? I'd pay for the ticket."

"Won't work. Could I come and pick it up and take it to him or her?"

"You are being cagey if you aren't identifying the sex. You're not getting yourself in any trouble are you?"

"And if I were, I wouldn't tell you on the phone. Of course, I could give it a try first."

Annie had Marc hold while she consulted with Janet and Roger, the latter saying, "It would be good to see the kid again."

They agreed that she would arrange for the last Geneva-Luton flight on Friday.

After Annie had hung up, Janet said, "If we find the USB thingies maybe we won't need this Marc person or his friend."

"If we find any sort of key, I'm sure it will be password protected too," Annie said.

Roger sat in a chair and let out a breath.

"Tired?" Janet asked him, which Annie appreciated. Her husband did not like being babied but would be more tolerant if it came from someone else.

"No, studying the room on how to start the search." After a few minutes he gave Annie instructions to start on the left side of the door, and Janet the right. "Feel down the walls, look behind the photos. When they got to the desk, he had them check the drawers for false bottoms. They felt under the desk. The process took two hours and then some.

"Nothing." Janet flopped on the chair behind the desk. Roger was still sitting. Annie was standing by the window. The sun was beginning to set outside.

"What next?" Annie asked and then said, "What about your bedroom? His clothes, his pockets: it's easy to stick a key inside."

They went into the couple's bedroom. The walls, which were painted a terra-cotta color, were covered with Janet's paintings, all except for one wall. It had a mural of a place where the couple had stayed in Italy during their honeymoon.

"Romantic," Annie said when Janet told her what the scene was.

"Not so much. After I painted it, Rod asked if it were a real place, even though we had been looking at it every day as we ate breakfast on a balcony. Of course, he was working on his laptop, a variation of the old days, when husbands read the newspaper while eating."

"Take everything out of the wardrobe," Roger said.

The women went to the large wooden armoire and removed all the clothing. Two-thirds belonged to Janet, the rest to Rod. Mostly his clothes were jeans, sweaters, and T-shirts. He owned one good suit, although Annie had trouble picturing Rod in a suit.

When the wardrobe was empty, they felt down the back wall and the drawers for a false bottom. Before putting clothes back in the armoire, they turned every piece of clothing inside out.

"Aha," Annie said as she pulled her hand out of a windbreaker pocket. She held up a small key chain, about the size of her thumb, that was shaped like a pig.

Janet and Roger looked at her. When she decapitated the pig by pulling it apart, it revealed a USB key.

"How did you know that?" Janet asked.

"I saw a whole bunch of animal computer keys on sale," she said. "I almost bought one for myself."

They went to Annie's room, where her laptop rested on the bureau on top of a lace runner. She inserted it into a slot. "Shit, password protected."

Before they went any further, she made reservations for Marc, then called him with the information. After Annie had hung up she said, "I feel as if I'm in a bad, bad spy movie."

"Just because we found one thing, doesn't mean there aren't others. Keep looking," Roger said as he sat on the bed, his back propped up with pillows against the headboard.

Annie thought he was looking too tired. "Let's break for dinner, and then we'll continue. Roger, do you want to lie down as Janet and I try and prepare a feast?"

That he didn't argue she took as a sign that he truly was overtired. At the same time, she guessed that he felt useful, at least for the moment, but she couldn't maintain emergencies for the rest of his life to keep him happy.

CHAPTER 26

Annie tiptoed up to the bedroom where Roger was sleeping, only he wasn't. He was sitting up in bed reading.

The house was quiet after dinner. Janet was downstairs doing some preliminary work on her new commission. At night, despite the MacKenzies having installed the maximum lighting possible, it wasn't strong enough for Janet's color work. Thus she found other things to do. This night she'd been sketching in the base of the portrait that she would paint from the photos she'd been given by her client. She'd sent Annie off to bed.

"You're not asleep," Annie said to Roger.

He held up his book. "I can't concentrate. I can't even say it's because it's in English, because it's in French."

Annie sat on the edge of the bed.

"Sleep with me tonight, at least until I start snoring."

Annie changed into her flannel nightgown and slipped under the thick, white duvet. Although the room was chilly, Roger had the bed well warmed.

He put his arm around her and she snuggled in. "I can't make love to you."

"I wasn't expecting it."

"What if I can never make love to you again? I'm so afraid I'll never get it up."

That Roger was admitting his fear was almost as frightening as the heart attack itself. She'd known when she married him that the fifteen-year difference in their ages might have some effect, not just on their love making but on things that interested them or things that one wanted to do and the other didn't that were age appropriate.

The impact of their differing interests had already led to a rocky relationship not just based on age differences. Thanks to her having lived in the United States, Holland, Germany and Switzerland and having worked in almost every European country, she was able to adjust to the cultural differences. She didn't care if Roger liked the fork prongs down at the dinner table or drank his morning tea out of a bowl—she could deal with it. Although he'd visited other countries, including America, he was slower to adapt. Then again, maybe it was just because he was a man, or then again, maybe he was just like that.

The sex between them had always been good, not just technically. When he was deep inside her, she had felt as one with him and that nothing else mattered.

"If we never have sex again, we can make love," she said. She looked up to find his eyes were overflowing. She brushed them away with her thumb and snuggled next to him after she turned off the light.

CHAPTER 27
EAST ANGLIA 640

Annie sat down at the computer with the notes she'd gleaned so far. If she didn't start, she would never make her deadline. Where she was really lacking information was in the small details. When she wrote her first book, she'd been able to visit the concentration camp and the streets of Hamburg. Even if it were seven and eight decades later, she could imagine what those places would have looked like in the 1930s or 1940s. Here in the 640s, she had less to go on. She started thinking about Etheldreda's mother.

Sawara padded along the wooden floor corridor holding a candle. All doors were closed. The only light came from the kitchen at the end of the hallway, not that the wooden slits in the wooden walls of the outer rooms would allow much light. Because the summer heat had not penetrated the building, she shivered in her light wool gown.

In the kitchen the smell of baking bread reinforced her hunger.

The cook looked up. There was a cauldron over an open fire in the middle of the room vented through a hole in the ceiling.

Annie had read about the Anglo-Saxon's home, but she still couldn't quite imagine a cooking system without at least a fireplace. It must have left the kitchen very, very smoky.

★ ★ ★ ★ ★

"May I help you, my lady?" The cook was younger than Sawara and was the servant who had been able to preserve their meat through the winter.

Annie guessed preservation was a problem but wrote herself a note to check it later.

"I wanted to tell you that my husband will be here for dinner." Sawara had not expected Onna back for another few days, but he'd sent a horseman ahead to announce his early arrival. Whenever he was away, the house took on a relaxed air, which Sawara preferred to the swirl of activity with too many men stomping about when her husband was in residence.

Onna had ridden to Mercia earlier in the week to meet with his ruling counterpart, Penda. Sawara thought it wasted effort. Penda wanted to be Bretwalda over all the Anglo-Saxon lands in the Heptarchy and she was sure her husband would in no way convince him to seek peace, not power.

The names and words were driving Annie crazy. It was like learning another language, one she found illogical. The names did not seem to survive that period of history—neither in England nor in Germany from where the Anglo-Saxons had migrated. She wrote a note—create a dictionary at the end. Include the words Bretwalda, Anglo-Saxon top leader, Heptarchy, the combined kingdoms. The book would also need a chart with who was who. Even a map might help untangle the history for the readers, if she could produce something worth printing. Never had she been so unsure of herself on any project and she didn't like it one tiny bit.

★ ★ ★ ★ ★

Fighting: that was all the kings of Wessex, Kent, East Anglia, Northumbria, Mercia, South Saxon and East Saxon ever thought about.

What did it gain?

An early death, that's what. Sawara was fed up with it. Sometimes she couldn't sleep for worrying that her husband would be killed. His death would be a catastrophe for her and her children.

Her husband had survived the last ten years as King of East Anglia, a miracle, since his predecessors had been killed in a short time one after another, leaving her in constant fear of his death.

She had not been that happy about marrying Onna, even though he was the grandson of a grand ruler, but with the exception of his loving to fight, he had turned out to be a good husband and not just because he presented her with gold rings, necklaces, bracelets and belts.

Annie had found enough pictures of Anglo-Saxon jewelry to be comfortable with at least this part of the story.

Admittedly, she loved these gifts and took great pleasure in wearing them. No, the reason that Onna was a good husband was that he never hit her. He treated her far better than her mother had been treated by her father or how her sisters were treated by their husbands.

His goodness was shown in other little things such as asking her if she were warm enough and getting a cover if she said she was cold, holding her hand as they took a walk on a beautiful day, or making sure he held something over her head when it was raining.

He listened to her ideas as well, something that many men of their class did not do. He supported her interest in making sure that the farmers in the area had the tools and seed they needed to produce the barley that went into beer making.

Although farming was an anathema to a warrior, he encouraged her when she told the farmers to plant wheat, parsnips, carrots, onions and cabbage. He said he ate better at home with more variety than anywhere else in the world.

Onna loved to eat and drink yet was able to retain his figure, a fact that she loved in bed. Touching his chest was like caressing a board. A board never reacted as he did.

She'd been a good wife to him besides keeping him happy in bed. She made sure that every cow was used from birth to death when it would become hides, glue and, of course, meat, but she would never have had a cow slaughtered just for meat. A cow could produce milk for cheese.

Annie stopped writing for a moment. Had she put in too many details? She knew she had a tendency to do that; when her research found something she wanted to use it no matter how well it fitted. She'd leave it in for now. She could always delete things later.

Onna said that Sawara's greatest gift to him was Jurmim, now a stocky four-year-old, who raced from the moment he woke until he fell asleep, usually wherever he'd been playing last. Whoever was nearest would pick him up and take him to his bed.

His two older sisters, Seaxburga and Etheldreda, had been quiet children. What the children in between would have been like, had they lived, Sawara had no idea. One didn't survive her time in the womb, two lived only through one moon, and another never saw her first birthday. She seemed to bear daughters; thus when Jurmim was born, his strength and good health were a blessing and increased her husband's satisfaction with her.

After the birth Onna immediately gave thanks to his god, while Sawara thanked Woden and Oestre. At times, she worried that the old gods would be angry at this new religion, which more and more people seemed to embrace. Or she should say new religions, although both talked about Mary and Jesus.

Religious conflict—Annie wondered how much she should concentrate on that theme.

The Celtic Christians had one set of ideas and those Christians from the continent had another. What made her laugh, although she would never admit it, both talked about only one true god. Well, if there was only one true god, why did they argue about how he was to be worshipped? No, she would stick with her own gods, albeit it more and more silently. If her husband wanted to think she'd converted to his way of thinking, it did no harm to anyone, most of all herself.

"Have you seen the children?" she asked the cook.

"I told them to go outside, all three of them. Jurmin was running around the fire. Driving me crazy, he was."

Sawara could not fault the cook for her concern. Last month Jurmin had reached into the fire to pull out some roasting nuts. Neither Onna nor she had punished him, figuring the pain of the burn was lesson enough.

Her children had spent too much of the winter indoors when the snow piled up outside. Now the trees were thick with light green leaves, and the smell of lilacs along the south side of the house almost overrode the odor of the manure spread in the newly planted fields.

She went outside. Onna's and her house, with its ten rooms on one level, was surrounded by fifty-two smaller houses, each one of which would have fit in the main hall where Onna received guests. Those houses were made of wood turned gray by the elements. The roofs were thatch and most only had a door. Windowless houses were better for retaining heat in winter and discouraging it in summer.

To the left of the village was a fenced-in area where some hundred sheep roamed. Within the week, their coats would be sheared and the spinning would begin. All the women did it together, catching up on gossip at the same time.

Before the forest began, Sawara saw men plowing and women following with their seed bags. But where were *her* children?

As she walked through the village she was greeted with slight bows. When she asked about the whereabouts of her daughters and son, the women in turn would talk about children as a worry as well as a blessing. More hands to help, more hands to cause problems, she'd heard as least three times, before one woman said she'd spotted all three going into the forest.

No matter that Jurmin was forbidden to enter the forest. He was small enough that an animal might consider him dinner. Sawara knew that there was a stream where they could dip their feet, although if any of the villagers were fishing, the children would be chased away for disrupting a possible catch. There was always the danger that they would fall in and drown or that they would catch cold from the icy water.

It was at the stream, full from the spring rains, rushing and tumbling over rocks, that she found her family. The bank had grass sprinkled with purple violets.

Jurmin was tied to a cross staked into the ground, his arms extended. His head held a wreath of twigs, but at least there were no thorns and his feet were firmly placed on the ground on each side of the stake making the center part of the cross.

"What are you doing?" Sawara demanded.

"Playing crucifixion," ten-year-old Etheldreda said. "Jurmin is Christ and we're praying to him."

Sawara marched to the cross and untied her son's hands.

"Seaxburga, you should know better. You should have stopped your sister," she said to her twelve-year-old daughter.

Seaxburga said nothing.

Sawara looked at her son's wrists. The leather cord had not been tight enough to leave too many marks. She lashed out at both girls, catching Etheldreda in the face and Seaxburga on the shoulder. "Go home both of you. Now."

The girls ran, but Etheldreda turned and said, "I'll pray for you, Mama."

Sawara sat on a large rock and pulled Jurmin in her lap. "Are you all right?"

"I like being Christ," the child said. "He is more powerful than any Bretwalda."

As Sawara rocked her son, she thought how much she hated the new religion that so captivated her family. She hated it, just hated it. What was wrong with Woden? With Thor? Despite what some people believed, she was sure her gods were far more powerful.

CHAPTER 28

Claude Müller and Martin Bruber ran the tape frame by frame trying to get any clues at all as to the identity of the intruder. He was big, big enough to be Johnson, Martin thought. Because the man was totally dressed in black, including a black ski mask, the clothing gave nothing away and just being big wasn't enough of an identification.

They watched as the man moved out of camera range. Martin wasn't sure if the man guessed there were hidden cameras. Besides Claude and himself, only Auer knew about them.

Auer often asked to re-watch the meetings that were held in the cabin. Sometimes he insisted Martin do it with him, asking for his opinion on nuances of body language or if there were speech patterns that could identify a person as untrustworthy.

Bankers are always untrustworthy was what Martin wanted to say, but he didn't. Although he was multilingual, his language skills were not such that he could pick up a variation of speech in English or French that indicated a person was lying in the same way he could in the Swiss German. He was aware that the other CEOs spoke English using different words and phrases, not to mention slang peculiar to where they lived. Even Auer, a far better linguist than most professionals, couldn't pick up on some nuances.

"We need to check everywhere the camera isn't filming."

Claude sighed. "That may mean we have to ask them to delay the afternoon meeting."

"Or move it," Claude said.

Martin shut off the camera. Claude clicked off the lights and together they locked the screening room located in a secure part of the basement of the Golden Aigle.

Martin was waiting when Christophe Auer came off the slope. His face was red as he pulled off his gloves. "This can't be good, if you're still here," the CEO said.

"There is a problem with the cabin." He explained in detail, watching a frown cross Auer's face and stay there.

"There's too much going on to delay the meeting," Auer said.

"Perhaps I should know."

"Not even you should know."

Martin wondered how he was expected to provide security if he wasn't aware of the full picture. "That does limit me."

Auer nodded. "I know. Do you think the room is safe for our meeting?"

"We've done a full sweep, but I can't guarantee it." He wondered what could be that important. Most CEOs attached much more importance to themselves than was merited.

"We could seal off the kitchen. You could meet there. That is a place no one would think to bug."

A smile almost hit Auer's mouth. "Can you guarantee *that*?"

"More so, even if not a hundred percent: no one would think that the CEOs of four of the biggest world banks would be conducting business in a hotel kitchen. Especially if you pretend it will be in the cabin up to the last minute." What Martin wasn't sure of was that the kitchen wasn't bugged, even though he had it checked the day before people arrived.

Claude could scan the security cameras that were positioned in the kitchen. "Don't say anything. Let everyone think you're going to the cabin. Then after lunch, lead them to the kitchen."

"I'll tell them they have to wash dishes," Auer said.

CHAPTER 29

"You must feel relieved with what the doctor said," Janet said as she parked across from the King's School near the arch where Rod had been hit by the bike. Roger was in the front seat and Annie in the back. Rain beat down on the roof of the yellow car.

"I'm glad the doctor says I'm coming along ahead of schedule," Roger said. "What I don't like is that he still thinks I should retire."

Annie didn't say anything. Once again she wished she'd stayed single in her studio loft with everything just as she liked it. There she could work at will and follow her passion of historical research or not, take off for months on some assignment, and not think about anyone but herself.

Hell, she'd even be content now if she could work on her current project without all the interruptions. At the same time, however, she didn't want a life without Roger, Gaëlle and even Hannibal, their German Shepherd. Nothing is ever a hundred percent perfect, she thought, only when she'd been single she'd thought it had been. Get over it, she told herself. It is what it is. You made the choice.

The house was a short walk from where Janet parked the car but with the pouring rain, they huddled under the one giant umbrella Janet kept in the car. When they'd left the house well before lunchtime, the sun had been out. Sometime while they were in the cardiologist's office, a storm front had moved in.

As they opened the door, Mercury slunk toward them on his stomach. "What did you do? Did you get in the garbage again?" Janet asked. The dog kept his tail between his legs.

They hung their coats in the closet.

"I'll put the kettle on," Annie said. "Oh my God!"

The kitchen cupboards had been emptied. Pots, pans and recipe books were thrown all over. Drawers had been pulled out and removable shelves had been removed.

"The dining room," Janet screamed. All the dishes were taken out of the buffet, many had been smashed. The drawers had been emptied of silverware, cloth napkins and placemats and had been left upside down.

Roger checked the lounge. All the books had been tossed from the floor-to-ceiling bookcases that were on each side of the white marble fireplace. The ashes in the grate had been emptied onto the tile in front of the fireplace. "At least they didn't put the ashes on the carpet," he said to the two women who'd joined him.

"My studio." Annie and Roger followed Janet into the studio. Anything that could have been emptied was. Paintings, which had been hanging on the wall, had been flung onto her worktable. Only one painting had been damaged: the one she'd been working on. The still wet paint was smudged. "Shit," Janet said. "The one time I work in oils, this happens. I swear to God, I'll only use acrylics in the future."

"Upstairs, and Roger, walk, don't run," Annie said.

All the bedrooms had been searched.

"We weren't gone *that* long . . . no more than three hours between the doctor and lunch," Janet said.

"We don't know how many people were in here, but it's obvious they were even checking for things like false bottoms." He sat on the edge of Janet and Rod's bed, although the mattress had been thrown to the side of the room opposite the door. "We need to get the police in here."

Janet ran into Rod's office. "His laptop and tablet are gone."

"The pig?" Roger asked.

Annie reached into her pocketbook and pulled it out. "I just hope Rod still backs up everything three times. If so this will be identical to the laptop. If not . . ." She shrugged.

Lake and Welch arrived within ten minutes of Janet's phone call. "What a mess," Welch said as he shook his umbrella just outside the door. He turned the umbrella stand upright and dropped his umbrella in it.

"They probably didn't find what they were looking for," Roger said as the men surveyed the chaos.

Welch looked confused.

"If they had found something downstairs, they wouldn't have gone up. If they found something in Rod's office, they wouldn't have needed to trash the bedrooms. Of course, there's no way of knowing where they started."

"They weren't looking for money."

Janet pointed to an envelope on a bookshelf. Before she could touch it, Welch picked it up but not before he slipped on a rubber glove. "£321 inside," he said. "Ordinarily we wouldn't bother to fingerprint for a B&E but since we're investigating . . ."

Lake held up his hand. Welch did not finish his sentence.

"This has to be connected to Simon's murder. And maybe even Rod's disappearance, not to mention his hit and run bike accident," Annie said.

"What bike accident?" Lake asked.

Janet told him.

"Rod and Simon obviously were involved in something that made them targets," Welch said.

Lake shook his head. "I'm getting a fingerprint crew in here." He pressed one key on his mobile and made the request.

"If they had any intelligence they would have worn rubber gloves," Annie said.

"Maybe not." Janet pointed to a broken plate that had blood on it.

"DNA if you ever find the perps," Roger said.

Annie looked at Roger, who was very pale and holding onto the back of a chair.

"My husband is recovering from a heart attack. Do you think he could lie down?"

"I'm fine," Roger said.

"I'll call Catherine and see if we can go over there," Janet said to Annie before facing Lake. "She lives next door. Frankly, I don't want to be here when your men tramp around my house." Then she burst into tears, but when Annie went to comfort her, Janet gave a wink that Annie read as Janet was issuing tears to help Roger rest without making him look like a wimp.

CHAPTER 30

Annie was frustrated that Marc was not coming until the weekend. She was frustrated that she wasn't getting the work done on Etheldreda as fast as she needed to get it done. She was frustrated that Roger wasn't as healthy as he had been or they thought he'd been. She was just plain frustrated and frustrated that she was frustrated. All of this she kept to herself.

Annie had never been interested in being a martyr, but at the moment she felt Janet and Roger had enough worries. Her acting as a spoiled child would add nothing.

She and Janet had spent most of Thursday returning the house to some kind of order. "At least, this gives me a reason to clean and throw out things I should have thrown out long ago," Janet said.

Roger was given the chore of making sure the teapot was full and lunch and dinner were made. When that didn't satisfy him, Janet had him put photos back into an album and file papers. "There's nothing in there that's secret enough for us to hide," she said when he worried that it would be delving into the MacKenzies' private affairs.

The downstairs living and dining rooms, the kitchen and the art studio, were fairly easy. The hardest part of righting the lounge was putting the books back onto the top shelves. Annie stood on the ladder while Janet handed books to her. Just to be sure there was nothing hidden she shook each book before shelving it. A couple of old cards with doctors' appointments were found, an unopened birthday card with a date stamp from four years ago and a shopping list or two, but nothing that would give any indication as to what might have happened to Rod.

"He doesn't read my type of books: nincompoopy romances and mysteries. He'll do thrillers, but most of his reading is technical." Janet shelved three more books. "Annie?"

The tone made Annie climb back down the ladder.

"I can't believe that he might be dead. I should feel it, shouldn't I?"

Annie had no idea. She hugged Janet.

Muffled by her shoulder, Janet muttered, "If he is alive and hasn't told me where he's gone, and I find him, I'll kill him."

Then they both laughed, not that it was funny, but it released tension.

Upstairs the cleaning was slower. Although Janet had put clean bedding on last night, they threw the sheets downstairs for Roger to wash. "Make him feel useful," she whispered to Annie, "without straining him."

At the entrance to Rod's office they stopped. "Wouldn't it be lovely if we found something the robbers missed," Annie said. They exchanged looks. If the people who broke in were robbers, something would be missing, but nothing was—except for the laptops.

"With all the replacement computer equipment we should be buying stock in the manufacturer," Janet said.

"Tomorrow, do you mind if I go out and try and get some work done?" Annie asked.

"Oh, Annie, I'm so sorry you're involved in all this."

"Oh, Janet, I'm glad we're here for you," and she was, but she still had deadlines.

CHAPTER 31
EAST ANGLIA 652

Annie was absolutely determined to make today a good working day. The only way was to leave the house and find a café with wi-fi where she could cross-check a fact, buy a cup of coffee and hunker down. It was good to escape, if only temporarily the worry, about Rod, Roger and even her parents' banking problems. Work and historical research had always been not just her escape but her solace.

There was another problem: she felt no bond to this historical period. She could imagine herself walking into a Greek temple, carving a stone for a medieval church, or even ducking a bomb in World War II. But even if she'd found descriptions of Anglo-Saxon buildings and tools from the 600s, the warring mentality of the period, even compared to all the wars going on currently, was an enigma to her. Settling down with her laptop, a cappuccino on the table, she tried to channel what might have been in Etheldreda's head.

Etheldreda was warm under the skins covering her bed. Outside she heard the wind and wondered how much snow had fallen during the night. When she had peeked through the shutters before going to bed, the snow probably had been up to her knees, judging by the cow herder trudging through the drifts as he headed from the barn to his own small house at the other end of the village.

Her sister, Seaxburga, slept next to her. While Etheldreda woke many times every night, her sister would close her eyes and not open them until morning. Nor did she move. If she fell asleep on her left side she stayed that way. If she fell asleep on her back, she would be on her back all night.

Etheldreda twisted most nights. Often she would fold her hands and pray, which was about the only thing that made her fall asleep.

Early morning sounds from the kitchen where the cook was preparing the meal to break the fast penetrated the wooden wall. The kitchen was in the next room and the cook was never quiet in banging a kettle or shouting to her helper.

The worse part of getting up in January was the shock of the air against her heated skin before she could dress, not that she complained. All she had to do was to think of how Christ had suffered on the cross and her small discomfort became tolerable. When it was as cold as today, she needed to pray away her sin of wanting to be warm.

The household was not a happy one. Her father, Onna, was pressing her to marry instead of letting her retire to a convent as she had asked innumerable times. He said he needed the alliance with Tonbert of Fennlander, Prince of Gyrwas.

Her mother wasn't much help. Etheldreda spent much time in praying for her mother's soul. No matter what she said or how hard she prayed, her mother would not give up the old gods. The threat of hell wouldn't move her mother to reconsider. Instead, she just waved her hand as if brushing away an annoying insect.

When Etheldreda gave up making her own case, she asked her mother to plead with her father to let her join the convent. Sawara had replied that as daughter of a king Etheldreda's duty was to marry whomever her father selected.

Etheldreda thought her first duty was to God, her second to Jesus Christ and her third to the Virgin Mary. After that came her father's wishes. Although she knew the commandment "Honor thy father and thy mother," she thought that God had not intended her for marriage. His message, however, had not been received by her parents.

One good thing about the storm, it would delay marriage negotiations.

Seaxburga woke. Even when she woke she was slower to move. Etheldreda felt her sister come to consciousness slowly. Only then did she stretch and say, "good morning."

Etheldreda knew her sister was as believing as she herself was, but for her sister, her belief seemed to bring an inner peace as she glided through the day seldom getting upset by anything. Etheldreda, in contrast, could never feel she'd done enough to honor her God, His son or Christ's mother.

Try as she would, Annie couldn't identify with Etheldreda's religious fervor. But if she wanted to show the woman as she probably was, she would have to add in all this have-to-pray-a-lot stuff. At least she could understand having goals and the frustration of not being able to reach them because of things over which one had no control.

Before falling asleep, Seaxburga and she had talked about the two of them forming their own convent in the event her sister's husband died and/or once her children were grown.

Etheldreda knew she didn't belong in her childhood home. No sooner would she be on her knees than her mother would find another chore to be done. "There's nothing unholy about making sure our winter meat is properly salted," Sawara would say.

Her friend and confessor, Wilfrid, would say it was also her duty to obey her parents. God would not consider making sure meat was properly salted a sin even if said salting took away from prayer. She and Wilfred had become friends when her family had stopped at Lindisfarne, where he had been studying.

His knowledge of the new religion had impressed her. He had written her when he had gone to study in Gaul and his letters had contained passages from his Bible. Although Onna had insisted that all his children could read and write, they did not know Latin, Hebrew, Greek or Aramaic, in which the holy words were set down, but Wilfred wrote to her in their own tongue.

Annie made a note to herself by marking the type on the screen in red to check to see if it would be possible that Etheldreda might know Latin; if so, then Wilfred could write her in that tongue.

"Good morning," Etheldreda said to her sister.

Seaxburga stretched under the bear skins. "It's good to be home. I've missed you."

"I've missed you too. I'm glad your husband let you come."

"What are we doing today?"

"After prayers, we can spend some time with Jurmin."

"Is he still driving father crazy with his woodworking?" Seaxburga asked. "I was afraid to ask last night at dinner."

"Alfred has a new lathe and pedal. Jurmin is there almost every day working with it."

"I imagine that makes Father unhappy."

"Father wants him improving his spear throwing, not wasting time with old, dead trees, as he says."

"My husband said he could be one of the best throwers, if he would practice." Seaxburga turned on her side and propped her head up on her hand.

"Maybe Father is worried about the next war."

"Which is precisely why you need to marry Tonbert," Seaxburga said.

Etheldreda didn't want to hear it. Her sister always was more practical when it came to politics and the various kingdoms. Etheldreda didn't want to deal with any of it. She only wanted to be free to practice her vocation.

When Etheldreda finished dressing she headed to the altar in the back of the house. Kneeling, she prayed to be delivered from marriage until her knees hurt, a small price to pay to communicate with the Holy Mother Mary.

Seaxburga joined her and the two sisters prayed side-by-side until the call came for them to eat. As they walked toward the dining hall, they smelled roasting venison from the deer her father had killed before the storm.

"I've an idea," Seaxburga said.

"And it is?" Etheldreda stopped to look at her sister.

"Talk to Tonbert. Tell him your vow to remain a virgin. He might understand."

More than once, she thought God was testing her. Could he have put the idea of talking to Tonbert into her sister's head as a way for her to fulfill her mission in life?

Annie closed her laptop after starting a list.
Find out what the weather was like that winter?
Did they salt meat in those years?
Where did the salt come from?
Was it expensive?

Writing while researching, then rewriting, wasn't the way she liked to work, but she had no choice if she were to meet her deadline. And at that moment, her choice was to head back to the house.

CHAPTER 32

The CEOs convened in the kitchen, although Masterson had protested loudly, saying it was too uncomfortable. Auer had quieted him, saying it was for security.

Martin could see them perched on the stools that the chefs used when peeling carrots and potatoes. The dishes and pans from lunch were piled in the sink, ready to go into the dishwasher, but the staff had been chased out and told not to come back until it was time to prepare dinner.

Martin took an aspirin bottle from his jacket pocket and reached for a clean glass. He poured himself water from a carafe. Although his head hurt, it did not feel as if it were one of his migraines. They were infrequent, but when they hit, the pain left him unable to function.

Claude came up behind Martin and reported that after an inspection of all the other rooms, he had found nothing.

Anne-Joëlle called and said she'd examined the download of the intruder. She'd picked up nothing distinguishing. She asked Martin to have someone check on where the man's head came on the wall in the video so they at least could get a reading on his height.

Martin cursed himself for not thinking of that.

"Did you check footprints outside the chalet?" Anne-Joëlle asked.

"There were too many," Martin said.

For a while he sat watching the swinging door to the kitchen until he was aroused from his almost trance-like state by his mobile. It was his wife's number.

"I suppose you might like to know how the search for my son is going." Her tone could have caused frostbite of the ear.

"Of course."

She didn't ask why he hadn't called, which Martin would have thought was the next logical question.

"We found him. He was walking along the river heading to the Opera House. The headmaster was the one who guessed where he might be."

"How?"

"Something Johann said about the Captain landing in Zurich from a time machine and he hoped he wouldn't get wet on landing."

This would have been funny had it not been serious. Until now Johann had enjoyed the retelling of episodes of *Star Trek*, but had not created his own dramas.

"Where is he now?"

"Watching television. *Star Trek.*"

Punishing Johann would do no good. First, he was getting too big, and even if he never had been violent, he was large enough to do real damage. Although Martin was in good shape, he wasn't sure he could control his son if he were caught unawares. The idea that it might be coming to the time when they needed to find a residential home wove its way to the top of his mind. Until now his wife would not even consider it, and this was not the time to bring it up. He would later.

"When will you be home?"

"I honestly don't know."

"Right now, I honestly don't care."

CHAPTER 33

With the exception of running to the small restaurant for a quick lunch of an egg salad sandwich and cup of tea, Annie worked solidly at the library all morning and half the afternoon. Like all libraries, it felt like home, with the tables, computers and shelves and shelves of books. She had given up on writing in the café because of the noise; however, she still needed to leave the house to accomplish even the most minimal word count.

In one corner several rug rats sat cross-legged on the floor as a woman in her mid-fifties read a story. Annie had to force herself not to listen, because she saw by the children's' expressions that the reading was dramatic. Nothing like making young kids love books, she thought, and pulled out another reference work on the Anglo-Saxons.

One thing she found particularly frustrating was names, although place names were easy. She knew a place described as *barrow* would mean it was once a wood, and a *ham* was a village.

Her problem came with the names of the people. She had a similar problem in trying to keep the characters straight when reading translations of Russian or Chinese novels. She solved it by creating an Excel spreadsheet with the main name and then all the alternative spellings. Even poor Etheldreda was also known as Æthelthryth. One source had modernized the name to Audrey.

When she found her muscles complaining about being in the same position for far too long, she debated heading over to the museum to make the most of her free time without dealing with Roger or Janet. Instead she decided to walk down to the river and look to see what had happened to Simon's boat.

The movement felt good. Already she had fallen in love with the shortcut through the field that flanked the cathedral. The church historian was on her list of people to interview, but she still had to make contact. Intellectually she knew there were twenty-four hours in the day, but at the moment they seemed condensed into five at most.

A few horses were grazing as she stopped by the fence. A small brown pony ambled up to her, checking if she had anything worthwhile to share. "I'm sorry. I should have brought some apples or sugar cubes. Maybe tomorrow." Bending down, she pulled some grass and held it flat for the pony. It nuzzled her hand with gusto as if the grass on its side of the fence wasn't the same.

Annie rubbed her hands free of horse spit on her jeans. Shouldering her laptop case she walked down the hill to the river. To get to the boat, she had to cross a small bridge. A conference of ducks was on the opposite shore.

She glanced down into the river to see if she could see any of the eels for which the town was named. From the time it was first settled, the abundance of the relatively repulsive-looking creatures had been a major source of nourishment. No mind how they looked: they tasted good. No eels were visible.

Simon's boat was in place: the crime tape had been removed. No one was around. Buildings on the other side of the bridge seemed deserted, but Annie had no way of knowing if anyone might be peeking out.

She stepped onto the boat. She called out. Of course there was no answer.

The unlocked door opened with a creak.

What she expected to find, she wasn't sure. One of her friends in France had a canal boat that Annie loved. Several times they had gone up and down the Canal du Midi. Annie had become expert at maneuvering the locks. This boat was even more luxurious than her friend's.

Why hadn't there been a struggle? But then Simon was on the toilet with his pants down. Why hadn't he locked the boat when he was inside?

Thinking back to when they were in Zurich, Simon had been very security conscious as far as his work was concerned. One team manager had been furious when Simon had password protected a shared file. "Habit," had been Simon's response without even a hint of an apology. No wonder he and Rod worked so well together with their identical attitudes.

The amount of equipment Simon had on the boat should have meant he would have kept the place locked. Looking at the door, she saw there was the regular lock plus two additional security locks and a chain lock. Since there were no marks of forced entry, Simon had to have left everything open. Could he have been expecting someone? If so, who?

Simon had been found on the toilet with his pants down, but the killers could have put him there after they'd killed him. She rejected that idea, because the only blood was in the bathroom, suggesting first that the killer or killers had surprised him.

Why hadn't they taken the computers? How did they have enough time to clean the hard drives? And why were there no CD-Roms, USB keys, backups or extra hard drives? Had they taken those?

The boat was now devoid of anything more high-tech than the electric knife on the countertop. Annie wondered when the police would return the computers. Rod had said the police told him the computers were totally empty, not even an operating system remained. The murderer then knew his way around a computer. Or murderers? One killed, one stripped? Or could it have been one very efficient murderer?

How was it connected with Rod's hit and run accident and his disappearance, if at all? Until Rod came back she had no one to ask.

Annie hated answerless questions.

The furniture was a black leather loveseat that made into a small double bed and a recliner. She sank into the recliner to think.

When they worked in Zurich together, they'd occasionally eaten at the cafeteria. Had they talked about anything that might make sense in relation to Rod's attack and Simon's murder?

Annie racked her brain trying to remember. Sometimes they talked about sports. She and Rod were tennis fans. When it came to sports Rod was chatty in comparison to his regular self, which meant he might add a comment now and then.

Somewhere from deep in her memory banks, she recalled that Simon described himself as not very sporty except for golf. He'd been almost embarrassed by it, explaining that his father was an avid golfer and he'd been forced to take lessons like some kids had to take piano lessons. As a kid he'd hated it. As an adult he loved it. Maybe Simon had golf clubs and maybe the police hadn't taken them.

Simon's bedroom was obvious the place to look. Annie found that the police had left his clothes scattered on the bed. Most were jeans, T-shirts, sweaters and underwear. Normal personal things were still there: a watch and several paperbacks, mostly about banks, finance, regulation or lack thereof and the recent crash. Several portrayed the major bank leaders as criminals. All the magazines referred to the financial crisis. She hadn't known that Simon had any interest in the financial world.

As she opened the door to the bathroom, she tried not to

think of Simon on the toilet. Rust-colored blood was spread all over. Simon's shaving equipment was on the rim of the basin. An extra roll of toilet paper was blood spattered. The murderer must have hit an artery based on the way blood painted the bathroom walls.

What would happen to the boat? Sharon, as Simon's ex-wife, probably had no rights to it, unless he willed it to her. Annie didn't know if Simon even had a will. UK law on what happens to property when a person who dies intestate was a complete mystery to her.

Annie went into the second bedroom. The bed had been stripped to the mattress, unlike the one in Simon's room. Maybe it never did have any bedding, or maybe there was something that had led to the police taking it with them for examination. The mattress was pristine. Annie struggled with the mattress to see the other side in case the murderer had killed Simon on the bed, then turned the mattress to confuse the police. The other side was so clean that she felt stupid even thinking of the possibility. The police weren't that stupid.

Annie's best guestimate was that Simon used this as a storeroom. His bike, which he used in place of a car, was propped up against one wall. Three suitcases were in a corner. When she opened them she found winter clothing and a pair of skis. She didn't remember him skiing when they were in Zurich, but the contract had them working Monday thru Saturday.

ZBPI never bothered to get the permits to allow anyone to work on Sunday. With the long hours, no one had much energy to do anything but collapse at the end of the fourteen-hour, six-day, work week. Since she was paid by the hour, Annie hadn't complained. She knew it would give her weeks of free time after the assignment ended.

Annie searched the suitcases, even though she thought that if the police had left them there was nothing important. What did she find?

Nothing important—just clothing.

When she checked the closet, she found Simon's golf clubs. Although she was sure that the police had checked the bag, she still took out all the clubs, noting that there were grass strands on several of the drivers when she removed their jackets.

There were two side pockets. Annie unzipped them and wasn't surprised to find a golf glove, tees and a package of three new and several grass-stained old balls.

There was a card holder on a key ring that had a laminated version of Simon's business card, giving his mobile phone number and e-mail address. The key ring itself had a rooster attached but no keys.

Annie put everything back together. Through the small portholes she noticed it was getting dark. Better be getting back to the house. She was halfway up the stairs before it hit her. She rushed back to the golf bag, unzipped the pocket and pulled out the cardholder and key chain. Pulling it apart she found a USB key. The men must have thought that animal key chains would be overlooked where computer keys would not.

Although she knew she should take it to the police, she attached her own key to it and dropped it into her bag. Since neither Simon nor Rod was the type for cute things like animal USB keys, it had to be a security measure. When Marc came, he could examine both keys, because Annie was sure that this rooster would be as password protected as Rod's pig was.

CHAPTER 34

"You know," Roger said, standing by the open car door, "the pig and rooster should be given to the police. It's evidence." A wind, strong enough to swirl the leaves, made Annie shiver.

"Go back inside, you'll get a cold." She adjusted the seat of Janet's car to where her legs could comfortably reach the gas, brake and clutch.

Roger had followed her. "And you don't know UK law. Maybe you could be charged as an accessory." He bent down, holding the door open.

"Maybe there are things on it that are confidential for his clients." Annie put the key in the ignition and glanced at her watch. She didn't want to be late getting Marc.

Janet had joked that the car knew the way to the airport without any driver, but Annie still wanted to arrive in time. Not that Marc was unable to take care of himself, but she still half thought of him as the kid who used to visit her in the evening to tell her about the things in which his parents had no interest.

As it was, Marc was one of the last people off the plane. He picked Annie up and swung her around. He'd turned into a really good-looking kid, muscular with long blond hair. All his gawkiness was gone.

"Did you bring your computer?" Annie asked as they walked to the car.

"In the backpack. Stupid one-bag rule. It's wrapped in my underwear . . . it's a mini."

On the way back to the house, Annie explained what they were looking for as well as the situation. "What's strange is that Janet seems in a daze, neither upset nor worried any longer. At first she was, but now—well, she's become almost zombie-like when it comes to her husband."

"Isn't that the couple you once said didn't have anything in common with each other: you didn't understand why they were together?"

"I think I've described several couples that way, and probably I'd describe Roger and me the same way too."

"But you love Roger."

"And I thought Janet loved Rod. At least in her way. And that he had loved her in his own way."

"You're drifting to the other side of the road."

Annie quickly corrected the car, but not before a horn blared at her. The wind had picked up and the skies were getting dark. "So tell me about you."

"I love my classes. I'm more and more politically active. I've come over to the UK to demonstrate and gone to Washington too."

Annie remembered how idealistic Marc had been when he was young, how he'd said "I want to make the world better."

A thought crossed Annie's mind, and she and Marc had always blurted out whatever they were thinking. "Marc? Are you involved with any of those hacking groups that go after the bad guys?"

"Ask no questions, I'll tell no lies." He looked out the side window for a few minutes. "No, Annie, I'm not, but I could be . . . I'm really good at it, although far from the best." He paused. "But I'm not sure I'm good enough to get into what you want me to . . . I mean, from what you said, those guys are super talented."

Annie wasn't sure if she were happy or disappointed that

Marc was politically active. She alternated between being a news junkie; despairing at the wars, environmental problems and inequality; and ignoring it all to concentrate on people around her, figuring there was nothing she could do anyway on the big issues of the day.

When Rod and she had worked at ZBPI they would talk about the different financial crises and the effect that they had on people's lives. "If it bothers us so much, why are we taking their disgustingly high rate per hour?" she had asked.

"Our getting poorer doesn't do anything for others," Rod had said.

Annie's next assignment was for a charity at a fraction of the pay rate—social balance, she'd called it.

By the time they reached the house, it was not just dark, it was pouring. Even though she'd found a parking place less than a block from the house, they were soaked before they reached the door. They found Janet and Roger in the lounge with a fire and Bach playing on the sound system.

Roger and Marc greeted each other with those shoulder slaps that men do.

"Welcome to my home," Janet said. "Get yourselves dried off. I'll put dinner on the table."

Dinner was a thick minestrone soup and an oatmeal bread that she'd baked while Annie had fetched Marc. The smell of cooking yeast hung in the air.

"So what is it you want me to do?" Marc asked as Janet served baked apples for dessert.

Annie ran upstairs and brought down the pig and rooster on their little key chains. Marc raised an eyebrow until Annie pulled them apart.

"Both Rod and Simon had these. We've tried to get in and they are password protected."

"What are the police doing?"

167

"Not enough," Janet said. "They seem to think my husband is a criminal who ran away after murdering his partner."

"They didn't say that," Roger said.

"They didn't have to, once they found his car at Gatwick," Janet said. "They think he must still be in the country because he left his passport here. When the police check, they might only be looking for an English citizen with an English passport."

"He could also use his Swiss indentity card and the police might think it was a different Rod MacKenzie," Annie said. "Or an R. MacKenzie who is Swiss."

Janet was briefing Marc in the same tone as if she were talking about buying a couch, planning a meal or any other irrelevant topic.

Although Annie had remembered Rod was a dual citizen with a Swiss mother, between his name and his ruddy coloring, he could have been the poster man on any Scottish tourism poster. Just put him in a kilt and hand him a bagpipe. She wanted to ask Janet why she'd been so calm, but she decided not to in front of the others.

*Annie couldn't shake the guilt she felt that whenever she worked on
her Etheldreda project, she was stealing time from Roger or Janet.
Nor could she shake the feeling when she was with Janet and Roger
that she wasn't spending enough time on the project. Sometimes she
thought of Roger as a small child, demanding to be read another
story or to have her lay down next to him while he fell asleep. She
turned on the computer and imagined how Etheldreda would deal
with a marriage she didn't want.*

The snows had let up to a point that allowed Tonbert and his
six-man entourage to arrive. They looked like snowmen as they
entered the house, shaking themselves until their real appear-
ances emerged. King Onna and Etheldreda, plus a serving girl,
went to the door to greet the men in response to their pounding.

At Onna's order, Sawara, who just yesterday had changed
from agreeing with her husband about the marriage to arguing
with her husband that forcing their daughter into marriage was
a bad idea, had been banished to her chamber. Etheldreda knew
that her parents seldom argued. She prayed for forgiveness at
causing the disagreement as well as for her pleasure that her
mother had stood up for her even if it had been useless.

Tonbert was the tallest of the six men standing at the
entrance, taller even than Etheldreda's father, who was a big
man by Anglo-Saxon standards. He was also in his mid-thirties,

old to be seeking a wife for the first time. Men of power who had survived various battles to reach his age usually had buried one if not more wives.

Sawara more than once had made the remark that men die in warfare, women in childbirth. She had not appreciated Etheldreda's comment saying God decided when to take someone to their heavenly home and had snapped, "I prefer to stay in my home on earth."

Etheldreda had given up trying to convince her mother that the Christian God was the only God: pagan gods did not exist. She'd also given up trying to get her father to deal with her mother's refusal to accept their religion by ordering Sawara to accept Jesus Christ.

He'd said that Sawara had to be responsible for her own soul, and all they could do was to show her the way. No one could force a person to believe something that they didn't want to believe. However, he didn't see the irony of using force against his daughter until she agreed to a marriage she didn't want. Thus, he'd ordered his daughter to come to the entrance of the house to greet the man that would be her future husband.

Etheldreda and Tonbert had met before. He had been at more than one meeting when plots and plans were made to attack this or that enemy of the moment.

Unlike many of the warring kings in the area, Tonbert preferred negotiation to the battlefield.

"Negotiations aren't any fun," King Onna had thundered. Etheldreda had heard her father despite his being two rooms away from the plotters. "The thrill is in knowing your weapons have destroyed your enemy and that his land will become yours."

She hadn't heard Tonbert's reply, but her father complained afterward that Tonbert was far more interested in having his people plant crops and build houses and barns for themselves and their animals than take up arms. "Not that he is a coward.

When we can get him onto the battlefield, he's ferocious," he'd added.

Tonbert did not look ferocious as he undid his cloak. He looked cold.

Tonbert stared at Etheldreda as she said to a serving girl, "Get these poor men some hot cider."

"That is kind of you." Tonbert and the rest of the men were blowing on their hands. "Our horses are outside."

"One of my boys will put them in the stable," Onna said.

The servant girl, who was not more than thirteen, arrived with a tray and a big wooden bowl of steaming cider. Six smaller wooden bowls were stacked on one side and a wooden ladle was on the other. She put the tray on a table near the door.

"Not here, girl," Onna said. "In the main room."

The main room had a huge fireplace. A log, the size of a small tree, created a fire, throwing warmth to all corners.

The servant girl set the tray with the cider on a table and scuttled back to the kitchen.

"If we need anything, we'll call you," Onna hollered after her. "She's terrified of me, but I don't know why. I've never hit her; I never tried to bed her." He laughed and the other men followed.

Etheldreda wanted to leave the room, which smelled of smoke, cold wool and dirty men gulping down the hot cider as they jostled for places closest to the fire. She started to withdraw but her father blocked her way.

"Where are you going?"

"To the kitchen to see how dinner is progressing."

Onna moved to one side.

In the kitchen there was the smell of onions and roasting meat. The smoke rose through the hole in the ceiling. Sawara, although disobeying the order to stay in her room, was already there directing the preparations. "Needed to escape, daughter?"

Etheldreda nodded. Escape not just the evening but the house.

"Marriage won't be as bad as you think," Sawara said. "And once you have children, you will realize that life is far richer than it would be in a convent."

Etheldreda did not answer.

The dinner had been consumed the same way a pack of starving foxes would have fallen on the residents of a chicken house had the door been left open.

Sawara, under threat of what might happen if she did not keep her mouth shut, was allowed to sit on the left of her husband and Etheldreda sat on his right. Etheldreda tried not to resent that her mother was saying one thing to her—do your duty—and another thing to her father—don't force her. She told herself that her mother's position was such that she had no choice.

Beer flowed. Three of Tonbert's men were slurring their words, becoming more boastful of their actions on the battlefield.

Tonbert leaned over and whispered in her ear. "We need to talk later."

The men drank more. One passed out. Two others, in not much better shape, maneuvered him to the room that they would be sharing.

Sawara excused herself to direct the kitchen help, which left Tonbert, Onna, Etheldreda and two of his men in the dining room. Tonbert dismissed his other men, who stumbled to their beds.

Etheldreda once again started to leave, but her father's hand shot out, stopping her. He had not consumed more than a horn of beer. He seldom drank heavily, especially when others did. He felt keeping his wits about him gave him advantages, and not just in case a fight started. Information could slip through mouths that would not have opened had the alcohol not loosened them.

"We need to talk about your marriage, daughter."

Etheldreda knew better than to protest in front of Tonbert, who, like her father, had not drunk much.

"I think, Onna, it might be best if your daughter and I talked together."

Onna frowned. "Let me speak to my daughter alone."

Tonbert stood. "I'll check the horses and be back."

Father and daughter heard his footsteps go to the door; a pause followed where they assumed he put on his cloak, then the door open and shut.

"Do not, I repeat daughter, do not try and throw yourself on his mercy to let you escape this arrangement."

This was nothing like the man who would sneak Etheldreda a spoonful of honey when she was little or even bring her a gold buckle for her belt. This was not the same man, Onna the father, that would take her on his knee and tell her stories that made her giggle or would tickle her until she cried, saying stop but meaning more, more, more. This was the Onna, her King.

This was her king, with alliances being far more important than her individual wishes. That he had humored her to this point was unlike how he would have treated anyone else.

His patience with Jurmin and his woodworking was non-existent; he often dragged the teenager out of the shop and thrust a javelin or bow into his hand. He would make him ride a horse, something Jurmin hated, screaming at the boy that he was his heir and he had to be ready to take over the kingdom.

Jurmin would scream that he neither wanted to be a king nor a warrior.

Any of his subjects who crossed Onna met with either beatings or death. Etheldreda always had escaped his fists and his whip, but now she knew that she had pushed her king and her father as far she could. She resisted saying that she'd given in: she merely nodded her head.

"Say it," the king demanded.

"I will do as you wish."

It was her father who gathered the young woman into his arms. "Know that I'm doing what I must, not necessarily what I want to do."

A smidgeon of hope ran through Etheldreda's mind. She pulled back but as she started to open her mouth, Onna put a finger to her lips. "I know how important your religion is to you. But God expects you to honor your father." He turned and walked out.

She stared after him, not wanting to face Tonbert. Her back was to her future husband when he reentered the room. Had she wanted to be a wife, despite his being older, he would have made an adequate husband. She felt his presence and when she did finally turn she saw he sat on the bench, his back against the wall.

The detritus of the meal was soggy bread trenchers and a few bones scattered about the table. One of the king's dogs, a black bitch about to deliver pups, came in and sat. Tonbert took the bread from his place and fed the remains of his meal to her piece by piece, then did the same with the food that the others had left.

"I know you don't want to marry me." When she didn't say anything, he said, "Am I that repulsive to you?"

"Not at all."

"Then come and sit next to me."

She walked slowly behind the table and sat on the bench next to him, leaving a place between them. When he reached for her hand, he held it tightly: not so tightly it hurt but not so loosely that she succeeded when she tried to pull it away.

The silence in the room was almost like an echo.

"Talk to me," he said.

"It's not you. It's me."

What her father expected fought against what she wanted. She said a quick prayer to the Virgin Mother asking for guidance. Although she couldn't be sure it was the Virgin speaking, her thoughts told her to tell the truth. "All my life, all I wanted to do was live in a convent where I could immerse myself in prayer. When I first took communion, I also took a vow of chastity."

He let go of her hand. "Now *this* is an interesting development."

She wasn't sure why but he smiled. "Your father wants this marriage for political reasons. He is right: it will be good for me and my kingdom."

With her head bowed she said, "I'm not a person, but a treaty."

At that he laughed. She stood up so suddenly that the bitch, who was chewing a bone near her foot, jumped and hit its head on the bench.

"Sit down," he said.

The dog sat.

Etheldreda sat.

"Well, at least you're as obedient as a dog, a good thing in a wife." Looking at her face, he said, "I see I've made you angry. I was only trying to make the mood lighter."

"How can it be light when . . ."

". . . when everything you want is out of reach. I know the feeling well. I would like nothing more than to be left alone. But to get any peace at all, sometimes I need to fight, although I hate it. But also, I need to make alliances such as this one with your father."

She had never heard anyone, except perhaps her brother,

argue against war.

"There may be a way we can both get what we want."

"How?" She was afraid she'd spoken too abruptly, but it didn't seem to bother him.

"I want an alliance. You, for whatever reason that I can't understand, want to remain a virgin and waste your time in prayer . . . no . . . no . . . I don't really care for the Celtic Christian, the Roman Christian or the pagan gods. If there were a good god or gods, he or they would never allow war. And if he/they did, he/they are not a god or gods to whom I would want to pray."

This was blasphemy. What he was saying was nothing like she had ever heard said by anyone.

"We will marry. I will never touch you. You can pray all you want."

"But you must want something?"

"I do: a helpmate in taking care of my people. And, you may want to be chaste, but I do not. You will say nothing when I find a woman so that I can do what men do. However, I promise never to shame you."

Etheldreda thought about what he'd said. She could honor her vow, and although she would not be cloistered as she wished, she still would be able to follow her prayer routine. What he asked of her was not unreasonable.

"I would like to build an abbey," she said.

"Not immediately," he said. "There are things you must learn first, mundane things compared to holy prayer." His lips twitched and she wondered if he were mocking her. "Right now, you have no idea how to arrange for stone or masons. Although the way you've dealt with me, I suspect I will be able to teach you easily how to negotiate a contract, but not every merchant will be as easy."

"What else do you want from me?"

"A friend," he said. "Should we tell your father that we will be man and wife?"

"Yes."

Annie glanced at her watch. She was running late—big surprise there. Hopefully she'd been able to explain how Etheldreda had remained a virgin during her first marriage. The why, she'd never understand. She was too twenty-first century.

CHAPTER 36

Annie couldn't sleep. Roger had said he wanted her next to him, but his snoring drowned out the noise of the rain beating off the metal roof directly over the door below leading to the back terrace. Before his heart attack, the snoring might have annoyed her, although she knew it wasn't his fault. Now that he was alive snoring was something to be grateful for.

Marc was ensconced in the spare room where Annie had slept earlier, cutting off any escape or hope of a restful night.

Still she was tired. Everything had taken a chunk out of her energy levels. Her wish that things would go back to normal and she could just work on her project was an impossible dream.

Not just Roger's snoring kept her awake. On a personal level, she worried about her marriage. Having fought so hard against it, she wanted her couple to work. That they might never have sex again was disheartening at best, but she knew that it would not be a deal breaker. Even when she tried, she could not picture herself being unfaithful. Even if she had fought taking marriage vows, she knew from the beginning that once she'd made them, she would keep them. Part of her was annoyed at herself for being principled.

She slipped out of bed and reached for the thick robe Janet had loaned her against the chill of the house. Part of her wished she liked warm milk, because that was supposed to put one to sleep. Just the thought of milk, warm or cold, made her want to gag.

As she tiptoed into the hall, she saw that Marc had shut off the light in Rod's office. He must have packed it in and gone to sleep himself.

As she went by Janet's room she heard crying. To avoid disturbing the other sleepers with a loud knock, Annie instead scratched lightly at the door. Janet told her to come in and lifted the duvet so Annie could slip in. The bed was a four-poster, of some dark antique wood. The rain was either lighter or not landing on anything, so the sounds were muffled in comparison to the other room.

Janet switched on the nightstand lamp. "Did I disturb you?"

Annie shook her head. "I couldn't sleep. I'm a good listener if you want to talk."

"I can't grasp it. The murder: Rod's need to disappear."

"And when were you required to make sense of a murder and a husband's disappearance? They don't have articles about how to do this in women's magazines."

At that Janet smiled. "Can you stay for a little while?"

Annie nodded and Janet turned off the light. Soon she was snoring, but not as loudly as Roger.

Still Annie was unable to fall asleep. As quietly as she could, she headed downstairs and turned on her computer. At least if she couldn't sleep, she could work on her project.

Chapter 37

Annie interrupted her writing to go to the bathroom. Between two in the morning when she had left Roger and then comforted Janet and now, just before dawn, she'd written drafts of three more chapters. She could go no further without doing more research, but she had made appointments with the church historian and the museum director, both of whom had left messages of time and place on Janet's answering machine. The only problem was that they had been for the same day and time.

Needing to be in two places at the same time just added to her frustration. This too will pass, she thought to herself. Everything that is happening is exceptional. Life will be ordinary again. Or at least it had better be, she thought, although she had no idea of what the alternative would be if it weren't.

Unlike when she was writing about Hilke Fülmer, whom she had admired, she really was annoyed at this seventh-century woman's attitude toward sex.

In those early morning hours, she'd gone from drinking tea to drinking honey, cinnamon and hot water and even if her nickname hadn't been "bitty bladder," the liquid consumed was taking its toll.

Mercury had come downstairs to keep Annie company, but he too was snoring on his blanket, which was protecting the couch from his shedding fur.

Just as she was going into the kitchen to make herself some toast, the telephone rang. She grabbed it, hoping that Janet,

Roger and Marc would not be disturbed. The dog opened one eye.

"I'm Anthony Barrow from *The Sun*. I'm looking for Mrs. MacKenzie."

She glanced at the clock. The nerve calling well before breakfast on a Sunday morning. "Why?"

"We want a comment on her husband's disappearance."

"She isn't available and she won't be."

Shit, shit, shit. Somehow the papers had become aware of Rod's flight. Annie was under no illusions that it would be only one paper. Sadly she was right.

By the time everyone but Marc had come down to breakfast, the phone had rung over a dozen times and an ITV news truck was pulling up in front of the house.

Janet disconnected the phone and tilted the venetian blinds so no one could see in, but they could watch the reporters hang around. "I guess we are back to bothering the neighbor if we want to leave." She reached for her cell to call Catherine.

Annie listened to Janet's end of the conversation.

"I'm sorry . . . I know that's what friends are for . . . no, nothing from him . . . Okay, I'll open the back door."

Catherine appeared within seconds, still in her bathrobe. She wore her brown hair schoolgirl long and it had been brushed and fastened with a barrette. She hadn't put on any makeup, but then she hadn't worn makeup when Annie had seen her before, when they'd used her house as an entryway or escape route.

Catherine poured herself a cup of tea from the pot and sat down. Although she'd met Roger they needed to introduce her to Marc, who still wasn't up.

"I love your French accent," Catherine said to Roger, then turned to Janet. "How about some toast and your homemade apricot jam?"

As Janet busied herself in the kitchen, Catherine pulled out two house keys. "These are for my front and back door so you can escape at will," she said.

Janet came back with a tray and a selection of jams, butter, toast and another pot of tea. "I don't know how to thank you enough." She turned to Annie. "Catherine is a painter too."

"And we painters have to stay together," Catherine said as the doorbell rang. "Should you answer that?"

Janet went to the door. She needed to stand on tiptoe to see through the peephole. It wasn't that she was short: it was that the hole was higher than normal. She opened the door and Lake and Welch, the two policemen that Annie had begun to think of as Tweedledum and Tweedledee, slipped in to the dog growling rather than his usual barking.

Mercury wasn't a growler, so he must have picked up on the tension that came in with the policemen, Annie decided.

Both men wore raincoats. They had already closed their black umbrellas and dropped them in the wooden bear-sculpted umbrella stand. "I see the newsboys and girls are back," Lake said.

"Did you have anything to do with it?" Janet's tone was hostile.

"We weren't getting anywhere in finding your husband, so we sent his photo everywhere," Welch said. "Now that they found that missing child, they need a new target."

Annie wanted to pour the remaining tea over their heads.

Marc tramped downstairs. That boy had heavy feet. When he entered the dining room, it was clear to see from his wet hair that he'd showered. He wore his EPFL sweatshirt, and Annie guessed that the police would not know this was a Lausanne school. "This is Marc Stoller, a friend from Geneva who has come to help me research some history for a project of mine. I've used him before."

Welch and Lake both frowned as Annie willed Marc not to say anything about the real reason he had come to Ely. She was also afraid the inner policeman in Roger would take over and he'd turn the pig and rooster over to the two men.

As if he understood, Roger put his hand over Annie's. "My wife is on a tight deadline and we alternate between supporting Janet and giving Annie time to work."

"Even if my husband hadn't had his heart attack and he could travel, I couldn't imagine leaving Janet alone," Annie said.

Lake nodded. "I suppose none of you has heard from Mac-Kenzie?"

"We would have told you if we had," Janet said. "He hasn't done anything wrong."

"We're worried something happened to him," Roger said. "As one policeman to another . . ." Lake scowled, but Welch nodded, ". . . we can't rule out foul play."

"We still would like to ask you a few questions, Mrs. Mac-Kenzie. We can do it in another room or you could come with us to the station."

"Not much of a choice with the press outside. Let's go into the lounge. But first . . ." Lake turned toward Catherine.

"I'm their neighbor."

They demanded her address as she explained that she helped everyone leave the house while avoiding the press.

"You might try coming through my house to avoid the press as well," Catherine said. "Unless you want them to see you coming and going." Her smile was sweet, but Annie suspected it was a dig.

When the door to the lounge shut, Annie said, "I'd love to be able to hear what they are saying."

She and Roger finished drinking the tea and cleared the table, with the exception of the toast that Marc had made for himself.

Roger glanced at his watch.

The door to the lounge remained shut.

Marc finished eating, cleared his place and put the dishes in the dishwasher. "I'd better get back to work," he said.

"Not until the police leave," Roger said.

"And go upstairs, please, and make sure the pig and/or the rooster aren't sticking out of your computer port," Annie said. "I should have thought of it earlier."

"Turn them back into key chains." Roger slumped in his chair. "I'm off my game."

"You usually are not trying to hide stuff from the police," Annie said and Roger didn't quite smile but his lips did twitch.

Annie took her laptop upstairs to the bedroom where she slept when Roger was snoring too loudly and which Marc now occupied.

Although she tried to work, her mind was on her friends. She closed the door so she missed the sounds of the policemen leaving until Janet knocked at the door.

Janet walked straight to the window and looked down. Annie joined her.

Below the reporters were shoving microphones into the faces of the police, who were pushing their way through the crowd.

"I suggested they leave through Catherine's, but they pointed out that the reporters saw them come in and if they didn't come out, they would discover the escape route."

"Decent of them," Annie said.

"Or maybe they wanted the media coverage: about the only thing they are convinced of is that Rod killed Simon, then did a runner, and that I know where he is." Janet sank down on the unmade bed. "I only wish I did."

Annie looked at Janet closely and knew for no reason other than instinct that her friend did know about Rod's whereabouts. The tension had gone out of her friend's body. It wasn't enough to bring up the topic and it certainly wasn't something she would share with Roger. He would either be the patronizing husband downplaying her "instincts" or he would become Mr. Policeman and want Rod to give himself up.

CHAPTER 38
ELY 655

Annie was relieved that she had an uninterrupted hour to write. Fortunately the book was to be fiction, but just because it was fiction didn't mean she could ignore the known facts. Outside it was raining. She would make it rain in the book.

Would it never stop raining? Already the Fens were overflowing. Etheldreda worried about the villagers who lived around the house that her husband, Tonbert, had provided for her as a morning gift. A good part of the Fens was in danger.

Annie made a note to herself to explain that a morning gift in Anglo-Saxon times was what a husband gave to his bride. She wasn't quite sure how to word it, so she planned to come back to it later, when she had more time. She marked the type in bold red so it would be easy to find.

Etheldreda had not asked for the traditional present a man would make to his bride, but she accepted it with pleasure and plans. The house might be the possible site for the abbey.

During her prayers she would ask Christ if she were over-reaching in the way she wanted to honor Him. Was she being too proud to think she could do such a thing? What did she know about the physical requirements of building any structure much less an abbey?

At times she felt that it would be enough to just be in a

convent where she could pray without daily responsibilities.

Tonbert had insisted she be aware of all the details in running his kingdom from the cost of goods to overseeing the birth of a lamb. He had complimented her on her bartering skills for materials and on getting workmen to do what he needed them to do, although sometimes he chided her on being too giving.

When he was away, she'd been in complete charge, something that she thought she would never be able to handle by herself, yet with each problem that she solved, she grew in confidence in her ability to meet any challenge.

Annie, whose dislike for Etheldreda didn't change the more she found about her, had to admit, albeit grudgingly, that the woman was extremely competent. Maybe in today's world she might have ended up running a corporation if she hadn't carried her religious fanaticism across the centuries.

Tonbert never criticized what she did, saying if he left her in charge while he was off fighting or just meeting with others, he had no right to disagree with her decisions.

Tonbert and Etheldreda were staying in Ely temporarily until the weather cleared and they could return to his house in South Grywas.

Etheldreda stood in the doorway and watched the constant drizzle. She knew the river was rising because her maid, who had arrived soaked through, had told her. The overflowing of the Fens was almost an annual event. The villagers knew that they shouldn't use all their seed in any one planting, or at least she so hoped. If they didn't, it would be a long and hungry winter.

Tonbert had not just given her the house but the area surrounding it. "The land will allow you to be independent of me, if I mistreat you or if I die," he'd said on their wedding night when they each went to separate rooms. Part of her was surprised at what a good man he had turned out to be, accepting that she would not share his bed because of her religion. God wanted her to stay a virgin and a virgin she would stay.

Although she could have lived alone in the house, overseeing the land, the couple went back and forth between his land and hers.

He never told her what to do, but suggested this or that, always giving her a reason for his suggestion. She learned more about when to plant the oats, wheat and barley than she ever thought there was to know. He knew more about farming and raising animals than anyone she had ever met and he shared his knowledge with anyone who would listen. When they were apart, she missed talking with him.

He loved music and played both a stringed instrument that the carpenter had created and a windpipe. Etheldreda was afraid that the pipe might influence bad winds. Her priest had warned against the instruments, but the sound was so beautiful coming from the instrument that she couldn't help but listen. It was like her gold necklace and belt, things that took her mind away from God, but she was drawn to their beauty.

Annie wished she could find out more about Anglo-Saxon superstitions. The Leechbook *had information on witchcraft, medicine and magic, but Annie couldn't figure out how to incorporate it into her story. She made a mental note to herself to never take an assignment like this again—she would have to love or at least like any future historical project.*

When Etheldreda confessed her sins to her priest, he had chided her for earthly desires, but in talking with her friend Father Wilfrid, she heard a different theory: if God had not wanted the music to exist, he would never have allowed man to create it. If

God had not wanted decoration, he would not have created gold.

When she'd told Tonbert what Father Wilfrid had said, he'd laughed so hard that she had started laughing and neither of them could stop. When they finally regained control, they both agreed it hadn't really been that funny, but the laughter had felt good.

At times she wondered if her husband kept a woman elsewhere. Despite his saying before their marriage that he would find comfort in the arms of other women, he now told her that physical relations no longer interested him.

Maybe that was his age. The skin on his arms when his sleeves pulled up was a bit wrinkled. What the rest of him looked like she couldn't tell, for she never saw him without his clothes. The only male she had ever seen naked was her brother when he was a baby and needed a change.

Her husband had a full head of hair, albeit it gray, which he bound in braids or in a knot on one side. As for his beard, he often asked her to cut it so it fit his face. He was not vain about his looks as some men Etheldreda knew. Mostly she found his face kindly with lines around his eyes carved by his smiles.

She headed down the corridor to the kitchen. The supper meal would be a soup made from eel and onion.

She wasn't sure when her husband would return. He was out trying to determine storm damage. Yesterday, he'd found several drowned sheep, he'd said. More than one villager's home was flooded, turning wooden floors into a mud sea. Many had taken refuge with friends and family living on higher ground.

Etheldreda loved how Tonbert cared for the villagers, making sure that all those working on her land had the animals they needed to survive as well as the tools to make their work easier. A well-crafted rake, spade and hoe were invaluable for the land to produce as much as possible.

The carpenter in Ely who produced almost all the tools for the area was as valuable as the man who wove the baskets that caught the eels. The two men were part of the hierarchy of the village and Tonbert treated them with respect, not as underlings existing only to serve his needs, although he did expect them to provide what he needed. Etheldreda had only to look at her kitchen with its wooden bowls, trays and spoons to realize how well the two craftsmen served them.

She regretted that Tonbert had not accepted her God. Strange, neither had her mother, even on her deathbed, which had brought Etheldreda great sadness. Her mother's soul would never live in heaven with the Blessed Mother. Yet her mother and her husband were two of the kindest people she knew— more so than many of the Christians from either the Celtic or the Roman side.

The door burst open. Tonbert stood in the doorway. His clothes dripped, forming a puddle where he stood. He sneezed and coughed.

"Stay there." She ran down the hallway to his bedroom where she grabbed a drying cloth and a change of clothing, which she carried to the kitchen.

While he changed, she turned her back, stirring the soup in the kettle over the fire in the middle of the room. One of the tinkers had devised a contraption that had a large tin cover and a chute that went up to the hole in the roof, thus reducing the smoke within.

Now clothed, Tonbert moved to the bench in front of the table and sat down. "I'm so damned cold." His teeth were chattering as he took the bowl of soup from his wife and drank a huge mouthful and spit it out. "Hot!"

She took a ladle and spooned beer from a bucket. "Here."

"Everything's too hot or too cold."

The servants had all been sent home to care for their own

places under threat from the floods. Etheldreda didn't mind. She liked the solitude. It gave her more time to pray. And she could not have lived with herself if something had happened to one of the servants over her own selfishness.

Nor did she mind doing the necessary tasks around the house. The main hall was usually closed off because they had few visitors. She spent most of her time in the bedroom, kitchen or chapel, a small area where she'd installed an altar. Wilfrid had consecrated it.

One of the few arguments she and Tonbert had had was when he had refused to allow an altar in his home, saying she could pray anywhere she wanted.

Etheldreda had not given up on converting her husband, preferring to lead by example in her own good works, but his good works were as many as hers if not more so.

"You're shivering." Gathering up some glowing ashes she put them in a metal pan with a top. This she wrapped in a cloth and carried to her husband's bedroom.

He followed. "Slip into bed. The furs and ashes will help warm you."

"One would think that you were trying to seduce me."

"You know better." It amazed her she could joke with him, but they had fallen so deeply into friendship that anything and everything could be said. Misunderstandings, although few, could be discussed until they were no longer misunderstandings.

From under the covers Tonbert gave her the report of which houses had been damaged, which fields would need to be replanted. When he finished, he said. "I feel terrible."

"I'll let you sleep."

During the night she heard him coughing. She went into his room to find him thrashing around. The animal skins were on the floor.

"Tonbert?"

"I'm so hot." He almost choked on the words. "My throat hurts."

She went to the kitchen to heat some honey to soothe his throat and sat next to him until he fell back asleep.

The next morning, two of the serving women came back to work. They took over all the chores as Etheldreda sponged down her husband when the fever became too much, and found extra skins when the chills racked his body.

CHAPTER 39

Martin groaned when he heard the ringing alarm. It couldn't be morning already: it felt as if he'd just closed his eyes . . . where was he? . . . at the Golden Aigle under a thick feather duvet that seemed to hold him down . . . the damned alarm kept ringing.

He opened his eyes. The clock read 2:22. Shut up clock . . . It wasn't the clock . . . who would call at this hour . . . Johann? . . . his wife? . . .

He knocked the phone onto the floor and leaned over the bed to pick it up. "Hmm?"

"Bruber?"

"Hmm."

"I know I've woken you. Auer here. Get down to the conference room ASAP."

The line went dead.

Auer had never, ever, called him in the middle of the night. What the hell was up?

Now that he was awake he staggered into the bathroom, peed, rinsed his mouth and washed his face. His black sweat suit, which he wore in his room when his work was done and he wanted comfort clothes, was hanging on the bathroom door. He pulled on the pants and top and left the room, making sure to double-lock the door behind himself.

On his way down the corridor to the elevator he had to pass Masterson's room. Through the door, which was a rather thick oak, he could hear the CEO yelling. "Severance? Are you nuts

193

after the way you messed up? I want you out of here as soon as you can get your stuff together."

Martin would have loved to know to whom Masterson was talking . . . or rather at whom he was screaming.

"It took you long enough," Auer said in a voice so low Martin could barely hear him when he entered the conference room. His televisions along one wall were on but muted, and from where Martin stood, he could read the news trailing across the screens. He could see that there were four different stations: CNN, MSNBC, Bloomberg and BBC.

He knew better than to say anything. The softer Auer's voice, the angrier he was. More than one employee had said they would have preferred he yell when he was mad, but the soft words thrust through clenched teeth were worse.

"What's wrong?"

"We've been attacked, electronically that is. Not ZBPI, but the other three banks here and many more. I suspect that we are on the list, just further down. Or maybe it is because we are a private bank." Auer shrugged. He was dressed in jeans and a pullover. He wore slippers without socks and Martin noticed he hadn't shaved. The CEO circled the table as he talked.

This was not characteristic of Auer, who normally sat quietly. The most movement he made during a briefing session was to twirl his pencil between his fingers.

Martin wasn't sure he understood. "Attacked how?"

Auer ran his hand through his hair. His accent bore the Zurich twang instead of his normal High German. "We've no idea of who or why, but it has to be coordinated. Whoever it was stopped all service. No one can get money out, use a charge card or use a debit card. Mobile banking is poof . . . gone. We don't know if records are wiped out or just blocked."

"How many banks?"

"At least twenty in the US, UK, Netherlands, Singapore and

Germany. The biggest ones."

Martin had no idea how to respond as Auer turned up the volume on one set, brought it down, then turned it up on another. The news was the same on all of them.

The Far Eastern financial markets had shut down, the ones in Europe were said to be not opening, and no one knew what the North and South American markets would be doing later on in the day once they opened, if they opened.

Talking heads wondering who had done it.

The presidents and prime ministers of the major countries—all were declaring a state of emergency.

Auer didn't give Martin a chance to say anything, even if he could have thought of something to say. His voice was almost a whisper as he said, "We need helicopters to get Masterson, Wang and Carter to the Zurich airport. Their pilots are waiting and ready to fly them home."

Martin did not necessarily understand how computer systems worked. He knew that the ZBPI VP of Technology was tops in his field and had put up every security measure possible, which might explain why they hadn't been attacked.

Auer sank into one of the two chairs located by the table.

The door opened and one of the wait staff, a woman who had been there longer than Martin, came in and asked if they wanted coffee. She obviously had been summoned out of bed because she was dressed in jeans and a sweater and her hair, which was normally in a chignon on top of her head, was in a long braid. "Do you need anything?"

"That's why I called you," Auer said. "Coffee, please." He turned to Martin. "What are you waiting for? Get those helicopters in the air."

As Martin was leaving, Carter and Masterson entered the conference room. On the way to the office he passed Wang limping off the elevator.

The village usually had three helicopters on standby. The CEOs did not like sharing transportation nor did many of the bigwigs that came through. In fact secrecy was part of the service ZBPI offered.

The first pilot Martin called took a long time to answer. His voice was slurred with more than sleep. Martin said, "Never mind." He would not reprimand the pilot, because he was officially off duty. He hoped he hadn't been drinking with the other two pilots, who also were officially off duty until the next afternoon.

The second pilot yawned into the telephone, but told Martin he could have the helicopter airborne in an hour. The helicopter needed to be checked out. Martin told him to do it.

His next call was to the VP of technology, who was wide awake. "I'm in our computer center. I arrived less than a half hour ago, but we've just been hit. Our entire system is down."

"*Scheiß!* Does Aucr know?"

"I just hung up from telling him."

Martin didn't bother to ask what the VP was going to do. He wouldn't understand the technical side of it anyway. The man was competent. He would have all his programmers and his technicians on the way into the center.

The assistants: damn he'd forgotten them. The helicopters only seated four people. Martin called his third pilot, who was in the proper condition to fly and said he was on his way to the field. Then he got two of the limo drivers out of bed.

The lobby was Martin's next destination, where the CEOs and their assistants waited with their luggage. All of them looked drained. All were stabbing at their mobiles.

Thinking it was over for the evening Martin watched the two limos carry everyone to the field. He debated following.

Auer stood behind him. "I suppose you know we've been hit too."

Martin nodded.

"As soon as one of the helicopters comes back, I need to be taken into the city."

Martin nodded again. What he wanted to do was to get back to bed. Even if he wasn't yet fifty, he felt too old for this life.

CHAPTER 40

Burt Johnson wiped down his room at the Golden Aigle. He was sure that he'd left his prints someplace in the hotel, but was equally sure that no one would have picked them up, not even that sanctimonious Swiss bastard Bruber.

He wanted to kill someone, and in the rage he fought just to maintain control, he had to think of Bruber as a likely candidate. But there were others he considered preferable, starting with his former boss, Masterson. And anyone Swiss, he thought. What a fucking country!

How he disliked the Swiss with their too clean streets and their play-it-by-the-book mentality. Christophe Auer was another example. Always trying to make sure everyone was comfortable. God damned suck-up, although he supposed Auer was better than his newly ex-boss Masterson. Auer was powerful in his head, but the man was a coward when it came to anything a real man would do. The asshole had actually flinched when he'd thought that he'd seen Johnson's gun.

Flinched?

What did he think a bodyguard carried? A water pistol?

Johnson looked thoroughly around the bathroom. No hairs at all. He'd take the towels. His DNA was his and his alone. When he ate in the restaurant he made sure that his dishes and silverware were taken into the kitchen and his napkin was switched with others. He didn't get where he was by taking chances.

By now he was used to the surgical gloves that he wore when he was in his room alone to cut down on prints. He even slept with the gloves on his hands, although they gave him a rash, which he ignored. It would disappear when he was no longer at the hotel.

He put the sheet, duvet cover and pillow cases into the bathtub and filled it with water.

Taking his duffle bag, which he carried in place of a suitcase, he slipped out of the room.

No one was in the corridor, but rather than walk through the lobby, even at this early hour, he went out the back entrance, where a security alarm would have sounded had he not disabled it earlier. The door led onto the parking lot.

Which one was Bruber's car? He was sure Bruber would be down at the helicopter pad dealing with getting the fucking bigwigs out of this phony, god-forsaken postcard place. Bruber would be tied up there till everyone was safely on their private planes and air-bound for their individual cushy offices.

Johnson wondered if Bruber would check the choppers for bombs. Maybe that had been done in Zurich, before they took off. If he were in charge, he'd check both places, but he'd seen much more action in his lifetime than Bruber ever had. Sure, sure, sure the man had been in the Swiss military, but had he seen action in real wars in Asia, Africa and the Middle East? That fuckhead probably wouldn't know what to do if a real bullet whistled by him.

Overhead the sounds of choppers beat their own melody, as if the heavens were corroborating his thoughts.

No more time to think, time to do.

Johnson had been a master car thief since his teens. He also was a master at not getting caught, so he took it for granted that he would be out of the village within minutes after locating Bruber's Volvo. He lived up to his own expectations, opening the lock and starting the car in less than a minute before heading down the mountain.

Not one regret did he feel in leaving this living, fucking postcard. What he did regret was that the asshole Masterson had fired him. One thing Johnson couldn't stand was being called incompetent, but Masterson had called him that—and worse.

Masterson had been shaking. The television had been blathering on in the background about hackers. He'd been hired to prevent the attack that Masterson was sure would happen, thanks to information from some United States government contact of the asshole.

Johnson had found out who was doing the planning, an unlikely duo, who should have been easy to stop.

His one regret was hiring Anderson to do the job that he should have taken care of himself. That was Masterson's fault too. Had he not insisted that Johnson stay with him, Johnson would have accomplished the mission. Shit.

Now, against all logic and his better judgment, he was honor-bound to somehow avenge the whole situation, not that it would do much good. It was stupid, even, but he couldn't allow any other course of action, even if nobody but he would even know about it.

Johnson was a perfectionist, and he couldn't allow any imperfection to survive—not on his watch!

His first decision was whether to leave the car in the next village or two villages away. He glanced at his watch. 5:05. Dawn was still awhile away, but the Swiss were ungodly early risers.

In the first village the train station and coffee shop were still closed, as they were in the second and third villages. It was 5:30 when he drove into the parking lot of the fourth station. The lights came on in the coffee shop. He circled around and parked next to the only two other cars in the lot.

He was hungry, but didn't want to call attention to himself by going into the coffee shop. Probably those fairy-fucking croissants wouldn't have been delivered yet anyway.

This village couldn't be more than three thousand people and probably the man who ran the shop would know everyone in town and would remember him when they found that bastard Bruber's car.

A car pulled in and a woman with a briefcase got out and headed for the blue ticket machine outside the entrance. She put money in the machine, took something, which Johnson assumed was a ticket and disappeared down a stairway. A minute or two later, she emerged on platform two. A recorded voice announced a train heading to Zurich in ten minutes.

During that ten-minute period seven other cars pulled in; the owners bought tickets and ended up on the same platform as the woman.

At least he had a choice of cars. The woman's was a bright red, but all the others were gray. A gray car would be less conspicuous and by the time the owner returned at the end of the day he would be out of the country.

What he didn't like was his lack of pre-planning. Sure, he could react with lightning speed to emergencies, but he also knew that the better the plan, the less chance there was that emergencies would arrive. And Masterson's unexpected, unfair firing of him two hours ago made pre-planning impossible.

He could thank his bastard father for his pre-planning ability. As he waited for platform two to empty, his father intruded on his thoughts much more than he would have liked. Johnson knew that his father had been the stereotypical demanding military father: a master sergeant on steroids.

Nothing less than perfection was acceptable. Even an A- was cause for punishment, although his father had never laid a hand on Burt. Push-ups, running miles, lifting weights and even extra studying were assigned. Johnson thought it was a good thing he was a natural at football, although he would have preferred to play basketball. If he dropped the ball during a game or made any other move his father deemed a mistake on the field, the same discipline was rolled out.

His final punishment was his father disowning him for the sin of not being accepted at West Point. That Burt enlisted and moved up the ranks to become a master sergeant like his father did not cause his father to seek a reunion, even when a military friend tried to intervene.

Burt had won medals in Iraq and during his last tour in Afghanistan: he decided he would never win over his father, so let the bastard rot in hell. It was at the same point that he realized that the military contractors made more in a day than he made in a month and he was better than most of them. His next move was a no-brainer.

When he got out of Bruber's car he could see his breath just as he had that day in Afghanistan when he'd made the decision to leave the army and become a contractor. He'd been on a mission and this kid, who had joined up believing all that patriotic shit about making his country safe from the Taliban, had been shot to hell and back, literally and figuratively and had died. He'd been a good kid with a wife and baby. It wasn't the first kid under him that Johnson had seen die, it was just the one too many.

By that point he had read enough and seen enough to have lost all belief in what he was doing there. He was the tool for a war machine that would profit on the blood of others. Now he was in it for himself and himself alone.

As soon as he could get out of the army, he got out. Even before the ink was dry on his discharge papers he'd signed up to work with one of the larger contractors. Since then he'd had contracts with the top three working in Afghanistan, Iraq, Somalia and countries that many people had never heard of, much less would have been able to find on the map.

His bank account grew to six figures and was working its way up to seven fast, but much of his wealth was in gold and silver. He wasn't going to take any chances of a bank stealing his money, and he certainly wasn't going to gamble on the stock market with its crooked products. In Latin America he'd made a killing on copper and turned his profit into rental property run by a trust that no one would ever discover.

Now, Johnson didn't need to work at all, but he couldn't imagine spending all his days doing nothing. He loved challenges and overcoming them. Boredom was unacceptable.

When one contract in Ecuador ended, he decided to go out on his own. Working for Masterson was his twenty-first private gig. And Masterson said he'd messed up. He used the same tone and words Johnson's father used to use. Johnson felt like he should drop to the floor and do push-ups.

What now?

He would finish the job on his own dime, centime, peso, kroner, franc. The train pulled in and out leaving the platform empty. It would be a half hour before the next train, according to the board on platform one.

Johnson chose a gray VW and was off to Zurich. He needed to get to his safety deposit box, change passports, get another set of credit cards, change his hair color and remove the lifts from his shoes.

He decided not to fly out of Zurich. He weighed Basel or Geneva. If his destination was Scotland, maybe the best route would be via Vienna. No, he would take the train from Zurich to Geneva and fly from there. He used his phone to book his flight. On his way to Zurich he pulled over alongside a lake, rolled down his window and threw the phone into the water. No one was around to see him do it.

As he drove down the mountain toward Zurich, he was smiling. He loved a challenge and there were challenges ahead.

CHAPTER 41

When Annie woke around two she realized that Mercury had snuck up on the bottom of the bed once again. No matter how she twisted she could not find a comfortable position. The dog would get up each time she turned. With the duvet she was too hot, without it too cold.

Roger slept through it all, curled up like a baby and for once was sleeping noiselessly. She touched him to make sure he was alive: he was.

Annie gave up, threw on Janet's robe, peed and went downstairs. Her early morning or late night movements were becoming a habit. She decided to work on the book—the onerous book as she'd begun to think of it.

Annie had never suffered from writer's block. As a tech writer with tight deadlines, writer's block was a disease akin to leprosy. You sat. You wrote. Full stop.

She'd already covered Etheldreda's mother and her subject's marriage to Tonbert. She'd verified that the Anglo-Saxon houses were made of wood and that the Fens were subject to floods. Now she needed to deal with what happened after Tonbert died.

She put her fingers to the keyboard and began to write. "The day the rain stopped, Tonbert died. The two serving women helped Etheldreda clean the body. The carpenter and eel basket-maker asked if they could dig the grave to honor him."

The dining room was cold. She debated putting on the gas

fire, but she felt that was a little nervy in someone else's house. She had no idea what Rod and Janet's personal financial situation was, but with such an uncertain future, she didn't want to run up any bills for Janet.

In the living room she found an afghan and wrapped it around herself before settling back down to write. She heard the clock strike 4:30 and looked up. At least she now had something concrete down on paper even if it needed editing later.

Maybe she could get back to sleep now. Mercury did not wake up when she shut off the light and headed for the bedroom.

When she slipped into bed, Roger half woke and pulled her to him. As he had done countless times before, he put her hand on his hard penis. One of the great enjoyments of their sex life had been what they called half-asleep sex. If he could have an erection, maybe that meant her sex life wasn't dead forever.

She kissed his neck and he responded. "I love you," she whispered as she put his hand on her breast. Neither of them ever had a problem letting the other know what they wanted.

For a too-short time they stroked each other, then Roger froze. "I can't."

"I don't understand."

"I can't. What if it brings on another attack?"

"It would be a great way to go." Annie hadn't meant to be glib, but the words slipped out of her mouth before she could stop them.

He pulled his arm out from under her head. "I'm serious."

She apologized. "The Internet has said people can have sex after heart attacks."

"They didn't say when, and you can't believe everything you read on the Internet."

"I don't want to be responsible for killing you with love. Why don't you check with your doctor during your next appointment?"

Roger didn't answer.

Annie didn't want to press the issue: she didn't know how to alleviate his fears or hers.

As Roger fell back asleep, Annie thought again of what she would write next but she didn't have the energy to go downstairs. Instead, she snuggled under the duvet but her mind wouldn't shut off.

Usually she loved the research. Parts of working on the Anglo-Saxon woman's life were fascinating, such as trying to figure out who used what tools, how things were made and of what. Anglo-Saxon information was scanty in comparison to later periods.

What annoyed Annie wasn't the dearth of minor details of the period, but information about Etheldreda herself, aside from dates, marriages and her religious life. Being married and still a virgin was not a concept that Annie found sympathetic, especially when her own sex life looked so bleak. And try as she might to smother these feelings, they kept coming back and back.

It wasn't like she didn't know that marrying an older man meant she would probably outlive him. She knew that on her wedding day. She knew it before her wedding day.

She had anticipated she would care for him in his dotage. "Dotage," now there was a word she loved, right up there with "peckish" and "gobsmacked."

Had Roger arrived at his dotage when he was in his mid-seventies and she was in her sixties that would be expected, but she was in her thirties for heaven's sake, much too young to be sentenced to a life of celibacy.

Annie was angry with herself that she was not the type to have affairs. Her celibacy was not out of a sense of purity or religion, but a sense of having made a promise. Good old New England ethics, her mother would call it.

Shit on ethics.

Ethics sucked.

As much as she would have liked to call her publisher to tell him he could take his book and shove it, she knew she wouldn't. Ethics again.

Instead she made a mental note to find a photo of the headgear that any good Anglo-Saxon warrior would have worn into battle.

CHAPTER 42
ELY 655

The day the rain stopped, Tonbert died. The two serving women helped Etheldreda clean the body. The carpenter and eel basket-maker asked if they could dig the grave to honor him. She said yes, and they found a place in a field to the left of the house.

Annie allowed a bit of sympathy for the widow to sneak into her heart as she wrote this, trying to muster up how she would feel had Roger died of his heart attack. And maybe she could add a bit of conflict here.

A small clay pot placed by the doorway held Tonbert's ring and belt buckle. Another was filled with bread and honey for him to eat in the afterlife, which Etheldreda was sure would be denied him as a nonbeliever.

Although she would have preferred a Christian burial, he had never converted. Nor had he held much to pagan beliefs either, but since he was closer to pagan, she decided to follow the pagan funeral customs. She prayed to God for forgiveness for not succeeding in showing him the true religion.

Note to self: Check the funeral pagan funeral rites and add a line or two. I know by location a sea burial won't work. Check out funeral pyres for Anglo-Saxon pagans.

★ ★ ★ ★ ★

In the weeks that followed Tonbert's death, Etheldreda knew a heaviness that she had never felt before. Although she was busy helping those that had been so hurt by the spring's flooding, at night she found herself crying.

Because she was so busy during the day, she had less time to pray, but she imagined Wilfrid saying she was doing God's work in helping those that needed it. In fact, when she wrote him about her worries, he wrote back using almost the same words she imagined him saying. What surprised her was when he said, "You must miss your companion, whom you loved."

When she read what he'd written, she realized that she *had* loved her husband in the pure sense. That she had relied on him not just for his knowledge but for his humor and his music. She missed his smile when she placed his dinner before him, his concern that she was warm enough, his willingness to listen to what she thought.

More than once she'd sat in his room, held his cloak and buried herself in the fur lining that still held his smell. At the same time, she felt a tremendous freedom to now put her plans for an abbey into practice.

CHAPTER 43

Burt Johnson walked through Edinburgh customs holding his British passport. Traveling by air was getting harder and harder as Interpol's database expanded, alerting airlines to phony passports.

Interpol's databases and/or biometric passports were making all the ones he'd collected over the years useless. Getting new ones was becoming next to impossible. He knew of too many people, like himself, who had paid a fortune for a fake biometric passport only to be bagged in the customs line. One could no longer trust those idiot border people to just glance at the passport and boarding pass and wave one through.

His first stop was at the electronic shop on the upper story to pick up a new burner phone, load it and then wait for the Airlink bus to take him to the Haymarket train station.

He liked Edinburgh. The outskirts were mainly family homes with tiny flower gardens in front. Others had used the same space to park their cars. Had he taken a different course in life, he might have ended up in such a house with a wife and kids.

From the time he'd first gone to Scotland on an exchange program his junior year of high school, he'd felt an affinity for the country, although he still preferred the woods and wildness of the north, where a man could get as lost as he wanted.

The suburbs gave way to the city with its two- and three-story buildings, the park and the castle on the hill. Because of the late hour, traffic was light. The stores were closed.

Restaurants were doing a final cleanup before personnel went home for the night.

Good thing he'd bought a sandwich, albeit a sorry excuse for one, on the plane. Right now, his strongest desire was to crash.

Shouldering his backpack from the Airlink, he walked off the bus at Haymarket and entered the Military Hotel across from the station. The current owner, a former soldier dressed in a kilt, was in the office. "Welcome back, Major Nigro. If you'd let us know you were coming, we'd have freshened your digs."

"Last-minute decision," Johnson said. He'd rented that room in the hotel, once a private home year round, for the past five years, using it as a base before going north. He'd seen it go through three different owners, which was fine with him.

Upstairs, he threw his backpack on the chair and turned on the TV. It was not a plasma screen but an older model, with only the UK channels. BBC News was talking about the economic problems with the banks and how people couldn't get to their money.

Talking heads raged on about trying to straighten out their systems . . . doing everything possible . . . economic terrorism . . . couldn't have seen it coming . . . blah, blah, blah. A real fuck-up that was, although none of them would have said "fuck-up" on the air. None of them could have known that it was Johnson's crew that had fucked up. Had they done their jobs, the job Masterson had hired him to do, there would have been no cyber-attack, or at least not this one. No one could identify all the hackers out there—no one.

On the other hand, he had to smile. Masterson must be shit-ting bricks at this point, as well as the other assholes who'd been at the Golden Aigle. They thought they were so smart, those damned bankers. Pumped-up little assholes.

He loved watching the chaos that had been created when almost no bank could operate. Stores were closing because debit and credit cards no longer worked and people were unable to get cash from their ATMs. One Sky reporter was talking to a mother who had run out of food.

He switched to BBC to see Nigel Carter say they were doing everything possible to get the IT systems up and running.

He admitted a certain sense of enjoyment that all those fucking bank big shots were so distressed.

Still, he should have prevented it by doing the job himself instead of contracting it out, but it had seemed so simple. He knew his targets. So much for trying to build up a stable of subcontractors; from now on he would do the delicate jobs himself.

He showered. The mildew around the edge of the shower stall didn't bother him, nor did the leak that hadn't been fixed, even though he'd asked it to be done when he'd been there over a year ago. Compared to the places he'd slept in in the Middle East, Africa or Asia, mildew and leaks weren't a problem.

After toweling himself off, he fell asleep.

The sun arrived late in the morning, as it always did in October. The three things about Scotland he didn't like were the short days, the long winters and the rain. At the same time in a perverse way it fit his mood.

Downstairs he walked by a mannequin dressed in a military uniform, which included a kilt. He noticed that Alice was still the waitress. For his last five stays, she'd been there putting out the hot water for tea, filling the bread baskets and delivering plates to the table.

She gave him a big hug. She was in her mid-thirties and he noticed that she'd frosted her hair. No one could call her pretty, but she was in no danger of breaking any mirrors. She carried herself well with an almost military posture. He'd debated asking her once had she been in the service, but he didn't want any questions in return. As much as he shunned attachments, every now and then it was a nice change for someone to greet him.

"Welcome back, Major Nigro. Long time no see. Staying long?"

"I'm not sure yet." He wasn't.

His next step was unclear to him and he hated to act if he couldn't think things through. He needed to find a new client, but not for money. Not like some of the idiots he knew doing the same thing he did. They blew everything they earned on fast cars, faster women and gambling.

He needed to stay on top of his game, wipe out the last failure with a success. He'd always felt superior to the people in his profession who would want to disappear into Latin America or some island with palm trees. His idea of wonderful was the rugged backwoods of Scotland, with its lochs and bracken, where he could hunt and fish and live in a cabin without anyone bothering him—that is until he got bored.

Up until now his greatest fear had been boredom. After X amount of idleness he found that he always needed a challenge and that need was what had motivated him to take Masterson's assignment. Well fuck Masterson. Fuck the hackers.

He'd finish the job he'd started as he always had and always would—with or without pay. He didn't even care if Masterson knew. He wasn't doing it for him. This would be for himself.

Alice brought him a proper fry-up complete with potato scones. She poured him a cup of coffee, which he knew wouldn't match the continental coffee. He loved the Scots but not their coffee-making skills. Still, tea was a drink for old ladies.

The perceived failure in his last assignment left a worse taste than the coffee. God damn it, his mind kept coming back to that. That had to be rectified. His motto had always been "don't get mad, get even," just like his father.

He didn't have to worry about his reputation. Masterson

could never admit his part in the cock-up without jeopardizing himself, although he suspected that swaggering idiot thought that he was invincible. That asshole had bought so many government officials that prosecution for his financial crimes was unlikely, but murder was over the top and even his connections wouldn't get him off. It was a moot point. It would never come to that.

On the other hand, Masterson might bad-mouth Johnson to potential new banking clients. That was a relatively new sector for Johnson. He dealt more with military problems and military solutions: drug lords in Afghanistan, crooked contractors in Iraq, a coup in Asia or Africa.

He'd done some work for oil companies and agricultural conglomerates.

What he needed to do now was tie up the loose ends from this debacle but first finish breakfast; then he would head up north, where he could once again change identities.

CHAPTER 44

"I really appreciate it." Janet stood at the front door. Outside the sidewalk had been reporter-free for the past twenty-four hours. A scandal had broken out concerning a mayor two villages away. He had run away from his wife with a man. Funds were missing. It was not as big a story as a murder with the suspected killer on the run. Yet it was enough to get the journalists to go elsewhere.

"It's the least I can do," Annie said. After wrapping a scarf around her neck she clamped a beret on her wild hair and stood behind Janet. Mercury looked hopeful that he would get a second walk that morning until Janet shook her head and pointed to his couch. On his way to the couch, he picked up his teddy bear and put it under his chin as he lay down.

"I'll make sure Roger gets his medicine," Janet said as Annie walked past, giving her a kiss on each cheek.

The breeze was just strong enough to pick at Annie's face as she ducked through the arch where Rod had nearly been run over. Instead of heading to his office, she walked toward the back of the school, where the car that tried to hit him must have been parked.

Although the hit and run accident had at first been considered a one-off, everyone now felt it was related to Simon's murder, although when Annie said "everyone," she meant herself, Janet and Roger. Oh yes, and Marc. The two detectives talked about coincidence, but Roger had said that they might be saying that rather than reveal what they really thought.

Welch had even asked if they thought that Rod killed Simon before Simon killed Rod, which caused Janet to ask, "Are you crazy?" The detectives had let it drop, but Roger was sure that they might follow up on it later.

Even if she thought the car must have parked there based on Rod's description of its direction when it hit him, any other information was long gone. She chided herself for expecting to discover anything new instead of doing what she had set out to do—see how things were working in Rod's company.

The cathedral rose in front of her. Annie could never look at an old building without wishing she knew more about the people who had built it and lived in it. Not their names so much as what they had had for dinner, were they happily married, etc., etc., etc.

When she arrived at Rod's office, the secretary, Maud, jumped up. She wore a short skirt, blouse and one of those sweaters that only had sleeves above the elbow. The whole outfit was a gray/silver. The high black boots made her look extra stylish, despite the extra pounds, unlike many of the computer nerds at the desks in their sloppy jeans. "Janet said you were coming." Then she led Annie to Rod's office. "May I get you a coffee?"

"Thank you."

She pulled Annie to one side where they could not be heard. "I'm glad you're here. William just doesn't have it in him to manage. The workflow is really catastrophic. We have enough work to do but things get reassigned and reassigned again, and no one has a chance to finish a project."

"Bring me all the projects that are in-house, if you know them."

"Oh, I do," Maud said. "Do you want me to print the work log out for you, or should I e-mail it to you?"

Annie looked around the office and saw a laptop. "Do I have access? Or do you want me to use my own laptop?"

Maud went to the laptop on the desk and turned it on. "Let's keep everything in the office."

Going over the work log, Annie saw the problem. The type of work was well explained, thanks to an excellent system, but moving the project from person to person meant that the work was being handled choppily. Daily assignments made no sense.

Annie realized that she would have to talk to each person, but she was unsure whether she should do it as a group or individually.

She needed to start with William. How she hated managing people, which was the main reason she loved how she normally worked. With short-term assignments there was no managing, no office politics to pull her down: much better to watch people turn themselves inside out from an emotional distance.

As William walked by the door, she called him in. She wasn't sure how to tell him he was doing a lousy job. Twice she opened her mouth and closed it.

He sat up straight in his chair. "I'm doing a terrible job, that's what you're not saying," he said.

Her first inclination was to make him feel better, but that wasn't going to help anything. Too bad: he seemed like such a nice chap.

"It's all right. That's why I'm a programmer. You probably chose me because I'm the old guy around here."

"I wouldn't put it that way," Annie said, although she knew both she and Janet thought his age would be preferable over the young bucks, as Janet had called the rest of the staff. "Who would you recommend if you weren't in charge?"

"Maud." When Annie said nothing, William said, "She's the most organized person I know and she knows all aspects of what's going on. It doesn't matter that she doesn't understand the techie part. Someone else can recommend the time a project might take."

He stood up. When he reached the door, Annie called him back.

"What can you tell me about Simon or anything he and Rod might have been working on that might not be in the regular work log?"

William sat back down. "I know they were doing something top secret. I'm not sure it was billable. The few times that Simon showed up, he and Rod huddled together in here for hours and no one was allowed to come near them."

Annie took the information in but it wasn't enough. "Why not billable?"

"I may not be a good manager, but I did have Maud show me all the billable projects. I was terrified we'd lose money and I didn't want that to happen on my watch. There was nothing for the two of them, nothing for Simon either."

"Didn't Simon get paid?"

"Sure. But it wasn't tied to any of the codes for any project."

This time when he stood up, Annie didn't call him back.

By lunchtime, Annie had Maud prepped for her new duties. Or rather Maud prepped Annie on the rearrangement of projects. Then they'd met with the staff.

Rather than head back to Janet's, Annie decided to go back to the museum to see if they had anything more on Etheldreda. As she walked down High Street, she wondered what the Anglo-Saxon woman would make of Ely today. She certainly wouldn't understand the lack of a religious climate of the early twenty-first century.

In her imagination, she had Etheldreda walking beside her and seeing the scantily clothed young girls. Annie pictured her being shown a porn site on the Internet. Mentally she slapped herself. She couldn't let herself slip into disliking Etheldreda but needed to keep her in the context of the time in which she had lived.

CHAPTER 45

Annie put down her teacup after finishing one of the best cups of tea she ever remembered drinking. The museum director had made it for her and offered a chocolate biscuit as well. Only politeness kept Annie from asking for seconds. After all, she was taking the woman's time, peppering her with questions about Anglo-Saxons in the area.

The director, who was probably the same age as Annie's mother, was quite stylish in a tweedy sort of way. Her dark hair had a streak of gray that framed her face.

"Do you have everything you need?"

Annie filed the document she had been using to take notes as the woman was talking.

"I know more about pottery, jewelry, clothing, food and housing than I did when I came in here." Under ordinary circumstances she would have loved ferreting out the information, but with all the problems and her almost impossible deadline every shortcut she could find was welcomed.

Once again, she cursed herself for taking on this project, then cursed herself for cursing herself.

Before leaving the museum, she thanked the director profusely.

It was already dark as she walked down High Street. Some shops were closing. The butcher's window, which had been full of chops and sausages when she passed earlier, now had empty trays. Likewise, there was only one cake, of indeterminate flavor, and a lone chocolate cupcake in the bakery window. She went in and came out with the cake. Janet hadn't said what she was preparing for dinner, but Annie still harbored leech feelings. How she hated to take more than she gave. The cake would help assuage these feelings.

Between her laptop and the cake her hands were full so she put the laptop case strap over her head so that it crossed in front of her chest, leaving her hands free to hold the cake box by the string wrapped around the box.

The evening was crisp and she wrapped her scarf around her neck with her one free hand as she cut through the passage by the cathedral. The stone wall was on one side and the field on the other side of the passage. In front of her she could see lights from King's School. No one could be seen at the windows nor was there anyone along the path.

The gray mare in the field sidled up to the fence. Annie leaned against the fence to pat her with the hand not holding the cake box. Out of nowhere, or so it seemed, an arm wrapped around her neck as someone tried to pull her laptop strap from her shoulder. Because it wasn't just on her shoulder but over her head crisscrossing her chest, it pulled against her neck.

Annie had taken enough self-defense courses to know that instead of stiffening, she should relax. The man, for she assumed it was a man both by the size and the smell of aftershave lotion, loosened his grip long enough for her to turn and knee him in the crotch. She ran screaming like a banshee, although she didn't know what a banshee really sounded like, until she ducked under the arch and was on the street where there were other people, who stopped to stare at her.

When she gasped out what had happened, a man probably in his mid-twenties dashed under the arch. The other bystanders asked if she was all right.

"Just shaken," she managed to say. Involuntarily her hand

rubbed her neck.

The man who had gone after the attacker returned. "He's long gone." He bowed and disappeared in the crowd.

An older man, although when she thought about it, he was probably around Roger's age, offered to walk her home after saying there'd been quite a few women roughed up for their purses over the past few months.

"I'm staying just there." She pointed to Janet's house.

The five people remaining turned and looked at where two press vans were once again parked. One whispered loud enough for Annie to hear, "The one where the geek disappeared," and then another said not quite as softly, "The murderer's house."

"Rod wouldn't hurt a mouse." Annie walked away.

The older man followed, "People jump to conclusions."

Annie knew that she had done that enough times but it was one thing to jump to a conclusion yourself and another thing to have your friends at the end of the erroneous conclusion. "I'm really okay," she said to him. "Besides, you don't want them to become aware of you."

"You're right." He turned and crossed the small park area and disappeared into the gathering night.

As she walked up to the front door four people, two men, two women, jumped from the press van.

"Who are you?"

"Are you a friend of MacKenzie?"

"Where is he?"

"Do you think he might be dead too?"

She pushed past them and ignoring them as best as anyone could with a microphone shoved in their face, she laid on the buzzer. How in hell did they have their equipment ready so fast? Had she not been so annoyed and upset, she might have admired their professionalism, but she wasn't about to give them any credit at all.

Finally, Roger came to the door. Marc and Janet stood behind him as Annie slipped through the door and led them to the living room.

Without even taking off her coat she told them what had happened.

"Do you want to call the police?" Janet asked.

Roger already had his phone out, but when he realized he didn't know the number, he pocketed it.

"The man is probably long gone. I didn't get a chance to look at him." She sank onto Mercury's sofa, her shaking legs not able to support her.

"He was grabbing my computer."

"A regular robbery?" Marc asked.

"Maybe, maybe not," Roger said. "From now on whenever you women go out, I go with you."

Annie wanted to point out that he wouldn't, shouldn't and likely couldn't protect them in his current physical state, but she lacked the energy. They could argue about it later. Instead she put her head back against the cushions and closed her eyes, letting the voices drift around her.

CHAPTER 46
ELY 660

Annie was still upset when she sat down to work. The attack yesterday had left her shaken, but her schedule didn't allow for shaken-breaks.

On a day where bird song filled the air and the sun was too hot, Etheldreda toured her holding in Ely. The water from the almost annual floods had receded. The silt would enrich the land for the crops just as when the farmers plowed the remaining stalks into the ground to nourish the soil in the autumn. Already the land that had been replanted showed green shoots for various crops. The houses that had been water damaged were being rebuilt or at least swept clean of mud.

Etheldreda's mare was a quiet little creature that preferred walking to galloping. It allowed Etheldreda to meditate as she rode from farm to farm. An apple orchard with all the trees in the last part of their bloom perfumed the air, drowning out the remains of the smell of the manure piles she'd passed about a half mile back. The breeze was an excellent messenger.

Her plans to build an abbey had been delayed by her work, which she considered two-fold. One was to help the peasants through their river battles. The second was to commune with her Lord.

She and Wilfrid, who had just been put in charge of a new monastery in Ripon, had exchanged plans for the building. He had been her spiritual leader, but his common sense approach to the management of whatever needed to be managed built on the teachings of her late husband.

The seasons since Tonbert's death had passed so quickly that she barely realized that a fourth summer was upon her.

As she rode along the banks of the Ouse, a few ducks swam in circles. Every now and then one would stand on its head in the water, with its tail pointed skyward, before returning to its normal position. Sometimes its beak would move up and down as it swallowed whatever goodie it had located.

Annie imagined the river probably looked much like it did now, only without the modern boats.

An eel fisherman put his long willow basket in the water.

"Good luck," Etheldreda called.

He smiled and waved.

It had taken time since her husband died for her to feel lighter, although the feeling was fleeting. She stared back toward the field where her house was. What a perfect spot for her abbey.

Annie let some sympathy for the woman creep into her writing. To want something badly and not be able to get it for reasons so out of one's control was not limited to seventh-century royalty. And from what she had gleaned so far, Etheldreda did help those she was responsible for—more than Annie could say for some modern leaders.

After talking with each villager, it was late afternoon before Etheldreda arrived back at her house.

She was famished. She'd taken some bread and sheep's cheese and an apple with her, but the fresh air had sharpened her appetite. The cook had promised her onion porridge for dinner and there were also dandelion leaves that the cook had picked and boiled.

A horse she didn't recognize was tied to the post outside the house. She opened the door and entered the big hall. Her father sat on one of the benches, his back leaning against the wall. There was no fire, and the windows were open, letting in sweet, spring air. He started at the sound of her footsteps and then jumped up. "Etheldreda, daughter."

"Father, how good to see you." She had heard that he had been in Mercia negotiating with Penda yet again, an event that matched—almost—the regularity of the sun coming up each morning.

She'd also heard that Penda was determined to attack Oswig of Bernicia, but she was not sure which side her father backed, nor did she care. She barely had time to learn who was king in one region before that king was replaced. Her father's longevity had a lot to do with his being able to pick winners. In that she was proud of him, although pride was a sin.

"Have you been here long?"

"Since this morning. Your maid told me what you were doing."

Etheldreda thought her father had grown grayer since she'd last seen him. His body, however, was still all muscle.

The cook announced that dinner was ready and Etheldreda noticed a chicken that had not been planned for dinner was on the table. She didn't ask which one had been slaughtered. One of the hens had stopped laying plus this year's crop of chicks was already hatched without that particular hen's contributions.

"I'll make sure that Tonbert's old room is ready for you. You *are* staying the night?"

Onna took another swig of the beer the cook had placed next to his wooden bowl. "For the night and we ride out in the morning."

"We?"

"You and I. Besides wanting to see you, it is time for you to come home."

"No, I don't think so."

Onna stood up. When he leaned toward his daughter his hovering caused her to lean back as if she feared that he was about to strike her. "You don't think so?"

"I belong here. This is my land, my life." Etheldreda knew that Onna was not accustomed to his wishes being denied. All he had to do usually was put out his hand and whatever he had asked for was put into it as fast as the person closest to him could do it.

"Your place is with your family in East Anglia."

"I'm a widow and my husband gave me this place as a morning gift. I'm staying."

Onna had long ago mastered the art of the tantrum as his tool of intimidation. He found it effective in negotiations with the other kings in the Heptarchy. It wasn't effective with his daughter.

His daughter did not move. Nor did her facial expression change. She sat on the bench with her arms folded on the table as she watched him pace and holler. She thought if she were pagan she would believe that the god Thunor was creating thunder within her father's body.

"I could throw you over my horse," he said after he had calmed down.

"You could." There was no sense in Etheldreda denying what was true. "But I don't think you will."

"Why not?" Onna's voice was hoarse.

"Because you've nothing to gain in making me your enemy, and everything to gain by leaving me in peace." She wasn't sure what he would gain just as she had no idea how to behave as an enemy to her father, but it felt as if it were the most logical thing she could say and that it just might move him.

"Would you kill me? Your own father?"

"Probably not. There is the commandment 'thou shall not

kill.' " Patricide would have destroyed her not out of love of her father, but because it would put her soul in jeopardy. This was one of the reasons she hated all the wars and couldn't understand how Christians could fight them and still believe in the commandments. The commandment did not read, "thou shall not kill except on the battlefield." She was not about to say this to her father.

Annie could find no reference that Etheldreda had been anti-war but it made sense that she would be. She had no illusions that many people would read the book, but the temptation to slip in her own anti-war point of view was too great to resist. Quentin could take it out if he wanted to when he edited the manuscript.

"This is an area of peace, not a place you need worry will raise an army to attack you. The annual floods make it uninteresting to the other kings."

Onna gaped at his daughter. "You are planning to be a king, daughter? Impossible."

"Yes, it is impossible. But I am a landowner. Just think about it."

In delaying her father's plans, she was allowing him to leave without losing. She knew how much he hated losing at anything, even something as simple as arm wrestling.

"She did nothing to encourage him to spend the night but he did. In the morning he'd left before she woke.

Annie thought how she might have chafed under the limitations for women that Etheldreda faced. Heck, she wouldn't have wanted to live in the pre–women's lib days when her only alternative would be a career as a teacher, nurse, secretary or wife. She'd never have the life she had now, even with the current problems. Glancing at her watch, she realized that she had no more time to write that day and even if she did, she was just too damned tired.

CHAPTER 47

Annie woke to the sounds of the shower running next door. She turned to Roger only to find the bed empty. She glanced at the clock: 9:51.

How had she slept so long? And so hard?

She'd almost fallen asleep when they'd been arguing for a second day about whether to tell the police about her attack.

Some people, when they are upset, eat. Annie slept her way through problems as if by being unconscious things would work themselves out around her. She barely remembered Marc, Janet and Roger urging her upstairs to lie down after dinner. Not all her tiredness was from the aftermath of the attack. Part of it was from being locked into her computer and working on the book until every muscle seemed frozen.

Good lord, she was still in her sweatshirt and her jeans, although they had been unbuttoned at the waist. Roger must have simply pulled up the covers and let her sleep.

She felt queasy. One of the problems of seeming calm outside was that the turbulence inside her body took its own toll.

Roger came into the room, a towel wrapped around his waist and his hair a mass of wet curls, just as Annie was standing up. His chest bore the stapling from the surgery. She thought it looked like a zipper. He kissed the top of her head. "I couldn't stand it if something happened to you," he said.

She shivered. "And you think I feel any differently about you?"

They stood hugging. Annie broke the hold. "My mouth feels like dead eels."

"And how do dead eels feel?"

"Like my mouth."

He hit her bum.

Annie went downstairs. Mercury jumped off the couch to greet her. She gave him a rawhide.

Outside, she could see the press contingent had disappeared. One of the arguments against calling the police was that the press would see them and that would probably increase the attention that the house had. Now she didn't have that argument.

She could hear Janet singing in her atelier, the "Zip-a-Dee-Doo-Dah" song. Had Rod not been missing, it would not seem so strange. Probably trying to keep up her courage, she thought.

Janet poked her head into the dining room. "I've waited for you to have breakfast. Let me do a real English fry-up." When Annie frowned, Janet added, "I know Roger is supposed to eat a light cholesterol diet, but one meal won't hurt him and Marc is a bottomless pit."

The earlier queasiness had disappeared. "Go for it. I'm starved. Need help?"

"Set the table."

Roger was the next one down. "I smell bacon. I thought it was on my no-no list."

"We decided to kill you," Annie said, then slapped her hand over her mouth at her slip.

"It's okay," Janet called from the kitchen. "I don't believe Rod is dead." She resumed her humming.

Roger and Annie exchanged glances that said they weren't so sure.

Annie went to the foot of the stairs and yelled, "Marc, a breakfast you'll love is almost on the table."

"I'm checking the news on my computer. I'll be right down."

He wasn't right down. Janet served up the meal and the three of them sat waiting for him. Five, six, seven, eight, nine, ten minutes went by and just as Annie was about to call him again, he thundered down the stairs. "You won't believe this, but hackers have done a DDOS on that Swiss bank you worked for."

Annie gasped. "Which one? I worked for several."

"ZBPI."

"What's DDOS?" Janet asked, pouring some tea for Marc as he sat at the table.

"Distributed denial of service. They go into the computer system and make sure that all of a company's, or in this case a bank's, computer system goes down. Thus, there are no deposits, withdrawals, credit card payments okayed, ATMs. Nothing," Marc said. "That's not all. At least ten other banks have been hit also. In the USA, UK and various other places as well."

All four of them rushed into the living room and put on the set. For the next half hour they frantically switched between CNN, Bloomberg, DW, MSNBC, ITV, BBC, Al Jazeera and RT—and all were covering the story and nothing else. The number of banks grew: fifteen, twenty, twenty-five. A few of the big investment houses were also hit.

By eleven in the morning the United States president, the British prime minister, the French president, the German chancellor, and probably more leaders that they just hadn't heard about had all appeared on television, calling it a state of emergency.

"What does this mean?" Janet asked.

"For one thing no one who has money in any of these banks can get at it," Roger said.

"It had to be a genius to pull this off," Marc said. "It's better than a bomb."

BBC said that the heads of the International Monetary Fund

and the World Bank were meeting even though it was before dawn in Washington D.C.

"A monetary 9/11," one station started calling it and others soon followed.

"How are we for cash?" Roger asked when all the stations seemed to be circling the same story. It was after lunch.

"I've only been using my debit card." Annie used her mobile phone to check with her bank in France. "A 'cannot connect' message comes up."

"I've money in the house that the robbers didn't find," Janet said.

"They weren't looking for cash," Roger reminded her as they walked back into the dining room. "At least one good thing has come out of it." He pointed to the sidewalk outside the house. Not a reporter was to be seen.

CHAPTER 48

"Is your appointment with the church historian still on?" Roger asked. Now that the television news was just recycling the same DDOS story, they had shut the television off.

Janet had cleaned up the breakfast, which they had moved to the lounge to eat while watching the news channels. Annie and Marc had pulled themselves away long enough to shower and dress. Roger was back from taking Mercury for a walk.

"He hasn't called to cancel."

"I'm going with you." Before she could interrupt him he held up his hand. "And I want you to show me where the guy went after your laptop."

"You're not planning to launch your own investigation, are you?" The last thing Annie needed was for Roger to start overdoing things. But more and more, she was aware that her acting like a mother hen would be as destructive to their relationship as when he did it to her. This was going to be a balancing act that she wasn't sure how to accomplish. She made a mental note to check in with her mother for advice.

He held his hands palms up. "Ely's not my territory, Madame Young-Perret."

At least her attack kept him from dwelling on his forced early retirement. Annie wasn't Pollyanna enough to consider it a silver lining, tarnished or not, but taking advantage of it—well why not?

"I suppose it would be good for me to discuss it," she said.

Roger cocked his head in the way he always did when he was surprised.

Rather than go into anything more, Annie said, "I'll get my things."

"It happened about here," Annie said. The spotted pony that was closest to the fence ambled over to look at them.

"They picked a good spot. It is rather hard for anyone to see. No windows in viewing range. Tell me again how you got away." When Annie did, he smiled. "That's my girl."

They continued to the cathedral. It was no wonder it was known as the Ship of the Fens. Considering how flat the area was, when the church was first built it must have been visible for miles.

The wooden doors with their carvings made Annie wonder about the lives of those who had worked on them. She glanced at Roger, who hadn't noticed them. He was not one to be impressed with the past unless it was recent past and a crime was involved. *Vive la différence,* she thought, and for a moment she wondered if they never had sex again would she be more tempted by another history lover with whom she could share her nonphysical passion—not a thought to have in a church. She might not be religious at all, but she did respect other people's beliefs.

A woman in a woolen pleated skirt, sweater set, pearls and what her mother would call "sensible" shoes was behind the table taking money from a family of four: father, mother, son and daughter. "The next tour will start in about ten minutes," the woman said. "Although with what is happening with the banks, I'd be surprised if there were many people. The last tour was empty."

"Thank you," the man said. Annie's initial thought that the man's accent was French was borne out when the family spoke in French as they moved toward a small group of other tourists.

"May I help you? Do you want to take the next tour?"

"We're here to see . . ." Annie wasn't sure of the title of the church historian. Father? Vicar, like in the BBC shows? "Father Marshall. The historian. We've an appointment." She looked at her watch. "I'm about ten minutes early."

"He's in the building just across the way." The woman took them back through the entry and pointed them in the right direction.

They found Father Marshall in a small office. He was probably about the same age as Annie with dark hair and eyes that couldn't seem to stop smiling. He was chubby enough to have made a good Father Christmas. "So glad to see you Ms Young, and . . ."

"My husband, Roger Perret."

"Mr. Perret." He nodded to Roger before turning to Annie. "I can't tell you how much I've looked forward to this meeting. I adore sharing information about the church and the area. Coffee? Tea?"

"Tea," Annie said.

"Coffee," Roger said.

Father Marshall picked up his phone and placed their orders. Within a few minutes a woman appeared with a silver tray and three cups and saucers, cream, sugar and a slice of lemon on its own little plate shaped like a lemon. There was a dark blue teapot and a French press.

"The tea needs to draw a bit more," she said.

Annie noticed there were no biscuits.

"If I promise to eat only one, Mrs. Williams, will you bring some biscuits?"

She laughed. "You caught me out, Father."

Father Marshall patted his rather rotund belly. "We, she and

I, are trying to help me lose weight. It is working. I've dropped a stone."

"That's about six kilos or fourteen pounds," Annie said to Roger. "That's good, Father."

"Why in the world can't we have one way to measure things? I don't understand; I mean you Yanks, with your different size paper compared to everyone else."

Annie bit her tongue rather than say not many places considered weight loss in stones.

As if he read her mind, Father Marshall said, "Did you know that the use of stones as weight measurements went back to ancient Hebrew times and in the Middle Ages stones were selected to get a certain standardization?"

"I'm going to like this man," Annie thought, but she noticed by Roger's eyes that he was starting to tune the priest out.

"How did you get to be a church historian?" Annie asked.

"By a miracle of God. Or rather my lack of ability as an ordinary vicar. I just wasn't much good at administrating to the souls of my parish. Didn't care about inter-floral committee battles. Always had my nose in a history book. I was lucky when the powers that be realized they could make far better use of me in this role than any other. Since I don't have much ambition to rise through the ranks, everyone is happy."

Mrs. Williams knocked and brought in a plate of frosted vanilla cookies. She offered it first to Father Marshall but holding up one finger at the same time. She looked at Annie. "Now don't let him talk you into giving him more." Then she left.

Father Marshall nibbled at his and closed his eyes as he chewed. "But you're not here to discuss weights or my diet."

Annie explained her project.

"What fun," Father Marshall said. "How can I help?"

Annie explained.

Father Marshall sat back. "First let me talk about the two

brands of Catholicism, a bit like Coke and Pepsi."

Roger concentrated on sipping his coffee. Annie guessed he was far, far away mentally.

If people's eyes really could twinkle, Father Marshall's did. "Competing. Of course, no advertising back then: but there was an Irish branch and a Roman branch and each of the kings, of which there were too many, and/or their women were vying to be the top church, so to speak."

"Weren't there still pagans?"

"Oh yes, but slowly the pagans were converting to one or the other brands. Like most of the time, the wars—and it seemed like the kings thought there was nothing better than going to war—never really got involved in Christ's teachings. None of this *love-thy-neighbor* stuff: more likely, *kill thy neighbor, take his land.*"

"A bit like today, only now it is *take thy neighbor's oil*," Roger said.

He was listening, Annie thought.

Father Marshall sighed. "Sometimes I despair for humanity. We aren't a very nice species. We foul our planet; we kill one another and always assign it some noble reason but those that have fought through the ages, including back in Anglo-Saxon times, really have died for nothing."

Annie debated whether she should confess how she was feeling about her subject—acute dislike for Etheldreda. Probably not, without giving part of the reason as fear of loss of her own sex life: TMI, too much information, as her mother would say. "Tell me about Etheldreda."

"As a member of the church, I suppose I really shouldn't poo-poo miracles." He took a sip of his tea. "I wish I had another biscuit, but Mrs. Williams is a tyrant. Would it be wrong for me to ask for one for you and you give it to me?" H could only be described as conspiratorial. "Your wife on the phone, Roger, that you were a policeman: you could rat me out."

"I've no jurisdiction in Ely, and I could be bribed with a cookie . . . er . . . biscuit, and another cup of coffee."

Annie sent him a grateful smile. Mrs. Williams may have been wise to Father Marshall's tricks because she brought just two biscuits.

"My, my, we are stingy with our guests," Father Marshall said.

"These are the last," she said.

"God has a place for liars, even those with good motives," he said after she left. Annie surrendered her biscuit, her payment for the information.

She opened her laptop, which she still liked better than her tablet even if it were heavier, as the church historian began to speak. What a storyteller he was. It was as if the room faded away. She felt that she was witnessing those past events in person as he told how Etheldreda, as she fled from her second husband, was exhausted, so she lay on the ground to sleep after planting her staff in the ground. Waking in the morning she saw it had turned into a blooming tree, according to legend.

She was at the opening of Etheldreda's tomb. It was as if she were standing next to Etheldreda's sister and the other brothers and sisters from the abbey, which had once stood where she was sitting or at least close to it.

"You can imagine," Father Marshall said, having no idea how well Annie did imagine, "what the pilgrims who came to pray at her tomb went through back then. Boat was the best way to arrive most times of the year when the area was flooded. Now, what else can I tell you, my dear?"

Annie shut down her laptop. "Offhand, I can't think of much."

Father Marshall used his hands to lift his bulk from the chair. "I'll give you my e-mail in case you think of something later.

Don't worry about bothering me. I love delving into any part of the history of this wonderful region."

Annie wanted to say all regions were thick with history if anyone bothered to dig into them, but not many regions could boast about Romans, Celts, Anglo-Saxons and Vikings, as well as an awe-inspiring cathedral from the Middle Ages that somehow survived Henry VIII and Oliver Cromwell to boot.

"And you will see I get a copy of your book," Father Marshall said, making it a statement not a question.

"Not just a copy but an acknowledgment."

CHAPTER 49
EAST ANGLIA 660

When Annie had started writing, she had tried to imagine how Etheldreda might have felt about children, knowing she wouldn't have any. Did the Anglo-Saxons relate sex to pregnancy? She knew that by 1300 in France, women would insert a peach pit in their vaginas to prevent pregnancy, but that was another country and several centuries later.

Was fear of pregnancy, at a subconscious level, part of the reason that Etheldreda was so opposed to losing her virginity and had she just used religion as an excuse? She thought she remembered that the gospels of Mark and Luke referred to Mary as a Virgin and at the 325 A.D. Nicean Council the virgin birth of Christ was accepted, so Etheldreda must have known the concept. Try as hard as she could, Annie couldn't decide what influenced Etheldreda but she knew that she didn't want to attribute twenty-first-century cultural attitudes to the woman.

Etheldreda watched her niece toddle across the floor of Onna's house, where they'd all been for the last week: her unhappiness at being removed from Ely had not abated. The heat, strong for June, was not stopped by the walls.

The two-year-old listed to one side and plopped down on her well-padded behind. Glancing at her mother Seaxburga, her face showed her indecision between crying and laughing, but when her mother clapped her hands, the child laughed.

Etheldreda swooped up her niece and danced around the

room cooing and singing. The child laughed and when she was put down cried, "More, more."

"Later." Her mother called for the nurse to put the little girl down for a nap. This time there was no doubt about her reaction. The toddler let out a loud wail as the older woman dragged the child away. At the door she grabbed ahold of the wood frame, but the nurse was too strong.

"Motherhood! Especially with a child as stubborn as that one, it is a lot of work." Seaxburga got up and poured some water into a wooden bowl and drank. She nodded toward her sister in offering.

Etheldreda shook her head.

"I've talked to Father. He won't change his mind about marrying you to Ecgfrith."

Not only did Etheldreda not want to marry again, she certainly didn't want to marry a boy of fifteen. "I'm almost twice his age."

Seaxburga dipped a piece of linen into the water bowl and wiped her face and neck. "You're only nine years older."

"Whose side are you on?"

"Yours, of course."

Before Etheldreda could answer they heard the sound of horses' hoofs pound up to the house and stop. Looking out the window, they saw their father jump off and hand the reins to the stable boy. A young man also dismounted and the stable boy took his horse as well and led the two animals to a field where there was a trough made from a hollowed-out, water-filled log.

Etheldreda went to get beer for her father and his guest. Despite the heat, the beer was kept cool by a chunk cut from the pond during the winter. The large squares were stored in a pit dug under a shed outside the kitchen door and removed as needed until the next winter's ice formed.

As soon as she entered the reception area with the beer she was almost overcome with the stink of the two men. Tonbert had been fastidious about bathing.

Ecgfrith stood next to Onna, who looked at his daughter, then at his guest. He pushed the young man toward Etheldreda.

"Hello." Ecgfrith didn't look Etheldreda in the eye.

Heavens, she thought. He is as ill at ease as I am.

"Well say something, boy." Onna slapped Ecgfrith on the shoulder.

Despite his awkwardness, Etheldreda found his features pleasing. His hair was a mass of brown curls and his cheekbones were sharp. So many Saxons had faces that looked as if they'd stuffed food into their mouths and forgotten to swallow.

"Seaxburga, come with me," Onna said and grabbed his older daughter by the hand, almost pulling her out of the room. Seaxburga looked over her shoulder and mouthed, "I'm sorry."

Etheldreda poured some beer into a wooden bowl and handed it to Ecgfrith. "You must be thirsty after your ride."

He took the bowl and gulped down the beer and handed it to her for a refill.

I'm the adult, she thought. She beckoned him to sit on the bench next to the long trestle table, then she sat opposite him.

"My father wants me to marry you."

She gave a long sigh. "And would I be wrong in saying that you aren't any happier than I am, although you are indeed pleasing to my eyes." If she had no choice but to marry him, she didn't want him as an enemy. Too many wives were beaten, she knew, and if that was what the Lord wanted for her she would have to accept it; but she didn't need to give him reason.

He reached across the table and touched her hair. "Your hair is beautiful, and the jewel clip just . . ."

Etheldreda waited for him to finish, but he didn't say more. Her hair clip *was* beautiful. Her love of pretty jewelry was one of the sins that she confessed to, but she was always tempted to add a hair clip, a broach, a pin or a gold belt when she dressed. Sometimes during the day she would return to her room to remove them, then pray for forgiveness for her vanity.

Thank goodness, Annie thought, I can give her some human weaknesses.

"It is not you that I object to marrying: I just don't want to marry at all."

He smiled and she saw that he not only had all his teeth, they were straight. "I don't want to marry yet . . . oh someday, of course, but marriage . . . it means not doing the things I want to do . . ."

"Like what?"

"Hunt, fish, fight, ride."

Onna came back into the room. "Good, you're talking. We need to set a wedding date."

Ecgfrith and Etheldreda exchanged glances that did not register any enthusiasm but did show maybe the seeds of a mutual understanding.

CHAPTER 50

"Do you have my money?"

Johnson couldn't believe that the asshole Anderson wanted money for half the job. They were communicating by e-mail using coded language, but he still didn't trust it. Those idiots at NSA should be able to break the code. "You have to come get it."

"Where are you?"

"Scotland."

"Fuck man, I'm in Canada."

"I hear they have planes that fly across the Atlantic. Bigger than Lindbergh's, too."

"Who?"

Johnson figured if Anderson was too stupid to know whom he was talking about, he was too stupid to understand the explanation. At the same time he took responsibility for dealing with the man. He'd ignored the warning signs when they worked together in Iraq a good five years ago; they'd been contractors at the same time, but for different companies. The man was too trigger-happy and shot too many people just for the hell of it. At the same time, the two of them had so little to do with each other, a trace would never be possible.

"It's up to you. You want your money, you come over." Johnson gave a gentle push on the red telephone icon.

Chapter 51

On the way back to the house from their meeting with church historian Father Marshall, Roger and Annie stopped at the tearoom, where Roger ordered more coffee.

The waitress, a woman in her fifties with tightly curled gray hair, brought it in an oversized rose-flowered mug.

Annie knew he was used to demitasse cups, but he didn't comment. For a man who thought the French were superior in almost everything, he seemed to be adjusting to the English way much better than she'd hoped. "Did you find it at all interesting?"

He waggled his hand back and forth. "Miracles aren't my thing."

"But you were raised Catholic. They have saints and miracles galore."

He sighed. "Being a *flic* made it really hard to believe in miracles."

Annie was sorry she'd brought the topic up. As the top murder detective in the famous station known to the French as just 36, he'd seen the worst of mankind. Losing his wife to a criminal, revenging his own imprisonment, made possible by Roger's good police work, did nothing to strengthen his belief in the goodness of humans.

Religion had no part in their life as a couple. Their faithfulness to one another had nothing to do with the commandment "Thou Shall Not Commit Adultery" but rather to the promises they had made to each other, Annie knew.

Roger swigged down his coffee much as if it were a demitasse. "Imagine being married twice and still being a virgin out of choice."

"Father Marshall is a good storyteller though," he said.

"Isn't he? I could almost smell the earth Etheldreda slept on and hear the oars in the water as pilgrims came to her shrine."

Roger fiddled with his empty cup. "Annie, I want to go home. I want to go back to work."

"You know the doctors said you should retire."

"Money will be tight."

Annie knew his pension would be more than adequate for their needs. Neither were big spenders, although she was much more thrifty than he was. That was mainly because she didn't want much.

The word "new" was never enough to entice her to replace something she already had. As for designer labels, if she bought something with a label she immediately covered it up or took it off, saying she wasn't going to be an advertisement without any reimbursement from the company whose label it was. When Roger had accused her of becoming a COW, Cranky Old Woman, she'd mooed.

"What will I do all day, especially when you take an assignment away?" he asked.

"Come with me."

"Gaëlle."

"She'll be off to university in another year."

"Unless Guillaume and she . . . I don't even want to think about her settling down with that boy."

Annie didn't want to go there: one step at a time. "Either way, she won't be our day-to-day responsibility much longer."

He was silent and she heard him sniff several times. When he spoke, his voice cracked. "I don't want to grow old."

She thought she understood his fear. The one thing she hadn't thought of when she married him was that he would grow old sooner than she would. Okay, she'd been so worried about the limitations on her freedom that the age difference hadn't really bothered her. He was so vital. Also there was the same difference in age between Roger and her parents as between she and Roger, and she didn't think of her parents as old. They led active lives and were always full of plans for tomorrow, next week, next year. "It's better than the alternative . . . dying."

"I'm not so sure." He could have posed for a photo illustrating the feeling forlorn.

"I am."

"But what do I do without my work?"

"A man who is clever enough to solve murders and other crimes should be able to come up with something." His expression told her that her words weren't working. And she wasn't going to bring up her own fears at the moment about a celibate life. "We're in this together," she said, thinking if her sex life was going to be limited to masturbation, so be it.

Damn it!

Chapter 52

"I love you too." Janet's voice could be heard as Annie walked from the front door to her friend's studio at the side of the house.

"No, don't call again, it's too . . ." Janet looked up and immediately fell silent. She was sitting on the stool in front of her easel. Instead of a normal portrait, she'd been working on an abstract. The colors on the canvas matched the ones on her smock. Next to the easel was a table with paint tubes and cans of water with different sized brushes sticking out. The rest of the room had paintings stacked up for what would be future shows or placement in three of the galleries that took Janet's work.

The expression on Janet's face was shock at seeing Annie. She shut off the phone and dropped it in the pocket of her smock.

"That was Rod, wasn't it?"

"My mother . . ."

"What was it you used to say? Lie to me, but don't insult my intelligence?" Annie raised an eyebrow.

"You can't tell anyone. Not even Roger."

How Annie hated these dilemmas.

"Please." There were tears in Janet's eyes. "You've no idea how important it is."

"Do you think Rod killed Simon?"

Janet's reaction was too fast a denial for it to be anything but genuine. "But if he's arrested, he'll never be able to clear his name."

"But his staying away makes him look guilty."

"What if I told you he was in danger?"

"From what?"

Janet got off her stool and began to pace. "I don't know. It has something to do with Simon's special project."

"Which was?"

Janet shrugged. "I don't know." She picked up one of her canvases, a clown in the center ring of an old-fashioned circus, and held it at arm's length before putting it on her easel. "Even if Rod explained, I wouldn't understand what he did. Maybe he had some shady client. Money laundering. I just don't know."

"If Roger finds out that I knew about Rod, he'll be really angry with me."

"And what will he do if you tell him now?"

Annie suspected he probably would call Lake and tell him what he knew. "Shit," she said.

Janet picked up her palette and began putting a spotlight shimmering down on the clown in the painting.

CHAPTER 53

Burt Johnson had searched for a place to meet James Anderson where there wasn't a surveillance camera. It hadn't been easy. Stores were reopening now that the banks were up and running again.

Anderson had been annoyed that Johnson refused to pick him up at the Glasgow train station after his flight from Toronto to London, but Johnson's trump card of holding Anderson's payment hostage won.

Johnson thought that he should have listened to his instincts about Anderson as not being too bright. He had trouble thinking outside the box. God, he hated that phrase but it really was appropriate in this case.

At best military men weren't as bright or as clever as he was, and he gave minimal thanks to his father for insisting that he be the best in everything.

There was a place behind a Glasgow mall where the cameras didn't reach. He'd given Anderson instructions on how to get there from the train station. Then he'd "borrowed" another car from long-term parking in the airport, one whose engine was still warm. Although there were cameras there, he had disguised himself so well that he didn't recognize himself when he glanced in the mirror. Padding added weight. Lifts added height. A wig and cotton stuffed in his cheeks changed his visage.

He wore the same disguise as he waited for Anderson. The two had not met for years. All their business had been conducted over throwaway phones and in code. At least throwaway from Johnson's side: he wasn't sure that Anderson would be that careful, but still . . . tracing anything back to Johnson would be next to impossible, even by the savviest investigators, which most weren't.

The car was behind a dumpster. Johnson's view was blocked, not the best situation, but he was ready with a gun between the door and his seat.

A man knocked on the passenger's side.

"Walters?"

Johnson smiled. He hadn't used that name since he'd been a contractor in Iraq.

The man was in his mid-thirties, had a buzz cut and was obviously in top condition by the muscles that were marked through his T-shirt. His jacket was open.

Johnson saw no trace of a gun anywhere in Anderson's clothing, which made sense if the man had flown in from the United States or flown in from anywhere. He was sure that he didn't have the connections to pick up a gun in the UK.

Guns were hard to come by. Possession of a firearm in the country carried huge penalties. He'd taken great risks to get his own arsenal on a market so black that it was almost as large as the biggest black hole in the universe.

There could be a knife he might have hidden somewhere. Anderson's reputation with knives was one of the reasons Johnson had hired him in the first place. The idiot used a video to show how he could hit a target with one as an advertising tool for his skill.

"That's me," Johnson said.

He leaned over and opened the passenger door. "Get in."

"I'd like my money so I can get out of here."

"Do you think I carry it around? Get in."

Anderson did.

"Buckle up. We don't want to be stopped by the police."

Anderson let out a sigh. "I don't like this."

Johnson pulled out of where he was parked, knowing that he would once again be filmed. Although any connection would probably never be made, he preferred to play it safe. "No luggage?"

"My plan was to come, get the money and leave."

"Well, let's do it." Johnson headed north until the city fell behind and they were in the wilderness.

Anderson kept shifting in his seat. Johnson noticed that he adjusted his right boot's shoelaces. He guessed that was where there might be a knife.

"Where are we going?"

"My cabin. I keep the money there. Most of your payment is in cash, six one-thousand-dollar bills but I've also put part of it in gold. Anyway it comes under the $10,000 exporting-importing limit."

"Shit, that is hard to deal with. I can't walk into a convenience store with a thousand-dollar bill."

"Fuck it, man, you didn't say how you wanted your payment, just that you wanted it." He pulled over to the side of the road and turned toward Anderson. "You're an ungrateful bastard. I've given you a good assignment and all you do is bitch."

"A deal is a deal."

"But you didn't complete your part of the deal. Never mind how you fucked up the timing."

They drove in silence. On both sides of the road were pine trees. No other cars passed them. Johnson broke the quiet. "At least you can tell me what happened."

"The second guy went missing. That's it. Nothing complicated."

Johnson knew that had *he* been doing the job, he'd have known where both men were. He'd have hit them one after another, on schedule. And then the banks wouldn't have made headlines all over the world.

"And you didn't find any of their . . ." Johnson pulled off the side of the road onto a narrow path through a wood thick with trees and bracken.

"I didn't find shit. I searched anyplace they might have had the information. When I couldn't get into Bartlett's files, I wiped them out. The MacKenzie house was clean. Hey, why are we stopping?"

Johnson didn't answer. He reached for the gun between the seat and the door on his side and shot Anderson three times through the heart.

The dirt road was one that he'd discovered about three years before. He drove the car for about another half a mile, going deeper and deeper into the forest. Getting out, he locked the door and headed through the brown bracken until he reached his own car, which he had positioned the day before, a good five-mile hike away, often through dense undergrowth. That day he'd worn another disguise, that of a much older man, hitching into the next town. He had told the truck driver who picked him up that his car was in the repair shop.

As he turned on the engine of his own car, he thought that even if Anderson's body were found in a stolen car anytime in the near future, which he doubted, tracing the murder to him would be next to impossible.

It was no longer his problem. He needed to finish the job he had been hired to do in the first place: not for Masterson, who would probably never know, but for his own sense of pride. Rod MacKenzie was going to be a dead man, as soon as he could find him, and he would find him.

Annie wiped up the tea she'd spilled, happy that none had hit the laptop. Try as she might she could not shake off her own lack of desire to work. For the first time in several days it was beautiful outside. Janet had abandoned her easel to go for a walk with Roger and Mercury. However, the dread deadline loomed. Just another reason to dislike Etheldreda, she thought.

Etheldreda never remembered being so content. She finally had what she wanted—life in a convent. She spent her days in prayer when she wasn't doing the chores of the convent.

The sisters took turns in the preparation of food. Two others, with the healing gift, served the ill who came to their doors, but Etheldreda lacked that talent.

It wasn't that she shunned away from touching those with sores or vomiting. She didn't know how to help them other than to call for the sisters who grew herbs and made them into liquids to relieve their suffering. They knew how to push bones into place and wrap cloth around the limb so the person might walk or use the injured arm again.

Mostly she prayed: prayers for the afflicted, prayers of thanksgiving for the life she was leading.

As she knelt in the chapel, her skin not only itched, but there were small red bumps wherever the rough woolen of her dress touched her skin, a penance she had chosen to make up for her earlier love of jewelry, especially the gold belt and bracelets that her father had given her.

The warmth of the day did not help, although the convent's stone walls kept out some of the heat.

She seldom thought of her family and even less often of her husband, Ecgfrith, who was now king after his father, Osiwo, died. When she did, she saw him as the boy of fifteen that she'd married ten years before. "Boy" was the correct word. His interest in her was even less than hers in him. In one of the rare conversations before she took her vows in the convent, he had said that he would leave her alone sexually. He wanted young flesh.

The agreement worked. He went off to hunt, to practice with his weapons, to accompany his father to this or that battle and to bed whomever he wanted, when he wanted. Despite her disgust at his rooting around in other women's bodies, she had finally found the peace she desired. Let him worry about his own soul.

The short time she'd shared Ecgfrith's home, or rather his father's home, she'd tried to stifle a dislike for her husband. His temper meant that a dog in his way might receive a kick, or a too-slow servant a slap.

He could not read. Any hope of an intelligent discussion not involving hunting, fishing or making war was as useless as a thick woolen cloak on the hottest of summer days.

Annie thought that not wanting to make love with a man like that made sense. Her research had given only slight hints into the characters of Etheldreda's two husbands. Quentin had said he wanted a novel, not a history book. She wished she could channel the dead. She would have so many questions for all her characters.

Still, despite her present life suiting her so well, there were nights when Etheldreda lay on her narrow board with no straw between her skin and the wood that she wished she could return to Ely and build the convent for which she had so long dreamed.

When Bishop Wilfrid came to the convent, which was often now that he had returned from Gaul and assumed his role as Bishop of Northumbria, she confided her dream. He cautioned her not to be too ambitious, that God would show her what must be done when the time was right, just as He had allowed Wilfrid himself to overcome the politics that almost cost him the bishopric.

One of the novice nuns came up behind Etheldreda as she prayed. She jumped when the novice touched her. "The king is here."

A shiver went through her body. She had not seen her husband in over a year. His presence could only bode ill. Perhaps something had happened to her sister.

She followed the novice to the entrance. A door with a metal bar the thickness of a working-man's arm prevented anyone from entering the convent itself. Etheldreda removed the bar and opened the wooden door with carvings of the Blessed Mother holding her Son.

There was a short corridor to the outside world. This was where visitors, few though they might be, would wait. Through the door she could see the trees surrounding the convent and heard birdsong trilling.

Two crude wooden benches were on each side of the corridor whose width would allow for handshakes for people sitting on opposite sides. Her husband was seated on the left. He stood when he saw her.

He towered over her. When she'd first met him he had not yet reached his full growth, but in the intervening years, he had taken on a height that surpassed many men. His body was muscular. Had she ever touched him, she thought he would feel as hard as the door she had just opened.

"Return to your duties." She turned to the novice, who was staring at Ecgfrith almost open mouthed. The young girl glanced over her shoulder several times until Etheldreda shut the convent door.

Ecgfrith and Etheldreda faced one another until Etheldreda broke the silence.

"Husband."

"Wife." Then he sighed.

"Now that we've established our roles, dear wife, I want you to come back with me."

Etheldreda motioned for him to sit. When he did she took the opposite bench. "You know that is impossible."

"Impossible? All you need to do is follow me out the door."

Etheldreda smiled. "That is not how I meant 'impossible.' Physically, of course, I could walk out, get on your horse . . . or have you brought me my own?"

"I have an extra horse."

"When I said 'impossible,' I meant I have taken my vows and Christ is now my husband."

"You took your vows as my wife."

She nodded. "And you promised that it was a mere formality and that I would not have to be your wife in any other sense of the word."

"I need a queen. Even more, I need heirs."

Etheldreda tried not to show the panic she was feeling. "Then marry another."

"I do not have time to find another wife."

Etheldreda translated this to mean he did not wish to let go of the lands and alliances her marriage had brought him. She much preferred him as the boy that he had been than the man that he had become; one who spent too much of his time in preparing for battle.

When her friend and spiritual advisor, Bishop Wilfrid, visited, he updated her on his activities. The only good thing Wilfrid said about her husband was that his new coinage of silver with the design of a wolf was making trade easier.

Annie was comfortable with the facts about the coinage, having found references in several places. As for the conversation between husband and wife, she imagined how it might have gone, and she was comfortable with that too.

Wilfrid was of the opinion that Ecgfrith could have done much for the spirituality, as well as the daily lives, of his people if he'd used his expertise toward developing the land and skills that were needed to make tools and trade. He had given up, he'd said, on Ecgfrith's soul. He was too attached to the old gods. He'd told Wilfrid that if he were to give any room to Christ it would be through the Celts, not through the Romans.

"No." The softness of Etheldreda's voice did not reduce the force of the word.

Ecgfrith's face turned red the same way it had in the brief time they'd spent together when they were first married, before she'd moved to the convent. His temper reminded her of small children who threw tantrums even if Ecgfrith didn't lie down on the ground and kick his feet. Instead, he was a danger to anything in his way.

"No? I'm your king."

"It doesn't matter. I won't go."

She expected anything: his slapping her, picking her up and throwing her across his horse. What she didn't expect was what happened. He stomped out of the convent corridor without another word. She saw him mount his horse and take off in a gallop.

Although she hoped that was the end of it, she was sure it was not.

CHAPTER 55

Annie checked the time. She was tired, having awoken in the middle of the night two hours ago. This sleeplessness was getting to her. Once again she was too hot under the feather duvet, but after getting up to pee, she was too cold not to pull the duvet up to her neck and snuggle close to Roger, who was breathing heavily.

It amused her that they were both dressed in gray pajama bottoms and sweatshirts. His had two wolves howling at the moon, while hers bore the emblem of the Université de Genève. She thought of the cliché "her heart melted" every time Roger got up, his hair going in thousands of directions and his eyes half open.

She didn't want to turn the light on to read, because it might disturb him. Nor did she want to continue trying to find a position that was comfortable. Instead she tried to figure out why sleep was evading her. What she could eliminate was that it had nothing to do with all that had gone wrong since she'd arrived in Ely. At least she didn't think it was that.

That Rod was still on the run and that the police didn't seem to be any closer to finding the murderer was also eliminated. Annie seldom let things she had no control over bother her.

However, that was only one aspect. She felt somehow that if she just thought hard enough, she'd be able to figure out if whatever Rod and Simon were doing had some bearing on Simon's death and Rod's accident. Although the police didn't make that connection, she did. Both men would have been too smart to keep any information on their hard drives or in the cloud. Those damned animal keys must hold the answer, but the fact that they were such good nerds meant that cracking the password was next to impossible. That's what Marc had said after working hours and hours going from pig to rooster and back again.

Annie didn't like not solving problems. In her tech writing, she loved figuring out how something worked and then creating words in such a simple language that anyone could understand.

Janet was already in her studio when Annie padded into the kitchen at seven. A pot of tea was still warm and she poured herself a cup before heading to the dining room table, where she had set up her laptop in one corner.

She'd felt that she'd combined almost all the information she'd found on the Internet with that from the local historians, the library, the church and the museum to almost finish the book, except she still hated it . . . hated it . . . hated it. Why did she ever think she could be a novelist, anyway?

She picked up her cup of tea, now cold, and took a long drink. Defeat wasn't a word she liked to use in terms of her own accomplishments.

Maybe, just maybe, it might be good for her to not push herself to accomplish everything she tried, her habit from the time she'd mastered Dutch when her family had moved from Massachusetts to Nijmegen and thrown her into third grade in a Dutch school. The language battles had continued when they did the same thing a few years later and threw her into a German school in Stuttgart and finally a French school in Geneva. She'd mastered all three foreign languages and had earned top grades in her studies.

Maybe, just maybe, this once it was okay to say, I don't want to try anymore.

Her watch said it was after nine. She picked up the phone and called Quentin Taylor.

"Hey Annie," he said.

"Can we meet for lunch?" she asked her publisher. "I'm paying."

CHAPTER 56

Annie found Roger and Marc in the lounge sitting side by side on the sofa. Both of them were leaning forward with their elbows on their knees. The TV was tuned to BBC news, but since Marc held the clicker in one of his hands, she guessed they'd been switching from station to station. She glanced at the screen to see a list being scrolled.

"Those are the banks that were hit with the DDOS attack," Roger said. "Again. Amazing."

Marc spoke without his eyes leaving the screen. "Some got back up, but half of those were brought back down an hour ago in a follow-up attack."

"But a few are still up."

"Has anyone taken responsibility?" Annie asked.

Marc just shook his head, but Roger said, "The main groups that do this are denying responsibility, but the biggies said they wished it were them because it was so brilliant."

Annie wasn't sure how brilliant it was to bring the banking world to its knees. Her feelings were borne out when she saw on the screen lines of people standing in front of banks and ATM machines. Marc switched the channel to CNN, showing different lines. The lines switched from the United States to Paris, to Germany, to the UK, to Holland, to Japan and to Australia.

"It's interesting that Greece and Spain haven't been hit at all," Roger said.

While still watching the set Marc said, "I'm not sure how I'm going to get from Geneva to Lausanne." He was due to leave the next morning. "I've no money for a train ticket."

"I can lend you some," Janet said. Annie hadn't noticed her come in. She was still wearing her smock, although she almost always took it off before leaving her studio. "I've a secret stash for emergencies." She beckoned for Annie to follow her.

They went to the third floor. Against a wall was an armoire, not an antique one like the rest of the furniture in the house, but a flat-pack. Books were interspersed with framed photos, many of which Annie recognized as the source of Janet's paintings.

Both women pushed the armoire aside, revealing a door. Janet hit the light switch and Annie saw a narrow staircase leading to an attic with the roof so low that it left little more than a crawl space. "I feel like the hunchback of Notre Dame," Annie said.

"You look like him too, all bent over, except you're prettier," Janet said.

Annie realized that the police had not searched the attic: first, because they couldn't have known it was there, and secondly, because Janet's and her footprints plus one set of larger prints were the only ones on the wide-board floor. Annie guessed by the size of the prints that the third set were Rod's. She sneezed several times.

As Janet made her way across the area, she had to bend even a little lower to keep from hitting her head on the rough wood making up the slanted ceiling. Like all attics it was cobwebby and filled with things that Janet and Rod probably had forgotten they had. "Do you know, when we moved in we found this trunk." She pointed to a rounded trunk covered with destination stickers that looked like the ones used on ocean liners in the early twentieth century. Annie noticed Southampton, Le

Havre, New York, Rotterdam, Hamburg, Miami, Alexandria. Some just had the name, two had maps, a third had a photo of a woman in the dress of the era. She imagined the stories behind each of the trips: people walking decks, shuffleboard, dinner at the captain's table, a cheating husband.

Janet broke into her reverie. "When we opened it, it was filled with wonderful old clothes."

"Wait a minute, you painted this trunk, draped with some of those clothes. I remember seeing it in that High Street gallery when we visited last year."

Janet nodded. "Took photos. Did three of those paintings and sold them all for four figures. Nostalgia is a winner. Help me."

Pushing with their hands and knees was not that easy but they managed to move the trunk three feet to one side.

Under the trunk there was a loose floorboard, which Janet removed to reveal a safe, or rather a long thick metal container five feet long. Annie couldn't see how wide it was.

"I feel as if I'm in World War II and you've hidden Jews to keep them safe from the Nazis," Annie said.

"They weren't that small."

"You know what I mean."

"I do." Janet spun the combination and opened the top.

Inside were piles of more hundred-pound notes, Euros and Swiss francs than Annie could imagine, but there were also bars and bars of gold and even more silver.

"Rod put this away for an emergency." Janet leaned back on her heels. "And there's a pile missing." She pointed to an empty spot. "He must have taken money with him. Good, that's one less thing I have to worry about."

Annie had been right. Those large footprints in the dust must have been Rod's.

"Thank goodness, I was worried about him having enough

cash on him," Janet said.

Annie picked up one of the gold pieces. It had been bought in Switzerland and had a sheen that gave it a beauty that had nothing to do with its market value. By contrast, the silver bars were square and lacked luster. They could have been taken for dusty doorstops. Perhaps in sunlight, there might be a slight sparkle but only slight.

"Rod was paranoid about us running out of money," Janet said. "He had this safe specially made. You should have seen the two of us trying to get it installed ourselves, because he didn't trust anyone else to do it. He thought at some point the banks would confiscate our money we had in our savings accounts like the Cyprus banks did to their depositors and that they would eventually destroy the world's economy."

This was a side of Rod that Annie could believe. He wasn't trusting. Once they'd been in the cafeteria when they were working for ZBPI. A new contractor sat down and tried to talk about the stock market.

"I don't play it because I don't understand it," Annie had said.

"I don't play it because I don't want to support corporations that aren't paying their taxes, or are hurting the environment or the CEOs are getting rich off the blood of their employees," Rod had said. "I don't trust them. Besides, I don't understand it either. If I were to gamble, and I'm not a gambling man, I'd want to know what I was doing."

Then he turned to Annie, "I hate to do this to you, but we're doing some major changes in the program you finished documenting last week. You'll need to do a complete rewrite." She'd groaned and thought of the days she'd spent on the translations but had forgotten about the conversation until now.

Janet took out two fifty-pound notes. "This should get Marc back to Lausanne." Then she reached for another. "And in case he still can't get into his bank account, he'll be able to get some food."

"He might not be able to change them," Annie said.

"How stupid of me." Janet said, and exchanged them for two hundred Swiss francs.

The two women went back downstairs to find Marc and Roger still glued to the set. "I know they're simply recycling the news, but every now and then something different comes on," Marc said without looking up.

As he spoke, they showed stores shutting down on High Street in London because people had no way to pay for merchandise.

"It's still genius," Marc said.

"You aren't saying you approve," Roger said. "Think of the hardship that ordinary people are suffering. Imagine you were at the airport and had no money for a hotel or food."

"I'm saying that the banks are crooks, and deserve what they get. Maybe this will make the politicians take notice."

"Marc, let's take Mercury for a walk," Annie said.

At the mention of his name and the word "walk," the dog jumped off the chair where he'd been half asleep and came back with his leash. Marc went to get his jacket.

"Diplomat," Roger said to his wife.

"I'm going to try and get Marc to stay. At least here he doesn't have to worry about money, and we still need his computer skills."

Annie had been disappointed that Marc had not been able to hack into either the pig or rooster USB keys despite hours and hours of trying. On the other hand, she was relieved that if he couldn't do it, his future as a hacker where he might get into real trouble was limited.

CHAPTER 57
NORTHUMBRIA 670

Annie tried to guess Ecgfrith's thoughts. His ambitions were understandable, but not admirable. Mankind always seemed to seek if not power then at least some portion of land to be its own territory. Humans at least weren't like dogs, marking their domains by peeing. At the thought Annie smiled. Peeing vs. making war—peeing had to be less destructive. She forced herself back to work.

Ecgfrith's head was spinning. He'd drunk too much beer and he was about to slip from a pleasant buzz to being drunk. He was in the eating room of his house. His favorite hunting dog chewed on the bones of the lamb that had made up his dinner along with an oat gruel.

He'd summoned Bishop Wilfrid several days ago. The damned man still hadn't appeared. One of his deacons had sent word that the bishop was visiting different places in Northumbria to instruct his flock.

Flock—that was what many Christians were like—a flock of sheep, paying tribute to men on earth supposedly speaking for a god. He, Ecgfrith, didn't need any men to speak to his gods for him. He could do it himself. Mostly they gave him what he wanted. They didn't charge him anything—no chickens, no parts of crops, no gold, no silver.

More and more of his people were converting to that damned religion and the real gods, his gods, might get pissed off at their defection.

More worrisome was his so-called wife. Why did he let his father ever talk him into that alliance? Okay, he hadn't fought all that hard. At first it seemed like a practical solution. They demanded nothing of each other. He did what he wanted: she did what she wanted.

Even when he'd taken over the kingship of Deira on the Channel coast to help keep the people in line for his father, he hadn't needed a queen.

Now he did.

One of the things King Onna had said when they were arranging his marriage was that Etheldreda's first husband had taught her how to get the most out of the land. She knew how to oversee the construction of a building. If she could do that as his queen that would leave him free to challenge the Picts, who seemed to be getting ready to question his power.

Only she hadn't done any of that. She'd cloistered herself in that damned convent. Actions made things happen, not prayer. He could pray for a nice piece of venison, and maybe someone would bring him some. Or he could go out and shoot a deer, guaranteeing his dinner.

He wanted a son, many sons. His sons from different women whom he'd lain with weren't pure royal blood.

A maid, one whom he'd slept with and who looked as if she might be pregnant, entered the dining room. "Bishop Wilfrid has arrived."

"Keep him waiting in the outer hall. I'll get to him when I'm good and ready."

The maid disappeared.

Ecgfrith poured himself another bowl of beer. He hated that sanctimonious bastard. He'd love to throw him out of his kingdom altogether, but that might give one of the other kings in the area an excuse to attack Northumbria.

He went out to the hall, where the bishop perched on a stool.

Nothing in his clothing marked him as a bishop. Well, maybe the cloth in his tunic was of slightly better quality than that of a farmer, and certainly cleaner. But he stank of sweat and horse just like everyone else, and that was the way Ecgfrith decided to treat him.

"I heard when I returned home that you wished to see me." Wilfrid rose slowly. At thirty-seven he was not showing his age but he still acted as if his age as well as his position gave him authority over Ecgfrith's twenty-five years.

Ecgfrith refused to kiss the bishop's ring; the bishop refused to bow to his king. The two men faced off, each waiting for the other until Ecgfrith said, "Follow me."

Back in the dining hall, Ecgfrith went behind the table and sat on the only stool in the room, leaving the bishop standing. "I want you to tell my wife she must come here and serve as my queen. I want to fuck her. Finally!"

"She has taken a vow of chastity."

"I don't care."

"She has taken the veil."

"I care about that even less. I'm her king."

"She responds to a higher authority."

Ecgfrith's head was spinning. He picked up the bowl that had held the beer and threw it at the bishop, who ducked. Any object he could put his hands on he threw at the bishop.

"I hope you're more accurate in battle with your arrows than you are with household utensils."

Ecgfrith upset the table and grabbed Wilfrid by his shirt. He was taller and in better condition than Wilfrid, who did nothing to fight back, which made Ecgfrith even madder. He pushed the bishop away from him. "Get out."

Wilfrid stumbled but regained his footing before falling to the wooden floor. "Willingly." He shut the door behind him.

Ecgfrith grabbed the stool and threw it at the closed door. The stool splintered. "This isn't over," he yelled at the closed door.

CHAPTER 58

Burt Johnson could not let go of his self-anger about his assignment from Masterson. He'd been wrong, wrong, wrong to give Anderson a chance, even though in the beginning it had looked like a good decision.

Things had begun to go wrong when Anderson had only injured MacKenzie, but he had dispatched Simon Bartlett without leaving any trace that the police could follow. It was after that when things went really wrong. MacKenzie was still out there doing damage daily.

Johnson decided to stay at his cabin north of where he had left Anderson's body. What he needed was just enough time to look into everything he had on MacKenzie, which comprised about fifty pages of information. He knew what the man liked for breakfast, the projects he had been on. He had been able to see his bank statements for the past two years, thanks to Jillian, god, small "g," rest her soul.

He had found this cabin ten years ago, a place to escape to, a place where no one would be able to find him, which was the way he wanted it.

Even the closest grocery store, such as it was, took a good hour to reach. He stopped at it to load up on enough to eat for the next couple of days. Even though he didn't go to his hidey-hole, as he thought of it, all that often, he seldom stopped here for groceries at the same place in case the same person would be behind the counter and would remember him.

273

Any attempt of his to fake a good Scottish accent made him sound like an American trying to fake a Scottish accent. He credited himself for many skills: marksman, woodsman, critical thinker, planner, fearless hunter capable of disguising himself, to name a few. Accents were one of his failures, not that he hadn't tried. Even took an acting class in accents.

No, it wasn't a failure. He would keep trying until he could do it.

CHAPTER 59

Quentin Taylor and Annie walked from Janet's house by the cathedral to a small restaurant. Annie was almost afraid to look at him because she found him so devastatingly attractive with his mass of curls over his shirt collar and the smile that seemed to constantly play around his lips.

He was one of those people oozing a charisma that Annie decided was something people were born with or not. It couldn't be learned. Maybe it was an odor that the psyche recognized but not the nose. She rejected that theory, because one could watch a person on television and still feel the charisma.

Quentin knew all the staff at the restaurant, which only had ten tables. He was ushered to what the waitress, a woman probably in her mid-forties, called his "usual" table. He introduced her as Virginia.

"Let me order for you. I know the menu backwards and forwards." He chose eel in a garlic sauce. "You can't be in Ely without eating eel."

Since Annie loved smoked eel from her teenage years in Germany, she agreed. One of her friend's mothers had served her eel without telling her. She'd been glad she hadn't known, because politeness would have forced her to eat it and prejudice might have spoiled it for her. During her teens, she'd been a very finicky eater, not like now, where she loved almost everything.

Quentin launched into a long history of Ely as a major eel

provider going back to the Middle Ages. Annie did not want to interrupt him as he talked, because although she'd already heard much of it, Quentin had the ability to make whatever he said sound like the BBC News on a hot news night.

"You should have been a history prof," she said when he stopped.

"Except I don't want to get all the credentials I need, so I'm doing the next best thing—spreading the historical word, so to speak."

Perfect time to quit, Annie thought. "I asked you to lunch for a reason."

"And since you offered to pay for it, it is one of two things. One: You think I'm so adorable you want to spend time with me. Two: you are having problems with the book."

"How about three: both."

"Thank you for the adorable agreement. Now let's talk about the book."

Roger had once described Annie as a victim of conflict avoidance and then when she agreed with him, he said it proved his point. However, her hatred of conflict didn't mean she ignored issues. "I hate her."

"Who?

"Etheldreda."

"You hate a woman you never met? One who died some thirteen hundred years ago?"

"When I wrote about Hilke, I liked her. I understood the frustration she must have felt living in a family where her strengths were not valued and whose own values she didn't share. I understood the terror she must have gone through in the concentration camp, and how she did everything she could to survive. I liked her. Had she still been alive, I'd have wanted to sit down and have a cup of coffee, some *Schwarzwälder Kirschtorte* and talk with her."

"I suppose it was easier because you had her journal."

Annie thought of how she'd sailed through the journal and the words for the biography had run out of her fingertips onto the keyboard. Had they been water she'd have flooded the room.

"I didn't expect a journal for Etheldreda. That isn't the problem. And I loved the research, or at least the process, despite all the problems around me." She thought of the woman at the museum and the church historian. "What I didn't expect was how I couldn't identify with her."

Quentin didn't say anything, just almost raised one eyebrow.

"I'm embarrassed to say this, but I don't understand why anyone would put such a price on virginity. Why fight nature?"

"Or is it that you don't share her religious beliefs?" he asked.

"Partially. I was raised with ethics, not religion. Sometimes I envy believers in their certainties." How do I say I want out of the contract, she wondered. She'd never reneged on a contract in her life. More than once she'd worked at home if she were sick, or wherever she was making her home when she was away on assignment, rather than miss a deadline.

She would give him what she'd done so far, but before she could make the offer, Quentin said, "I understand."

Damn, he's being nice, which makes this all worse, Annie thought.

"Let's see if we can find something you like about her."

Annie thought hard. The woman had been a pawn of her father, who used her to cement his power: not that that was anything new for rulers. She did try and make the best of what she had to work with.

For rulers, marriage was a form of treaty. Even for peasants, the son of one farmer would marry the daughter of a neighbor to increase their holdings. The idea of marriage and love didn't matter. When did love come into play? Oh, she knew the literature: *Tristan and Isolde, Romeo and Juliet,* etc. Hormones existed throughout history.

Deals were always a part of power games; only in modern times the deals were between businesses rather than having a CEO's daughter marry another CEO's son.

"She was a strong woman, who followed what she believed," Annie said.

"See," Quentin said. "What else?"

"Obviously competent enough to found an abbey."

Quentin smiled and moved his hand in a circle. "More . . ."

Annie laughed. "I see what you're doing."

Quentin tilted his head. God, he was cute. "That is?"

"Getting me to be more sympathetic? Are you worried my book will be too negative?"

"Not at all."

"Or offend true believers?"

"That is possible." He smiled. "Which might boost sales. Remember what being banned in Boston did to *Lady Chatterley's Lover's* sales?" When Annie didn't answer, he said, "Skyrocketed."

"I know. That book is mild now, although at the time it was over-the-top sexy. This book is about sex avoidance. The only way it would be considered steamy would be if you melted it down and boiled it."

The waitress arrived with their salads.

"And another thing." Annie poked at a lettuce leaf. "Isn't it disrespectful to put down a saintly woman?"

Quentin waited until his mouth was empty to answer. "It's all in your point of view. If you can make her likeable, that would be a solution."

Annie wasn't sure how she would make Etheldreda likeable by twenty-first-century standards without a massive rewrite of what she had already done. "I don't suppose you'd give me another month?"

"I can't do a month: a day or two, maybe. But, Annie, I know you can do it." He reached across the table and patted her hand.

Shit.

The words, "I know you can do it," had always been the catalyst that had pushed her to get on with whatever she was having trouble. Hell, she even had eked by in algebra when her teacher and her father said those words to her. Granted, her grade had been the lowest passing grade possible, but she'd still pulled it up from a failure.

She swallowed the feeling that she was being manipulated into finishing instead of quitting.

How was she going to twist her mind to think more as an eighth-century Anglo-Saxon than as a twentieth-first-century woman?

Realistically, how many copies would the book sell? A thousand? Two? She was an A-list author only with Quentin. At any other publishing house, she'd probably be a C or D or even an E, if publishing house lists went that low.

"I'll do my best," she said without any idea how. As he smiled, she also gave him credit for being a master at manipulation.

Chapter 60

Annie had slept fitfully, despite being exhausted when she'd crawled into bed. Marc and Roger had danced around each other verbally on political issues throughout dinner, although there was no reason she should have been surprised that they would hold different opinions.

As a *flic,* Roger was conservative.

As a student Marc was trying out radical ideas. Also Marc had seen his mother's firm cheat on drug tests. She'd been a scientist. She was still a scientist/researcher, but at another drug company after she had stopped a dangerous drug from being released. Annie detested his mother, who was self-absorbed and certainly not a good mother to a kid as great as Marc, but Annie admired her ethics.

On the other hand, Annie sometimes found Roger almost naïve when it came to justice. He'd been a good *flic,* but Roger in retirement would not be a pretty picture.

The sun threw a bit of light through the small crack in the drapes. Roger was already downstairs.

Today, she needed to get at least thirty pages written and another ten rewritten to reflect a more likeable Etheldreda. And she didn't even want to think of how she would deal with miracles that she didn't believe in.

To make it harder, she felt lousy, not quite like she had the flu, but close to it. At least she didn't have any appointments today, although tomorrow she needed to check back with Rod's office. Maybe Marc could help out there, as he'd decided to stay for a couple more days or longer if he was needed, he'd said.

She rolled over and pulled the duvet up to her neck.

Rod.

She didn't believe for an instant he had anything at all to do with Simon's murder, but it made no sense for him to go into hiding. At least now she knew he was okay.

If she could convince Janet to tell her where he was, she could go talk to him and find out what was going on. If she were being truly honest with herself, which she always tried to be, part of her desire to find Rod was to leave the book, Roger and Marc behind, at least for a few days. Then she'd retackle everything.

She heard Janet walk by the door and called to her. Her friend, still in her red fuzzy bathrobe, entered and sat on the chintzy chair.

"Why don't we go look for Rod?" Annie asked.

"Are you mad?" Janet asked. "What if we're followed?"

"Who would follow us? Maybe we can sneak out like we did when the reporters were hounding us out front and catch the train. Or take the car? Wear a disguise?"

Janet laughed. "A disguise? You are too much."

Annie sat up in bed. She felt a little dizzy, but she hadn't eaten last night. Maybe she was crazy for suggesting this when she had so much more to do, but getting away had more merit by the minute.

"Leave Marc and Roger here with Mercury and their political battles."

"It did get a little hot last night. I thought you defused it well," Janet said.

"Come on . . . just us girls. Wouldn't you like to see your husband?"

281

Janet sat down on the bed. "What would we tell the boys? We were going shopping in London? Staying over?"

"Roger would never, ever believe I was going shopping. He would believe I needed to do some research in London and we wanted to take in a play or something. Besides, this is a perfect time. The police are being kept busy with the lines at the banks."

When Janet didn't rule it out, Annie stayed quiet. She thought her bank point excellent; even though a number of banks were back online, customers had been spooked and wanted to withdraw as much money as they could in case there was another DDOS. The banks did not want massive withdrawals so things were still unsteady.

Janet paused. "All right, tomorrow or the next day. But we have to be careful."

CHAPTER 61
NORTHUMBRIA 670

Annie wanted to get as much done as possible before she and Janet left on their Rod hunt. She even felt better about her subject, but not by much.

At first Etheldreda thought she was still dreaming, although she had awakened with a start. A man was standing over her saying, "Hurry, hurry."

She sat up on her cot and rubbed her eyes. Why was a man in the convent? Then she realized it was Bishop Wilfrid.

"Get dressed. You have to get out of here."

She struggled into her woolen dress and almost staggered into the hall. From the narrow opening in the wall, she could see that it was still night. No birds were singing. Two other young nuns stood next to the bishop.

"I've horses outside. You must ride to Ely starting now. There's food in the saddlebags." He turned and walked to the door and the two nuns followed him. They looked back and beckoned for Etheldreda to follow.

Outside, a breeze bordered on being a wind. Etheldreda shivered in her dress and cloak.

The horses, all black mares, whinnied. Although Etheldreda was an early riser for prayers, she'd never done well being woken in the middle of the night. Bishop Wilfrid, who carried a lantern, must have noticed the confusion on her face. "Ecgfrith is planning to come at dawn and take you back with him."

"He wouldn't."

"Not only would he, he wants to make you his wife in every sense of the word."

Etheldreda shuddered as Bishop Wilfrid helped her into the saddle and handed her the reins. Then he helped the other two nuns onto their horses.

"You're going with me?" Etheldreda asked the sisters.

The women said yes at the same time.

Bishop Wilfrid hit first one horse, then the second and then the last one on the flanks. The beasts took off down the path heading south. "Follow the coast," he called after them.

Etheldreda had always been a good rider, although she had not been on a horse since entering the convent. She knew she couldn't make the animals gallop long distances day in and day out without killing them. One of the other nuns was as good a rider as Etheldreda: the other was not, but Bishop Wilfrid had given her the best beast for a lesser rider. Still she lagged behind.

They rode until the sun was almost setting, when they found a beach. The tide was out and there was a raised island where they could find shade. Together they agreed that would be a good place to rest and eat. The three women crossed to the spit of land, the horses' hoofs splashing in the shallow water.

Once dismounted Etheldreda found her legs and rear end sore from the ride, but she refused to complain. Instead she said a silent prayer. Together they looked at the provisions: bread, the first apples of the season and a wedge of cheese.

Etheldreda wished it wasn't necessary to eat at all. As a child, she had loved anything with honey and was more than happy to consume not just everything in her bowl, but anything her sister and brother had left as well. She'd been chubby, but now she ate as little as possible, selecting things she disliked to show her God the sacrifices she would make for Him.

★ ★ ★ ★ ★

Annie debated taking out Etheldreda's self-sacrifices. Yes, it showed her faith and determination, but did she come across as too fanatical? She marked the passage in blue to remind herself to come back to it and make a decision about its removal after she'd finished the entire book.

"How many days do you think it will take?" the older of the two nuns asked.

"At least seven," Etheldreda estimated, "with straight riding." She'd made the trip often as a child with her father and later with her first husband. The time estimate was a guess, because they'd never been able to manage "straight riding," but rather they would stop at other kings' places for maybe a night, maybe for several days, depending on what her father and husband wanted to accomplish diplomatically.

"We should divide the food to make it last," the younger nun said.

"There are places that we can stop along the way, houses where I can stay and they will feed us," Etheldreda said, hoping that those places would not have heard of her escape. Returning an errant queen could provide political advantages.

They sat on the ground to eat. The blue sky began to change hue until it was almost as black as night. Then the clouds unleashed the water they had been holding.

The women tried to find shelter as best they could in a copse of trees. Even if they had wanted to ride on, they couldn't, for the tide had come in and the waves were much too high to risk riding the horses through them.

The rain continued throughout the night and all the next day and all the next night. Etheldreda couldn't remember ever being so cold, wet and miserable, but compared to the suffering Christ must have gone through on the cross, she told herself she could bear it if He had been able to bear his pain.

On the third morning the three women awoke to the sun, soaked to the skin and stiff. The spit of land had shrunk, covered by the extra high tide between them and the shore. When they looked, they saw that King Ecgfrith was camped on the shore opposite with six men. They had erected two tents. Their six horses were grazing a bit inland.

If captured, would her husband make her walk back rather than ride for fear that she would try to escape? Would he sling her over the horse? Or maybe he would assign her to one of his men, none of whom she recognized, but it had been awhile since she'd been under the same roof with her husband so she knew no one who served him currently.

The wind kept the waves high. Their crashing made any attempt of Etheldreda and Ecgfrith to call to each other impossible.

"We're trapped," the older nun said.

Etheldreda knelt and the two nuns followed her. They prayed until they could no longer see one another in the dark. Before the sunset, their clothes had dried, but the wind left them chilled. Without the wind, they would have been quite comfortable. They slept, their bodies touching, sharing what warmth they could.

The next day, which was also sunny but still windy, kept the water between the nuns and King Ecgfrith high. And the next. And the next. And the next.

Etheldreda watched her husband pacing on the opposite shore and looking toward her. He waved his arms as if trying to communicate in a sign language that she understood to mean that she must go to him.

The nuns chose to eat one meal a day. Berries extended their rations. They prayed in full visibility of the men, waiting for the high water to abate. But it never did.

The seventh day when the nuns woke up, King Ecgfrith was gone but the tide and wind remained the same.

"Do you think they gave up?" the younger nun asked.

Etheldreda did not know, but she led the sisters in prayer for still another day. No matter how stiff they were from staying in the same position for so many hours. No matter that their knees were pocked from gravelly stones.

Two days later the wind stopped and the nuns were grateful for the warmth. Another two days went by and the tides were reduced enough to allow the horses to walk through the foam.

Etheldreda found it hard to believe that her husband would give up. She didn't dare go too far inland. By keeping the coastline on her left, she knew that she would eventually reach Ely.

Every moment she expected Ecgfrith to appear. Each waking moment she alternated prayers of thanksgiving with prayers begging God to let her husband realize the futility of his plans and return to Northumbria.

She made a decision to stay in convents and churches along the way when they were close by, rather than any of those houses that might be on Ecgfrith's side. With shifting loyalties, it was difficult to know who supported whom. On nights that they could find nothing, they slept in the woods, sheltered by trees.

The weather, at least, stayed on their side. It was late enough in the summer that the days were warm and if the nights were cool, they were nothing compared to the nights on that spit of land with the rain pouring down.

It was late on the tenth day that they rode into the village of Ely, where Etheldreda was not only known but loved. She was home. This was now her time and nothing would stop her from doing what she'd wanted to do all along—build her abbey, which would house both a monastery and a convent.

CHAPTER 62

After Janet agreed, she and Annie didn't tell Roger that their goal was to find Rod. They said they'd be staying overnight or maybe two or three nights while Annie did some research.

Annie told herself it wasn't a total lie. She was researching where Rod was and what he was working on, knowing that Roger would never buy the idea that she knew where Rod was and didn't inform the police. As much as she tried to finesse the point beyond where she could feel not guilty . . . okay, she felt guilty for lying to her husband. Even thinking she didn't want to worry him didn't help alleviate the feeling.

Any worry she had about Roger being alone if he had any physical problems were eliminated because Marc agreed to stay until the women returned. He was more than happy to miss a few more days of classes.

He had been sitting on her bed, watching Annie throw a few things into a suitcase, while Roger was out walking Mercury. Walking was one of the things that the doctor had recommended, and Mercury was more than happy to oblige with his company, especially if Roger picked up a tennis ball on the way out the door.

"And you think your profs will buy it that you were stranded?"

"Probably not." Marc gave her the grin that she'd loved since he was a little boy who visited her after school to tell her about his day when his parents weren't interested.

"If you flunk out of the EPFL, I won't be held responsible," Annie said.

"Make up your mind, do you want to go away without worrying about Roger or not? Taking your laptop?"

"Of course, why?" As soon as she said "why," she regretted it.

"Because I don't think you're doing research. You said the other night you'd got most of what you needed: it was just that you didn't like your subject."

Annie kept her back to him as she unplugged her laptop and put it in its case. "Maybe I was wrong? Or maybe Quentin made me rethink the situation?"

"You know what I think?" Marc spoke to Annie's back.

When she didn't answer, he repeated the question. "I think since Janet's going, you'll be looking for Rod."

In the many years she'd watch Marc grow from kindergarten to manhood, Annie had never lied to him, something that had cemented their relationship. Thus she said nothing.

"I knew it. At least make sure you keep your phone charged in case I need to reach you."

Annie turned around. "You won't tell Roger?"

"Tell him what?"

The women left while it was still dark. The rain was pouring down and there was absolutely no one on the street as they put their backpacks and Annie's tablet in the car's trunk, or boot as Janet called it. Janet turned on the bum warmers as they waited for the vehicle to heat.

"You haven't told me where we're heading," Annie said.

"If I did, I'd have to kill you." Janet giggled. "I know how serious this all is, but in a way I feel like I'm on a road trip with a college friend. And I hope you won't mind if I tell you that I only think I know where Rod is."

Annie mulled that idea over for a few minutes. "As long as

we don't end up like Thelma and Louise," Annie said. She kept looking in the rearview mirror. "Doesn't look like we are being followed."

"We shouldn't use our credit cards in case someone flagged them." Janet pulled out of the parking space without putting on the lights until they were several blocks from the house.

"Maybe the bank mess might make it harder for the police to trace credit card activity," Annie said.

"I took enough cash from our stash."

"Shit," Annie said.

In the light from an oncoming car, Janet looked confused.

"I forgot the food we packed. And my stomach is telling me to put something in it."

"No problem. I'll go via Peterborough. We'll eat breakfast and pick up stuff for later on. Then we'll only need pee breaks on our way north."

"Want to at least tell me how long?"

"Probably around nine hours or more the way I drive and as-suming no traffic and not many stops. Rod always complained I had an allergy to putting my foot to the pedal."

When they arrived at the rest stop, the rain had ceased. The horizon had a slight band of light and the moon was dipping. They parked and entered the building. A man was washing down the beige tile of the central corridor using a string mop and a dirty-looking liquid in a metal pail. They walked around him to look at the number of fast-food big names in stalls on each side of the corridor.

There was a store selling sandwiches, biscuits, chips, bottled drinks, juices, candy, apples and pears and similar items. Grab-bing a shopping cart, they went up and down the aisles until they decided that they had enough to eat without having to stop again. It all looked pretty repulsive to Annie, but she knew she'd feel better after she had eaten something.

They were still ahead of the breakfast crowd as they picked up coffee, juice and croissants in the coffee shop and headed for a booth for four toward the back of the eating area where they could watch the door.

"Maybe this is dumb. If we were being followed and someone came in here, we wouldn't know what he or she looked like." She pointed to a woman in jeans. "If we were paranoid, we'd say she was an undercover cop."

As Annie put her tray on her table and sat, she frowned.

"What?" Janet's mouth was already full of croissant and she put her hand over it to not spit crumbs at Annie.

"I had a horrible thought. What if the police put a tracking device on your car?"

"Would they do that?"

"Maybe, if they thought you could lead them to Rod." The juice tasted sour and artificial although it claimed to be one hundred percent real orange. Maybe the manufacturers meant to say a hundred percent real orange color.

"Do you know what one looks like?" Janet asked.

Annie thought back to when the Argelès police had been ordering three of the devices for a just-in-case situation. About five years ago she'd done a technical manual for a tracking device but she had no idea if tracking devices all looked alike or if they'd changed in the interim.

The coffee shop had wi-fi. Annie left Janet sitting at a booth while she went back to the car to get her laptop. Coming back, she was glad that they had chosen a place where no one could see over their shoulders. Equally fortunate, she thought, was that she had remembered to bring a set of headphones. The last thing she wanted was to be overheard by God knows who all that might be drinking their morning coffee. Granted no one was nearby, but several people were in line and there was nothing to stop them from deciding to sit at a neighboring table.

Within minutes, using her favorite search engine, she'd found the information she wanted. Gesturing to Janet to come around the table next to her, she restarted the video on how to install a GPS tracking device. She listened as Janet watched, then Janet listened as Annie watched.

At the end of the twenty-two minutes it took for the video to run twice, Janet asked, "Does that mean you have to take the dashboard of my car apart to check if we have one of those little suckers?"

Annie hushed her and said in a low voice. "Before we do, we could check other places in the car, but I suspect that it has to be something like this."

The wi-fi signal reached out into the parking lot. Annie found a website that told where to look for a tracking device other than hidden in the dashboard. One place was under the car, although those were usually the older devices that didn't send signals very far. The two women walked around the car, looking underneath with a flashlight, not that they expected to find anything.

A man, probably in his late thirties and totally bald, watched them. "Anything I can do to help, ladies?"

"We just had an oil leak fixed and we wanted to make sure that it was really done right," Janet said.

"Check the ground for an oil stain," the man said.

"Now why didn't I think of that," Janet said.

"Women aren't supposed to know much about cars," the man said with a large enough smile that it negated the sexism of the remark. He headed into the restaurant.

"What now?" Janet asked.

"I take the dashboard apart." Annie leaned against the passenger door.

Janet shook her head. "I've doubts. My lovely car . . . you want to . . ."

"I *should* be able to put it back together."

"Should?"

"Should." Annie looked around. "We need to be someplace that the CCTV cameras won't pick us up. What do you have for tools?"

"The video said you would need a knife, tape, those pincher things. Rod insists I keep a toolbox in the car in case I break down, not that I would know what to do with any of the tools, if I did."

"Let's drive around to the back."

Janet did until they found the employees' parking lot. There was no gate keeping out normal traffic, but it was far enough away from the building so that they couldn't be observed.

Annie left the car to look for surveillance cameras while Janet stayed behind the wheel. Just in case there were any cameras watching, she stretched as if she needed to move around after a long time in the car. When she didn't see any equipment that might be photographing her, she opened the passenger door and said to Janet, who was still behind the wheel, "I guess employee cars aren't as important as customers' are."

"Or employees' safety as important either." Janet left the car and popped the trunk where they'd put their backpacks. There was a red metal toolbox and when they opened it they saw that they had some, but not all, of the needed equipment talked about in the video, but Annie decided there was enough. She could improvise, or at least she hoped so.

Annie picked out this and that and following the video's directions popped the dashboard as Janet grimaced at the perceived destruction. "Are you sure you can get that back together?"

"I hope so. Look." There was a little black rectangle box toward the top of the area behind the dash. "Lake is cleverer than we thought."

"So what do we do now?"

Annie wasn't sure. There was a make and model number that she used to find the manufacturer online. "It says it's active only when the car is on. It also says if we cover the top with metal then they won't be able to get any readings, but they may come looking for us if they don't get any readings for a long time. The police know your license plate number."

"Do we know if they are actively following us?"

"I've no idea. And they might already be alerted that we've left Ely."

"So we rule out covering it with metal, anyway," Janet said, "not that we have any."

The women sat a few minutes more saying nothing.

Annie looked around the employees' parking area. Two of the twenty cars parked side-side-side in two rows were old models, although Annie had no idea what kind of make they were.

She knew they were old because they looked beaten up. Cars had never interested her and the only thing that interested her now was if one of them was unlocked. Chances are if any were, it would be one of the older models. Maybe the owners even hoped they would be stolen, but then she doubted that the insurance money would go far in buying a better car.

She got out of Janet's car and tried to open the door of the blue vehicle. It was locked, but the gray and rust one was open. A closer look at the door showed that the locking mechanism was missing.

Annie carried the tracking device along with the tools to the gray and rusted car. Shaking as she worked slowed her down, but she managed to reinstall the device under the seat.

Grabbing her tools, she rushed back to Janet's car and managed to get the dashboard back in place just as five men and two women left by the employees' exit. "Drive," she said.

Janet headed back to the main parking lot. They watched as

several employee cars left the parking lot, including the gray and rusted one now equipped with a state-of-the-art tracking device. It looked as if the driver were a college kid behind the wheel or at least a boy of college age.

"So now, if I did it right, the Ely police will think we are wherever the owner of that car goes," Annie said. "I can imagine that poor kid when the police ask him about us."

Janet ran her hand over her dashboard. "And we look guiltier because we disabled the device." She began to laugh. "I can't believe you did that."

"I couldn't have without those step-by-step instructions. Thank you, Internet. And I can't believe we were so close to a shift change. Two more minutes and I would have had to explain what I was doing to whoever owned that car."

"What would you have said?" Janet continued along the route until they were back on the highway heading north. When Annie didn't answer within five miles she repeated the question.

"If it took me this long to answer your question, I can't imagine what I might have said to the owner of the car."

The women rode along for a few miles.

"Shit," Janet said.

"We forgot the sandwiches we bought."

CHAPTER 63

Burt never thought of himself as having a home. As an army brat he had moved every few years. His mother had died when he was ten and he and his older brother were pretty much left on their own on army bases in Germany, Japan, South Carolina and Ohio. Sure, sometimes women who lived in the same block of army flats would take pity on them and bring meals to the door.

He and Tom would usually eat whatever casserole there was, often cold, straight from the pan before his father got home, wash the pan and return it and make the women promise not to tell their father, who despised taking charity. "Stand on your own two feet," was the byword of Burt's reduced family.

His father had been killed in the Gulf War. Tom had died in a traffic accident. A short stint with an aunt and uncle who were college professors in the Midwest was more of a culture shock than changing countries, because most of his life he'd lived on the base, not the local economy of wherever they were stationed. His father had always put down civilians as being lazy, weak, stupid, unable to defend themselves or their country.

Meals at his aunt and uncle's house were times when people sat down together and talked about books, painting and movies. And, yes, leftie politics. His aunt and uncle had not approved of his mother's marriage to his father. Sometimes he didn't see them so much as different politically, but as a whole different species. They didn't know anything about the need for force.

If Burt Johnson had any home at all it was this cabin, a rebuilt nineteenth-century croft in all its primitiveness in the wilds of Scotland near a small loch. Although he might have to go outside to take a piss, the generator and the satellite dish he had installed gave him a first-rate communication system. If he were the type of man who joked, he'd have said that even his coffee pot was encrypted.

He thought of himself as a tough guy, but he had been able to go to his aunt and uncle's college free of charge as one of their benefits. His major had been computer science, but he left before he got his degree, feeling he'd learned all he could there. The rest he would teach himself. He prided himself on being as good a hacker as he was a strong man, although he preferred the latter.

Next he'd gone into the army, but found it too soft. Some might have said that he'd gone rogue. Burt thought of himself as an independent.

What he loved now was the thrill of the job—and what he hated was having any failure at all.

He caught a fish for dinner and had just gotten the fire going in the old iron stove when he heard a car pull in, followed by a door slam, footsteps and a knock at the door.

"It's Stewart, let me in."

Burt opened the door. The man who entered was somewhere in his mid-thirties, dressed in jeans and a heavy cabled beige sweater. He wore boots. "Good God, you are out here in nowhere and then some."

Burt thought it had taken Stewart long enough to get there after being summoned. "I like my privacy."

The man walked to the rough wooden table in front of the large fireplace and sat down without being asked. "Any chance of coffee?"

Burt took a metal coffee pot and pumped water from a long-handled pump over some coffee grounds. He slipped on an asbestos glove before putting the pot on the coals. He then removed the fish that was on a grill over the flame. "Fish?"

"Why not?" Stewart looked around the room. Besides the table and two wooden chairs, blackened with age as well as from the smoke emitted from the fireplace, there was a sink with a pump, and a single bed with a brass headboard. A blue sleeping bag was half on the bed and half on the floor. Gasoline lamps lit the room, barely throwing enough light into the corner next to the door and under one of the two windows that flanked the desk, which held a computer, printer, and scanner. Burt saved his generator for his electronics.

He divided the fish in half, putting it on two mismatched and cracked plates, then poured two cups of coffee and set a plate and cup in front of Stewart. "There's no restaurants within fifty miles, so if you don't like it, tough."

Stewart's tucking into the fish showed it was fine with him as it was. "Had I known your supplies were so low, I'd have brought bread and beer."

"I care more about the information you brought."

Stewart rubbed his sleeve across his mouth. He went to his backpack, which he'd left by the door, and pulled out a USB key and a folder. "All here. Those guys were amazing with what they pulled off."

"Amazing" wasn't the word that Burt would have used. It was his job to have stopped them. He'd failed. Now he was making up for it. He took the USB key, fired up the laptop and inserted the key.

All the information he needed to know about where Rod MacKenzie had gone after leaving Ely was there: every train ride, his overnight in Edinburgh, his going onto his boat and his leaving Edinburgh, and where he was now. Stewart had completed his assignment perfectly.

"Who have you talked to?"

"Only those I had to." Stewart spoke with his mouth full of fish but then washed it down with coffee. "Not even the wife."

"How did you do it?" Burt had to admire that Stewart got information the police had failed to get.

"I paid a shitload to get film from the cameras and even more to get it wiped out before the police could recognize what they had. I don't think they even know the films have been tampered with."

"Any more copies?" Burt held up the key.

Stewart shook his head. "How 'bout my money?"

Burt got up and opened the door to the armoire, although "armoire" seemed much too fancy for the piece of furniture that was little more than uneven boards hammered together. Inside on the bottom was a small safe.

He knew it wasn't smart to turn his back on anyone, but until Stewart had his money, Burt knew he would be safe. Once the safe was open, there was danger. He angled his body before he spun to the fourth and the final number so he could see Stewart's reflection in the window. The man seemed to be ignoring him.

Still watching Stewart, he pulled out a stack of bills. "Two thousand, we said." They had agreed on one thousand five hundred.

Burt noticed that Stewart opened his eyes just slightly before asking, "Two thousand?"

No honor among thieves, Burt thought. Stewart was a small-time operator, but still good, which was why he'd contacted him from Zurich before he left for Scotland. He stood and counted out two thousand in fifty-pound bills slowly, so Stewart could see he wasn't being cheated. That cheaters expected to be cheated was one of Burt's observations of the human species.

Stewart snatched the money from the table and checked just

the same as if he hadn't seen Burt count it out.

"Don't you trust me?"

Stewart's smile might have been sheepish, but more likely Burt thought it was a smirk.

"Anything else for me to do?" Stewart stood up and put the money in his backpack and pulled out his car keys.

Burt knew he would never use this man again. "Maybe next month. Depends on my client."

Stewart held out his hand. "Pleasure doing business with you."

"The pleasure is mine." He walked Stewart to the door. As soon as Stewart was outside, Burt went to his bed and pulled his Glock from under the mattress. By then Stewart was unlocking his car door.

"You forgot something," Burt called and started toward Stewart's car. When he was within ten feet, he shot Stewart four times, even though the first bullet in the heart more than took care of the job.

"Idiot," Burt thought. Then he considered what this inconvenience had cost him. He needed to get rid of the car and the body. Mentally, he ran through the places he could drive the car with the body in the trunk where it wouldn't be found until poor old Stewart was a skeleton. Even better would be to bury Stewart, remove the car's identification and drop it in the loch.

CHAPTER 64

By the time Annie and Janet reached Edinburgh it was early afternoon and a steady drizzle left their moods as heavy as the weather. Janet found a parking place. The car at this point was littered with papers from the snacks they'd bought on route.

"Why do you think Rod's here?"

"I'm not sure he's here now. When he called me, I thought I heard our niece and nephew in the background. Of course, I could have imagined it."

Annie hesitated to ask the question she'd been resisting asking, then headed into it. "Why didn't you ask him about the codes for the pig and rooster?"

"Two reasons. It was too quick. He said to me, 'I'm alive. I love you,' and hung up."

"And the second?"

"Had we talked more, I probably wouldn't have thought of it. I was too shocked."

She found a parking place along a side street. "No parking near Ute's and Duncan's house."

"Ute doesn't sound like a Scottish name." Annie hadn't budged from the passenger's side.

"She's German. Rod's brother is a computer nerd and a contractor like Rod. Ute and he met when Duncan was on assignment in Munich."

Annie wondered why she hadn't known that, although in itself the information wasn't all that important.

The two women got out of the car and walked up a narrow path, too narrow for even the smallest car to drive down. On each side were attached brick houses with tiny yards, most of which had been fixed up with potted plants and flagstones. One was filled with garbage cans. At 52 Bright Terrace, Janet bounded up the stairs, followed by Annie. They huddled under the overhang until a woman answered.

"My God, Janet, what are you doing here?" Only it came out, Mine Got, Yanet, vat are ewe doink here.

"I was hoping to find Rod."

Ute drew the two women in, took their wet coats and insisted that they have a hot cup of coffee. Inside it seemed that no expense had been spared to create a modern kitchen. Original brick walls had been exposed. The furniture was either antique or top quality new, creating an ambiance of a home worth far more than the neighborhood. However, Annie was aware of what could happen when a neighborhood was being gentrified. Or maybe Rod's brother, who as a contractor earned a good living, was being a typical frugal Scot in buying downscale and turning it upscale. It was not a question she would ask.

Off the dining room two children played. The little girl with bright red curls had a dollhouse, while the boy, with hair that matched his sister's, only shorter, was constructing something out of cardboard boxes.

Janet and Annie seated themselves at the kitchen counter on one side of an island as Ute dropped a capsule into her coffee machine. "Duncan is away on assignment. He's vorking in Germany for a month."

Annie turned to Ute. "Since he's a contractor, I imagine, he's away a lot."

Ute put the first cup of coffee in front of Janet and put in a second capsule. "Ya, he is, although he does try to get back at least veekends."

"Is it hard for you with him away so much?" Annie immediately felt embarrassed. It was too personal a question to ask. She apologized.

Ute waved her hand as she poured the final cup. "No madder. Sometimes it's easier. One less child to vait on."

"About Rod? I thought he was here. When he called I thought I heard the kids speaking German in the background."

"He vas. He had a lot of vork to do he told me, but he didn't feel he could stay here." She frowned. "Is he in trouble? Are you two in trouble?"

"Not really," Janet said.

Ute nodded. "As I told you he said he couldn't stay here. Imposition, he said, as vell as the kids being too much of a disturbance."

Annie wondered how Ute could not have known about the murder. If she had, that would be one of the first things she would have asked. One's brother-in-law is not the subject of a nationwide manhunt without relatives knowing about it. When Ute left the room to answer the telephone, Annie asked Janet about it.

"Ute doesn't watch television. Look. There was no television in the living room. And if Duncan is out of the country, he probably doesn't even know about Simon's murder. They aren't close, the brothers. As wives we do the birthday and Christmas cards and that's about the only contact unless there's a relative's funeral or a cousin's wedding." She sighed. "We did take a couple of holidays on their boat, all of us, after the boys finished assignments together. We said we should do it more often, but never have."

Ute came back into the room.

"Where did he go?" Annie asked, "Rod, that is."

"Rod seldom tells me where he is, but I really wanted to surprise him. It is our anniversary this weekend," Janet said.

303

"I thought you vere married in the spring," Ute said.

"The anniversary of our meeting."

Janet's quick, Annie thought with admiration.

"He asked if he could use Duncan's boat." Ute turned to Annie. "Duncan has a boat, a thirty-eight-foot cabin cruiser that he keeps just off shore. It picks up vi-fi if the boat is close enough to the dock. My husband tried to explain things but Vsat and telecommunications and most terms don't mean much to me. They are just empty letters and words."

"So Rod went there?" Annie blew on her coffee and the steam danced in a pattern.

Ute nodded. "I knew Duncan vouldn't mind."

"Do you know where he's docked?"

Ute gave them the address.

In the car, Janet said, "I'm so stupid. We've been on the boat. I should have thought of it before."

But when they arrived at the dock, the boat was gone.

CHAPTER 65

Ute did not seem all that bothered that Rod had taken the boat when the women returned to Bright Terrace and reported the boat wasn't in its slip. "He said he might go fishing. Vat's vhere he is, I'm sure," Ute said. "He'll be back in the morning most likely."

Because they were so tired, they accepted Ute's suggestion to stay the night and get an early start in the morning.

Ute had moved the children out of their bedroom, putting them in her bed and taking the couch, despite both Janet's and Annie's declaration that it was too much. Ute would hear none of it as she apologized for the simple dinner of eggs and toast that she'd planned for the children. Janet and Annie won the round that stopped Ute from rushing out to buy a better dinner or at least a take-away from the Indian restaurant around the corner.

The thought of Indian food turned Annie's stomach, which she chalked up to exhaustion. Normally, she wolfed down anything Indian whether at a restaurant or homemade by one of her Asian friends. Mostly she wanted to sleep, even if the kids' beds meant she couldn't stretch out full length. The fetal position would be just fine.

Janet had brushed her teeth after Annie had crawled under the duvet and tiptoed into the bedroom.

"So where's Rod?" Annie asked.

"I think Inverness, but I'm not sure. Or maybe Nairn. I was

hoping Ute or Duncan would know where he was exactly."

"Why?"

"He worked in Inverness. While we were assigned there we went up to Nairn. Rod knows both places and likes them."

"I'm willing to go look." Annie decided not to worry about the book. Maybe she could work in the car on the road. "Why wouldn't the police have questioned Rod's relatives?"

"Probably if they'd known about them, they would have. They never asked me."

CHAPTER 66
ELY 679

Annie woke in the middle of the night, and tiptoed out of the children's bedroom. Since she couldn't sleep, this was her chance to get a bit of writing done. Not wanting to disturb Ute on the couch, she went into the bathroom. By sitting on the toilet, she could put her feet on the bathtub, making her lap a place to work.

Bishop Wilfrid rode as fast as he could toward Ely after the messenger barreled into his office.

Along the way he'd changed horses when one beast tired, leaving the previous mount to be picked up on his return trip. The latest was a gray mare that he'd exchanged for this stallion only three hours ago.

His thighs were sore from gripping the different horses as he galloped over the countryside, passing farms and pounding through forests. Normally, his travel was leisurely, but the messenger had said there was not much time. Forty-six was much too old to be making this strenuous ride.

Until yesterday the June weather had been anything but springlike with cold and rain. Both he and his horse were sweating. He prayed that Ely would not have had floods preventing him from reaching Etheldreda's abbey before it was too late.

Without warning, the horse slowed and wandered off the path toward water. Wilfrid had to duck to keep tree branches from hitting him in the face until he could rein in the beast and slip off. The stream had obviously overflowed its banks for several trees were half submerged. Although not wanting to take the time, he knew he had to let the horse drink. He scooped up fistfuls of the icy water. As he gulped, the water ran down his chin. The horse had known what they'd both needed.

He wished he could have jumped into the water to cool himself. Instead Wilfrid led the horse back to the path, mounted and kicked the animal in its sides. Instead of speeding up, the horse slowed down.

Wilfrid wanted to curse the beast, but he was afraid that it would cause even more problems. He knew the route well enough to know that there were no more stops between here and Ely to exchange the damned animal for another.

Rather than gallop, the stallion picked up speed, not to a point that Wilfrid was happy about his progress, but it was better than a slow walk. The stableman at the church told him he had to show who was master. Wilfrid knew the answer. The horse was the master.

The sun was lower in the sky by the time he approached Ely. The roads were only slightly muddy, showing that whatever floods had happened in May, the water had receded.

The land was flat, but then he spied the top of the abbey above the trees. That Etheldreda had accomplished its building was a miracle in itself. Granted, he'd helped by wheedling materials and gold out of the richer of the kings and their minions for her.

She'd supervised the building as if she were a Roman architect and an engineer. What had amazed him was that the workmen listened to her. Although she was a woman, she'd won their respect. He'd thought she'd been too gentle with the workmen, making sure that they had food and water and time to rest. "They'll take advantage of you," he'd warned her over and over.

She'd told him that he was wonderful as a friend and as her spiritual advisor, but she knew how to get the best from others.

When the abbey was built in record time, he admitted he'd been wrong. She'd only smiled and had said, "I know."

As he arrived at the abbey, there was a crowd of whom he could only guess were locals outside the abbey.

As he dismounted, a little boy came up to him and asked, "Do you know how Sister Etheldreda is?"

An older boy, possibly his big brother because their faces were almost identical but their heights differed, hit the younger on the head. "Stupid, he's just arrived. How would he know anything?"

Bishop Wilfrid was greeted by a sister who then led him to Seaxburga, who was sitting outside a closed door. As he passed by the other sisters, they were moving their lips in prayer. The nuns had loved Etheldreda. Her abbey was one of the best he'd seen not just for the efficiency, but for the example she set for being kind, almost a female Christ, he'd once thought, even though the idea of a female Christ was heresy.

"Thank goodness you've got here." Seaxburga stood up so quickly, the three-legged stool tipped and crashed.

"I came as fast as I could. How is she?"

"Very weak."

Seaxburga opened the door. Her sister, Etheldreda, was on a narrow cot. One of the nuns was wiping the sick woman's head with a cloth dampened with water from a wooden bowl on a small table.

"Wilfrid. You came." The voice was barely a whisper. When Etheldreda saw Seaxburga she frowned. The speech must have exhausted her because she closed her eyes.

Wilfrid knelt by the bed, more of a board and barely the width of the patient. Even under the cover, he could see how thin Etheldreda was, except for the huge growth on her neck.

The room smelled of sickness. In his other visits to the abbey all the sleeping places had smelled of fresh straw and herbs.

He knelt by the bed to pray.

CHAPTER 67

Inverness was gray, but not raining when Annie and Janet drove into the city. They drove down streets where it seemed every other house was a B&B, many with vacancy signs swinging under the names. They had looked at every dock along the coast, but had not seen Duncan's boat and had decided to give up for the day.

"I've selected this one scientifically," Janet said, pulling to a stop before the Laughing Cat. "It was the third on the right."

Inside there was a plethora of cat art, cat statues and books about cats, but not a real cat to be seen.

The only word to describe the room with the two twin beds was "cozy." A fireplace had an electric fire. Violet, blue and green dominated the walls and duvets. Outside they could see the last of the light dipping over the horizon.

"This is perfect," Annie said.

"Breakfast will be between seven and nine," the owner, a woman around Annie and Janet's age, said. "If you need anything, just come downstairs and there's a bell in the dining room."

Annie thought how great this would be if they weren't on a mission. "So how do we find Rod?" she asked Janet when the owner had left the room.

"He gave me a number of a pay as you go telephone, but I don't dare call him from mine. I thought I'd buy a phone tomorrow."

"Or we could find a telephone booth." Annie opened her suitcase and took out a sweater. Cozy or not, the room was chilly.

"When Ute said Rod wanted to go fishing, I nearly blew it. We both know Rod is not a fisherman."

"So what next?" Annie asked.

"We'll go on to Nairn. He always loved it."

"And if he's not there?"

"Oh, Annie. How in the hell did all this happen?"

Annie had no answer.

CHAPTER 68
JARROW, NORTHRUMBIA
708

On the drive to Nairn, Janet was silent, leaving Annie mental space to plot out the last chapter of the book. Thank God, the project was almost over. She knew when she got home, she would be able to polish it and give it to Quentin. Glory Hallelujah! She wasn't sure Quentin would like the literary device of bringing in Britain's first historian, but it was the only way she could think of to explain the alleged stories of what happened after Etheldreda's death.

The thirty-five-year-old Bede left the refractory, humming as he went. Through the window he could hear a bird singing. He saw the little fellow in the lilac bush whose scent pierced the open windows. Now that spring had arrived the winter shutters had been removed.

He nodded to the other priests as he left one building for the other. A slight breeze lifted the hair that fell into his eyes. He tilted his head toward the sun, enjoying the smell from the nearby forest.

He'd been looking forward to his tasks today: writing about the exhumation of Etheldreda's body—sixteen years after her death. Writing, be it prose, poetry or song, was what he loved most. Words danced in his head, and he could not look at a blade of grass, a flower, or even the heavy stone rocks that made up the double monastery of Jarrow and Monkwearmouth without composing sentences.

Once he started, he would be able to work uninterrupted. He

had already prepared the parchments, this batch made of the finest calfskin. He would let no one but himself stretch it on frames. And he scraped each one with a semi-lunar-shaped knife to make sure not the smallest hair remained.

A small amount of pumice powder had been sent from Coldingham. He had rubbed that into the flesh side before removing the material from his frame. The last thing he'd done was to rub a starch paste into the material, which would allow his pen to fly over it.

For once he had a satisfactory supply of ink, having cut and dried enough hawthorn branches for its bark, which he'd pounded to powder and then soaked for a week. The water, spiced with a dab of wine, was boiled until it thickened and blackened. Just yesterday he had collected the bags into which he'd poured the mixture; he then hung them in the sun, being careful to watch the weather to make sure rain didn't soak the bags.

The room where he worked had shelves stacked with parchments both rolled and between leather covers.

He'd slept badly last night. Words kept him awake. This was often the way when he was about to start on an important chapter.

Wilfrid, now promoted to being the Archbishop of Canterbury, had been at the exhumation. For the last two weeks he'd been talking to Bede, who tried to contain his excitement. Granted, he'd had the written statement of Cynefrith, Etheldreda's doctor, who had also been at the exhumation. Their accounts matched.

Part of Bede's excitement was that he felt their findings proved that Etheldreda had, in fact, been a virgin despite being married twice.

Bede seated himself on his stool and tilted his table to the best angle to catch the light. His work area had three windows:

one in back, one on each side. Over his head, if he needed more
light, there was a chandelier with room for twenty candles,
although how many he burned depended on how much light he
needed.

He picked up his pen and began to write.

The decision had been made to move Etheldreda's body from
the graveyard to inside the chapel. The new burial site had been
prepared.

In attendance were Cynefrith, the physician who had thought
after he had lanced the tumor on her neck sixteen years earlier
that the forty-three-old virgin would recover.

Two days later, she had developed a fever and had left this
world for a place of eternal peace.

The gravediggers had dug into the earth, revealing the top of
the coffin. Four monks jumped into the hole and struggled to
get ropes under the box to lift it to the surface.

Bishop Wilfrid and Etheldreda's sister, Seaxburga, who was
now abbess at Ely, watched, as did several nuns. Those who had
known and loved her wept. Those who had taken their vows
after Etheldreda and knew her only by her reputation prayed.

The coffin was carried into the chapel where five other nuns
chanted prayers. At first, no one knew what to do: Bishop Wilfrid asked the monks to remove the nails from the coffin top, so
that the bones could be shifted to the blue-wool-lined white
marble casket.

The top of the wooden box was shifted to one side.

A combination of deep intakes of breaths and "Holy Mother"
and "a miracle" were whispered.

The nuns moved closer.

"She looks like the day we laid her to rest," said one of the
nuns who had nursed Etheldreda in her final illness, "but better."

Etheldreda's face was serene. Her hands had not lost any flesh. She was dressed in a black robe. Her hair was covered in a black hood pulled tightly around her head.

"It is as if she could speak to us," one of the younger nuns whispered but was shushed by an older nun standing next to her.

"Lift her up," Bishop Wilfrid said, but Cynefrith held up his hand.

"I would like to examine her."

Bishop Wilfrid nodded.

Cynefrith approached the body and bowed his head in prayer before reaching for the hood and slowly, ever so slowly, moved it back.

"Our Father, who art in Heaven," he said.

"What is it?" Bishop Wilfrid asked.

Cynefrith pointed to Etheldreda's neck. "When she died, this was still an open wound. Look."

Everyone gathered around to see that there was barely a scar on the body.

The youngest nun carried in a bowl of hot water and soap to wash the body. New clothing made of black wool was ready to redress their former abbess before laying her to rest, this time for eternity.

Bede sat back and reread his work. Now he needed to rework his words in Latin. There were times when he wrote using prose and other times poetry. He wasn't sure how to proceed.

For many years he'd doubted that any woman could live with two husbands and remain a virgin, no matter how much she desired it. Men had more problems controlling their physical urges.

Also men needed children to serve them, especially those who were warring to become the Bretwalda. They would want their own sons, rather than other kinsmen, to take over their territory. Usually, therefore, even the most devout virgin would surrender her body to her husband rather than be taken by force.

Etheldreda's body had been purified after death of its affliction, which Bede doubted would have been possible had she not been pure throughout her life. Had he just read eyewitness accounts, he might have doubted the event, but Bishop Wilfrid had assured him it was so.

Had he used all his God-bestowed talents to tell Etheldreda's story? He reread what he had written and was satisfied.

Annie knew that many copiers in medieval times always ended a manuscript with "Finished thanks be to God," or some other phrase of similar content. For her it was enough to type, "The End" but she was afraid to add "and good riddance" in case Quentin took it the wrong way.

CHAPTER 69

Burt pulled his car into Nairn. He sometimes felt like one of those dancers scattering flower petals, but he installed trackers on anyone and everyone who might be of help to him. The one he had put on Janet MacKenzie's car had become almost useless. She seemed stuck in Peterborough rather than Ely. Maybe the police had been giving her a hard time and she was trying to put some distance between them and herself.

He'd demanded that Anderson install tracking devices in the cars of the major employees of Rod's company, but they too seemed locked into home-store-work trips, useless to him. He also had them installed in Rod's brother-in-law's car and even the brother's boat, which he had learned about when he started his research for the project. MacKenzie would turn up unless he was already dead or had skipped the country.

At least Anderson had gotten the installations part of the job right. Granted, the device on MacKenzie's car was useless after he'd parked it at Gatwick. He called on his own network of hackers to determine that if MacKenzie had left the country, he would have had to do it under false identification, and he was positive that his victim did not have the wherewithal to do that. Only once did he think he might be on a wild goose chase when he followed up on the brother who was out of the country.

If Johnson were the type to bask in self-praise, he would have broken his arm patting his own back. The boat had been the key. He'd driven up the coast as MacKenzie had moved the

318

boat to Inverness and later to Nairn.

All Burt had to do was to wait for MacKenzie to return to the boat, which he did. Burt had been sitting in his car as Mac-Kenzie hobbled down the street and swung himself onto the deck. Rod did not give Burt a second look.

With the baseball cap, fake mustache, blue jacket and dark glasses, Burt had no worry that MacKenzie would tie him to the long-haired man in a gray jacket that had been following him earlier in the day. His trunk was always filled with clothes and different wigs to alter his appearance if need be.

Just as he arrived at the water, he saw *The Waiting* leave the dock.

Chapter 70

Renting a boat, and leaving his car, would be going with his instincts, Burt thought, and once again he was sure his instincts would be correct.

He'd try to outthink where else MacKenzie might go. Taking out his smartphone, he researched the local towns with ports. Burt prided himself on his ability to second-guess his targets, but this one was difficult. He had no idea how aware of the area MacKenzie was. Sure he was a Scot, but he'd lived in England and wherever his contracting took him since he'd gone to university. How often he'd gone back to Scotland was a mystery. Burt didn't like mysteries of any kind.

He found a garage and left the car before heading to the water. Then he saw it. The boat's name, *Pair-of-Dice,* appealed to him. The owner was on board looking a bit worse for wear. The smell of alcohol from the man's body did not dissipate in the sea air. The man wasn't all that old, maybe in his late twenties or early thirties, although his sun-weathered face already sported a few broken veins. Burt was usually accurate within a year of guessing someone's age, even those that didn't exhibit the normal characteristics.

"Ahoy." Did people say that in Scotland? Since he couldn't pass for anything but an American, let him play it to the hilt. A dark ponytail was under his baseball cap and he had padding under his jacket so that in case anyone saw him on the boat with the man and wanted to identify him, the major parameters wouldn't match.

Since the weather would have made dark glasses seem strange, Burt had put in brown contact lenses. He neither liked the color-changing way he saw things nor putting anything into his eyes, but caution was caution.

The man, who had been slumped in his deck chair, looked up but stayed sitting. "Aye?"

Burt had spent enough time in Scotland to work his way through many of the thick dialects. He wasn't sure how thick this one would be, but when the man said, "What do you want?" that was all it took to let him know it would be thick.

"Like the name of your boat. Bet when you pull into any port, the name helps you to find any action."

"Ya got it."

"Dice good to you?"

"Sometimes."

"Any chance I could rent your boat for a couple of days?" He was counting on the man needing money.

"If you rent it, I can't go fishing. If I don't go fishing, I don't earn any money."

He needs money, just as I suspected, Burt thought. "I'll make it worth your while." How desperate was the man? Maybe his offer would be too low-ball, but if he had the man make the offer . . .

Silence—a tool that worked well—would it work this time?

The man stood up slowly as if his head hurt. "How worth my while?"

"Fishing can be tricky. One day a good catch, one day nothing."

The man stared out to sea. Instead of speaking, he merely nodded.

"You work alone?"

"Most of the time."

Burt applied the old rub-the-chin trick as if he were thinking. The money wasn't the problem. But the man was. How well known was the man? "This your home port?"

The man shook his head. "Hail from Edinburgh. Go up and down the coast. Put in when I get tired of being out there."

"So you aren't in Nairn often?"

"Maybe a couple of times a year."

"Any friends here?"

"Couple of people I gamble with. Don't even know their last names."

An aha moment if there ever was one, Burt thought. "Going out today?"

"Thought I might."

"Want a hand. I love to fish."

"This isn't a sissy, 'throw your rod in the water' type of boat."

"My dad was a lobster fisherman off the coast of Maine." Burt's father's idea of catching a lobster was pointing to one in a tank at a restaurant and then telling the waitress how he wanted it cooked.

"How does £150 sound?" Burt thought he might be successful lower, but he didn't want to make the man suspicious. If he were too low, he could up the offer.

The man stuck out his hand. "Me name's Malcolm; welcome aboard."

As Malcolm cast off, Burt scanned the shoreline. Almost no one was around other than two gray-haired women, one with a cane, walking slowly and talking; neither paying attention to anything around them.

The sea was churning a bit, making the boat bob. Malcolm's hangover seemed to dissipate in the sea air and the rocking of his craft didn't seem to bother him. Burt was not a sailor by nature. He didn't particularly like the water, although he was a top-notch swimmer and as part of his self-training he'd learned how to navigate on water.

Burt scanned the horizon for MacKenzie. Nothing. He'd taken too long, but he wasn't going to give up. He didn't want to pull out his tracker.

Malcolm turned the boat toward the open sea. Burt wanted to stay closer to shore. As Malcolm stood behind the wheel, Burt asked, "Want that I make us some coffee?"

"Aye. You'll find everything you need down below."

The cabin had a small galley and an unmade bed and looked as if Malcolm had an allergy to any cleaning product. The metal coffee pot was encrusted with grime: dishes were piled in a small sink.

When Burt turned on the water faucet the pump groaned, but enough water came out to rinse the pot and then fill it. He found the bag of ground coffee among the cans, some opened and moldy and some unopened.

While the coffee was perking, Burt washed two cups. "Take milk and sugar?" He called up to the deck.

"Just black."

Into one cup he dropped three tablets.

On deck Malcolm pronounced the coffee good. "Always better when you don't make it yourself, and—" He dropped in mid-thought, unconscious to the deck.

Burt looked around and found some weights that were used to sink the fishing nets. He cut them loose and stuffed Malcolm's pockets before throwing the man overboard.

Taking over the wheel, Burt pulled his tracker out of his backpack and followed his prey, who was heading back to port.

Chapter 71

Rod MacKenzie had come back from his test run and docked in Nairn. Much of what his brother had taught him had come back to him, so if he had to head for Norway he was sure he could make it.

What a mess this was, but he didn't regret a minute of what he'd done. After working for four different banks, he'd seen how they rigged the system. It was the program for the off-books accounting done for Harrison, Harrison, Jackson he'd been hired to write that had convinced him that he had to act. While he was working in New York, a homeless man had come in and robbed a branch of $100. He was hungry.

The next day that same man returned the money. He was sentenced to twelve years for the theft, yet those in management in the bank were operating a shadow system, not to mention that their subsidiary was foreclosing on homes right and left. He'd seen the instructions telling the staff not to negotiate.

He'd never understood why the world had run amok. Activism wouldn't do anything. Protests were like mosquitos that might—at best—merely annoy those who could make a difference.

He'd moored *The Waiting* in Nairn, a coastal town with more people in the short summer than the rest of the year, toward the end of the River Ness. He wanted to be nearer the Moray Firth in case he had to make a run for it.

Rod's brother had given the boat a name that Rod thought

was both dumb and terribly appropriate to his circumstances. He was waiting to be no longer a fugitive or at least no longer a person of interest in a murder investigation.

No one knew his real crime: his and Simon's. Poor Simon. He and Simon saw too much, overheard too much, when they were contracting at two different big banks in New York, but at the time they'd had no idea that they could make any difference. They would share their frustrations: frustrations that went beyond seeing the CEO be driven off in a limousine, while they were writing code to handle products that even as non-bankers they could see were worthless.

At first Rod thought it was just his lack of financial knowledge, but one Saturday, he and Simon got together for a late-night beer, and Simon had mentioned, "Ever notice all those ads on the Internet offering mortgages with no salary check? That's crazy." And when Rod heard that, a click went off in his head.

The men began to research banking practices as best they could and the more they looked, the more convinced they were that the system was rotten. Over and over they asked themselves what they were missing. Surely, minds better than theirs would have discovered what they were discovering. The business television channels must be on it, except that they weren't. Nor was there anything in the business press.

As a kid, Rod had seen what had happened to his father as he was ground down when the company for which he'd worked for years had shut down. It had been one of the first to shift its operations to Asia.

His mother had tried to support him and his brother as a social worker, but she didn't earn enough to stop the bank from repossessing their modest-by-all-standards house.

It was on yet another assignment together in Denmark that he and Simon talked about the banks and the government's re-action to the crisis. Financially, as computer contractors they were both doing well and considered themselves lucky that they happened to have trained in, and loved, a skill in such demand. They could have as easily been in some other job that wasn't in demand.

"I guess being a plumber, doctor, nurse, dentist, electrician or a beautician are about the only jobs that can't be shipped overseas," Rod had said.

"Our jobs can still go to India," Simon had said.

It was at that point that Rod and Simon decided to set up their business helping people learn different software and installing systems. They would earn less than as contractors, but they needed to be physically on-site.

Once settled in Ely, their anger at what they knew grew. When the two of them were at the pub, they would find a corner table and play what-if games. At that point it was only a fantasy until one day, Simon said, "Why not?"

"Why not what?"

"Do it. Bring the system down."

The planning had been intense. They'd started with dry runs into Harrison, Harrison, Jackson's computers, then had moved on to others. None of the systems had the protections they should have had. One of their big worries was that they themselves could be traced from their forays into the systems.

Strange—that sequence of events that had led Rod to be here, at this moment, on this boat, as his refuge.

He and Janet had done one small trip on *The Waiting* after an assignment in Aberdeen, along with Duncan and Ute. It was just the four of them, before Duncan and Ute had had kids. His brother had showed him how to handle routine activities: docking, undocking, filling the tank, and speeding up and slowing down. They'd never gone out of sight of land. Yet, if he had to now, Rod would try to flee for Norway. Thank God for GPS.

He had no immediate plans to do another cyber-attack. He

planned to wait and see what the fallout would be, the investigations. He had a hope, albeit, a far-fetched one, that the regulators would crack down. If they didn't, he'd try again.

And thank God that the newspapers had lost interest in Simon's murder, going onto the next event. Strange that they wanted him as a person-of-interest in a murder he hadn't committed but knew nothing about the crime that he had. Only, he didn't think of it as a crime. He saw himself as a hero defending the little person against the powerful; Robin Hood with arrows or David with his slingshot.

He'd been moored in Nairn for the past three days, having moved the boat from Inverness when he'd wondered if he were being followed. Being on crutches slowed his movements, but he needed to go out to buy food and he thought there had been a man behind him. Rod had stopped a couple of times to look in a window. The man had stopped too.

Rod lost him by going out the back of a grocery store. He'd hobbled back to the boat and had taken off.

It also occurred to him that he might be a bit paranoid.

He hated his present circumstances because he constantly needed to look over his shoulder in case someone came after him. He needed the freedom from worry to do his work. He needed Simon. God, how he missed that man.

Men don't cry, his father had told him, but his father had told him a lot of things, including that education wasn't necessary and that it's good to beat up on others. His mother, who often was bruised, had countered his father's messages with stories of Robin Hood.

He hadn't cried when his father died, hit by a car on his way home from the pub. Rod had told his mother that now he was the man of the house, but she'd countered that she was the woman of the house, and it was his job to get a good education.

Rod never figured out how his parents had ever gotten

together, although he suspected it had to do with sex. His father had been a handsome man, one who could have turned a young girl's head even if that young girl was from a better class. "Don't rebel for the sake of rebelling," his mother had told Rod so often that it became a mantra: "Rebel for a good reason."

Maybe her marriage was a rebellion against her parents, who shunned her after her marriage. She continued to be a rebel, going to work for a social service agency where she fought for her clients to obtain their rights. She never dismissed those that didn't seem to want help, but concentrated on their children.

Rod was one of the many children from council homes, where they moved after their house was taken by the bank. Unlike most of the other kids he and Duncan were dragged to museums, the zoo, the castle perched above Edinburgh's Royal Mile. He'd cried when his mother had died, far too young, from cancer. And he'd cried when Simon was killed. Both times, though, he had waited until he had been alone.

Rod was in the cabin of the *The Waiting* when he heard footsteps on the deck above.

"Anyone home?" It was a male voice, one that was distinctly American.

Rod swung himself up on deck using his arms along the rails leading up the five stairs to the deck and leaving his crutches below. His cast was visible.

The man was probably in his mid-forties, tall and built like a bulldozer. He could have appeared in any war movie as the toughest, meanest sergeant on the planet.

"Nice boat."

"Thanks. What can I do for you?"

"Looking for a man named Rod MacKenzie."

"I'm not from around here. Just on a little holiday. Is he a local?"

"No. I heard he had a broken leg."

"Poor devil. I can certainly feel sorry for him." Rod pointed to his own cast.

"How did you do that?"

"Stupidly. Fell off the roof fixing some tiles. Next time I hire someone."

The man nodded. "If you come across MacKenzie, can you let me know?" He handed Rod a piece of paper that said "Brett Long" along with a mobile number.

"Well, if you'd excuse me, I was making lunch."

The man looked in the direction of the street that ran out to the docks. Despite the coolness, it was busy, mostly with women and children. He then turned and looked out the Firth toward the sea. There were two small ships.

"Sure." He hopped onto the dock and ambled away.

Rod went below but he could still see the man who had walked around the corner and disappeared. Then he started the engine and headed toward Norway.

CHAPTER 72

When Burt Johnson approached MacKenzie on the boat, only women and children were around. Johnson had given up waiting until the area was empty. As they were talking a man carrying fishing tackle appeared and meandered down the dock. When he left the boat, he deliberately turned the corner until he found a deserted alleyway to change clothes and put on a wig, which he'd stuffed into his backpack.

He could watch MacKenzie from the end of the street. As tempted as he was to buy a coffee in the coffee shop, which offered a good view, he decided he needed to be ready to move fast if MacKenzie took off.

When he saw MacKenzie go below deck, he walked back to the *Pair-of-Dice,* docked three boats away from *The Waiting.* Although he could just as easily have shot him, Burt was not about to chance killing MacKenzie near possible witnesses. Waiting was his course of action. He laughed thinking how his actions matched the name of MacKenzie's boat.

With MacKenzie gone, both hackers would be dead, not that other hackers in the future might not be as dangerous or try other attacks on banks. But the two that he knew had brought down the financial system while it was under his watch would at least be out of the picture. He doubted that anyone else in the world knew what he knew, not even that asshole American banker.

Burt admired the hackers' cleverness as much as he admired

his own. To this day he wasn't sure what had been Masterson's exact sources in finding those two men, either before, during, or after they'd pulled one of the most audacious crimes in history. Even then, discovering exactly who and where they were, Masterson had needed *him*—Burt Johnson—who alone had been able to find out in advance through his network. He'd done it—he'd located them.

He had to stop mulling over his mistakes, but he couldn't. Even if he hadn't been a hundred percent sure that the hackers represented a danger to his client, his decision to take them out, thus eliminating any possibility, had been the right one.

Burt's mistake had been counting on Anderson. Damn him for bungling the hit and run against MacKenzie. If he'd done his job right, Burt would be enjoying his time in his cabin while waiting for another job that might catch his interest, not here, trying to rescue his self-respect.

Johnson had no respect for the police. No policeman had the intelligence to look beyond the obvious friends, family or colleagues. Their minds were not wired for international intrigue despite all the terrorist-this-and-terrorist-that and a-terrorist-under-every-bed propaganda that had people so scared that they believed whatever lie the government might circulate.

Burt had to laugh. Fewer people died from terrorists than bad doctors, bad food, bad water, car crashes or their own stupidity. No hysteria on any of those problems.

Maybe his life would be easier if he didn't have to finish everything he started. Not just finish, but finish well. If he were the type to go to a shrink, the shrink would probably tell him it went back to the huge model plane he and his father were building when they were stationed in Japan.

Night after night they would work on it when his father wasn't doing field exercises. Then one weekend he'd had a sleepover with a friend. When he came home the next morning, his father, in a drunken rage, had smashed the model to smithereens.

Johnson shook himself mentally. Looking backwards except to avoid repeating the past was useless. He had to stop. Get on with it.

By using his binoculars, he saw *The Waiting* leave. Following in a boat was nothing like following in a car.

Pair-of-Dice had a small electrical heater in the cabin. Burt had no idea what comforts were available to MacKenzie, but he was sure the man, who had never served in the military, wasn't into discomfort.

He hadn't worried he would lose track of *The Waiting* because of the tracker. He was about to leave when he saw two women heading toward the dock. He was positive one was MacKenzie's wife based on photos he'd seen. He never forgot a face.

CHAPTER 73

Early in the morning Janet and Annie entered the breakfast room, which held four tables. The cat theme was carried over with a cat clock on the mantle and cat pictures on napkins. They were the only ones in the dining room.

"I think I should purr," Annie whispered to Janet as two other women walked in and went to the buffet laid out to the left of the fireplace.

Then a man came in.

Annie's reaction was that a man didn't belong in this rather feminine environment. He was probably in his mid-thirties, dressed in jeans, a forest green turtleneck and a navy blue jacket. When the owner, this time wearing an apron with cat designs, came in, the man ordered a full fry-up.

Annie and Janet indicated they would select from the buffet with its dry cereal, fruits, cheeses and eggs.

No one else joined them.

From the conversation of the women at the next table, Annie gathered they were retired teachers, exploring Scotland. One took out a camera with a large lens and took a photo of the ceramic cats serving as curtain tiebacks.

As for the man, she worried about whom he might be. It was strange to be so suspicious, but with Simon's murder and Rod's running away, not to mention the tracking device, caution was more than called for.

As soon as they finished breakfast they headed for the docks and then drove up and down any place where boats would be anchored.

Nothing.

"Maybe we should ask?" Janet said.

Annie shook her head. "Not yet."

She took out her laptop and went onto the Internet to Janet's frown.

Annie's first search led her to a site that showed where cargo ships, cruise liners, and tankers were positioned, but nothing for tiny cabin cruisers.

"What now?" Annie asked as they walked by a closed café with tables and chairs linked by a chain. Janet sat in one, Annie in another.

"I don't know. I feel it's a wild goose chase." Janet sighed.

"We won't know until we check the harbor."

The women headed for the Nairn harbor. They drove down narrow streets with small brick houses. The day was overcast and the smell of salt hung heavily in the air. At the water's edge many small boats were either anchored at the dock or bobbed at various distances from the shore.

"I don't see *The Waiting*," Janet said as she paced up and down the dock looking out over the water.

Neither did Annie. "Maybe we were wrong about Nairn."

"Can I help you ladies?"

They turned to see a rather good-looking man with an American accent. He was standing on a 30-foot fishing boat, and looked as if he had been about to cast off. They had not noticed him before. He was wearing jeans, a heavy sweater. A windbreaker was thrown over a deck chair.

The boat was named *Pair-of-Dice*. The deck was covered with nets. A new coat of paint would not have gone amiss to replace the chipped blue. Neither Annie nor Janet knew enough about boats to tell what kind it was.

"We were looking for a friend," Annie said.

"I've been here all day."

"Did you see a boat called *The Waiting*?" As Janet spoke she intercepted Annie's glance that maybe they shouldn't have said anything.

"Are you a tourist?" Annie asked.

"My accent give me away?" The man gave a huge smile.

"You certainly don't sound like a Scot," Janet said.

"I saw *The Waiting* leave maybe ten minutes ago, if that."

The two women exchanged glances.

"I was just about to go out fishing; would you like to come with me and we can look for *The Waiting* if it's really important?"

Annie pulled Janet to where they could whisper without being overheard. "I don't like it."

"Neither do I, but can you think of another way to catch up with Rod?"

"He's American, so he probably hasn't heard of Rod."

They returned to the boat and the man helped them climb aboard. "I'm Burt," he said, sticking out his hand. He went to start the boat and fumbled. His smile was sheepish this time. "I rented it. I guess from the name, the owner might have over-gambled and needed some money."

The engine turned over, and Burt maneuvered the boat away from the dock. He set up a GPS on the area behind the wheel.

Overhead clouds looked like they were going to release a lot of water.

CHAPTER 74

Burt watched the women's body language. Janet MacKenzie stared into the horizon. He guessed she was looking for her husband's boat. The redhead, on the other hand, was keeping her eye more on him. The women had only given Burt their first names.

Burt concentrated on the wheel, opening the engine to full throttle. The boat shuddered a complaint against its unaccustomed speed. He felt that if he engaged the women in conversation, he just might increase their nervousness.

The wind had picked up and the water was getting choppier and choppier, throwing the boat around.

"I think I see it," Janet called.

Burt had the throttle out as far as it would go. Even if he could increase the speed, the engine seemed almost to the point of exploding. He thrust the throttle back only slightly. The boat ahead was not moving as fast.

The distance between the two boats narrowed as the sky darkened. Although it looked as if the heavens were about to open, the rain held off.

"It's Rod," Janet hollered.

"Does he have a radio?" Annie yelled.

"I don't know."

"Doesn't matter, we don't have one," Burt said. "I'll try to get alongside."

They were almost on top of the other boat. Janet climbed to

336

the front of the deck, and holding onto the rail screamed as loud as she could. Annie joined her and together they hollered.

The wind carried their voices.

Rod looked around then waved madly and cut the engine.

It allowed Burt to pull alongside of *The Waiting*.

As their sides hit they made a banging noise when the fiberglass struck wood.

Janet started to jump onto the other boat until Annie put out a hand to stop her. "It's not safe," she said.

Rod had come to the rail. His words, "What are you doing here?" were lost in the wind. Then he staggered back, a red stain expanding on his chest. A second red spot appeared on his forehead just as he fell onto the deck.

CHAPTER 75

When Annie knocked Janet to the deck after Burt Johnson fired his third shot over their heads, she twisted her leg. She tried to process the information as fast as her brain allowed. Rod was dead and this man was trying to kill both of them with no one anywhere to help.

When she looked up she saw that the pitching of the boat had thrown him off balance and he was grabbing for a table, which, although tacked down by one leg, still moved back and forth. He still held the gun in his hand. Annie guessed it was a Glock, but she wasn't sure.

Why she cared about the manufacture would have amused her if she'd been able to think more clearly, but her only thought was how to get the gun away from him.

Janet's screaming meshed with the wind, making it difficult to separate the sounds.

Burt stood up.

Annie got to her feet and grabbed a pail and threw it at him. It ricocheted off his shoulder. He dropped the gun.

"Get the gun," she hollered to Janet, who ignored her as a keening replaced her screams.

Annie lunged for the gun at the same instant that Burt did. He reached it first, but as he stood up, she head-butted him across the deck, over the rail, and into the sea, still holding the gun. He hit the water hard, disappeared and resurfaced empty-handed.

As he swam toward the ladder hanging over the side of the boat, Annie pulled it up. She looked around for a weapon, anything that could be used as a weapon. A tackle box was to her left.

Burt had reached the side of the boat, but the rail was too high and he was not able to pull himself aboard.

Although Annie wanted to throw the tackle box at him, she knew it would be impossible to aim with the boat bouncing in the water, assuming she could have hit him if there was no motion, which was unlikely. With the boat rocking as it was, there was a greater chance that she would go overboard.

Could they just leave Burt in the water and head back to shore? She wasn't sure—not that leaving him bothered her. He would kill them if he could, but how to get the boat into port?

Annie tried to keep her eye on Burt flailing against the boat as he tried to get aboard as she went to Janet and slapped her not once but twice. "Shut up. I need you."

Janet stopped her keening.

As the boat dipped, Burt's hands grabbed the railing. Annie picked up the tackle box and smashed it against his hands. In doing so she almost went over the edge, but another wave tossed her across the deck. She grabbed onto the table.

The hands had disappeared. She thought she'd heard the words, "You bitch," but she wasn't sure.

"Stand up," she screamed to Janet.

Burt was trying to swim between the boats. If he could make it, he would be able to use the ropes dangling over the side of his boat to pull himself up, but the boats were too close. It would be too easy for them to hit each other, either knocking him out or crushing him.

"Do you know how to start this thing?" Annie asked. The rain was coming down faster.

Janet shrugged. Annie took her by the shoulders and shook

her so hard that had Janet been a baby, she might have suc-
cumbed to shaken infant syndrome. "If we are to get out of
here alive, shape up. I asked, do you know how to start this
thing?"

"I don't know. Rod would know." As she spoke Rod's name,
she choked.

"Try." Annie brought her hand back as if to slap Janet.

"I'm okay. Don't hit me." She went over to the wheel and
turned the key in the lock. The engine coughed. She tried a
second, a third and fourth time. On the fifth try it caught.

Annie stayed at the rail holding on and watching Burt. When
he heard the engine she was able to make out the panic on his
face.

The boat began to move forward, bumping against *The Waiting* as they went, catching Burt between the two boats, just as
she'd hoped might happen. Janet was able to maneuver the boat
away from *The Waiting* away from Burt. When the *Pair-of-Dice*
moved away, Burt was face down in the water. He looked
unconscious.

Neither woman said anything until both *The Waiting* and Burt
were lost from sight.

"Good on you," Annie said to Janet. "Any ideas on how to
navigate?"

Janet shook her head. She was shaking, as was Annie. It didn't
matter if it were from the cold, the rain or the shock of Rod's
murder and Burt's attack. Both women were soaking wet.

Annie didn't want to ask about how much fuel they had or if
there were any provisions on board. "I'll check for a radio."

"That man said there wasn't one."

"He could have lied."

Down in the hold, she located a radio, or parts of a radio,
laid on a table to be put back together. She slumped onto the

bed and forced herself not to cry. She had no idea what to do next.

"Annie, I found a compass." Janet's voiced drifted below deck.

Annie took the five steps up to the deck to see Janet holding up a compass. Her friend's clothes were sopping, her hair plastered to her head. "Right now we are heading northwest. We want to be going southeast."

"Can you turn his thing around?"

CHAPTER 76

"You have to go to the police," Roger said to Janet and Annie as they sat in Janet's living room. The women had arrived back in Ely less than an hour before. Both fulfilled the cliché about looking like something the cat had dragged in. They had changed into dry clothes, but there were deep circles under their eyes, having driven nine and a half straight hours, stopping only to buy coffee and take a potty break.

They'd taken turns, although the one not driving had stayed awake to make sure that the driver did not fall asleep behind the wheel.

Roger had staggered downstairs at 4:17 in the morning to answer the bell that didn't stop ringing and to quiet the dog that wouldn't stop barking.

Mercury was a mass of happy wiggles as he jumped on Janet.

Roger was not a mass of happy wiggles. "I'm thrilled you're okay, but what the hell is going on?"

"Make us some tea, and we'll tell you," Annie said. While he did, she went upstairs to get everyone's bathrobes. Janet started the gas fire, warming the room.

"And Rod's dead." Janet broke into sobs after they'd re-assembled. They both held her until she subsided into hiccups.

"We can't go to the police," Annie said.

"They'll connect you to that man's disappearance."

"We wiped the boat clean. No one saw us get on or leave."

"And the license plate of the car?"

"We were in a car park and not all that long. Would there be a reason to notice?" Annie asked.

"This country has CCTV cameras everywhere." Roger used his sensible voice, the one that usually drove Annie mad.

She hadn't even thought to think they might be caught on camera. It dawned on her she didn't know for sure if the man owned the boat. He didn't seem all that familiar with it. And if he hadn't been the owner, where was the owner? Maybe he'd come back and never guess what had happened while he was gone.

"I'm not saying lie to the police," Annie said. "I'm saying, don't say anything. We have no idea when or if Rod will be found. And the other man probably drowned."

"And if the man got on *The Waiting* and brought it back to shore?"

"With a body in it? Of someone he'd killed? He doesn't want to call attention to it any more than we do."

"He'd need only to throw the body overboard." Roger's upraised eyebrow said it all.

"I think he was dead, crushed by the boats, but no—I am not absolutely certain," Annie replied.

Roger let out a long sigh. "I don't agree, but I give up. I am only an old, retired *flic*. What do I know?"

Gäelle and Guillaume were putting the last of the decorations on the Christmas tree. Annie's parents had come down from Geneva, and Christmas dinner was in various stages of preparation.

"Roger seems to be doing better with retirement," Susan Young said to her daughter as she basted the roasting duck.

"More or less. He's bored, but at least he's trying to find things to occupy his mind." His body had recovered, she thought, enough that they had resumed their lovemaking. Annie was so grateful that she did not have to be celibate like Etheldreda.

She'd received the preprint copies of *Etheldreda, the Reluctant Queen* that Quentin had sent along with the first mixed reviews. Some felt she'd not treated the Anglo-Saxon abbess with the proper respect: others said that Annie had truly captured the spirit of that period or at least as much as had been known about it. She was complimented on her details in describing the household contents, the jewelry, the meals.

Quentin was talking about another book contract, but Annie wasn't sure.

Her agent wanted her to take an assignment in Schwyz working with a family cookie factory that had been in business since the 1800s, but she wouldn't take another assignment for several months. She put her hand on her growing stomach.

That she was going to have a baby was still a shock. Children happened to other people, not her. The sonar showed it was a girl. Having gone through the teen years with Gaëlle, Annie thought it might, just might, be nice to have a small child. "Sorta like getting a puppy or a kitten after only having grown cats and dogs," she said.

Roger at first was shocked. "I'm too old. What if I die?" he'd said.

"Then I take care of our daughter," Annie had said. When he still wasn't convinced, she asked how he felt about an abortion.

He didn't like that alternative.

"Adoption?"

"What would people say?"

"Doesn't matter," she said. "It's up to us."

As it turned out it wasn't up to them. Once Gaëlle learned she'd no longer be an only child, albeit one on the verge of adulthood, there was no way that either could have convinced her to accept either adoption or abortion of her sister.

Roger found a new reason to grumble over Annie's away assignments. She was pregnant. But now that the morning sickness had stopped, Annie had so much energy that he decided it was better to have her working. Because of his retirement he would go with her and Annie's parents would stay with Gaëlle, something that suited all concerned.

The Youngs were still unsure of what they were going to do. A majority of their American friends, who were dual nationals, had either renounced their nationality so they could have ordinary banking relationships or had moved back to the States.

"We'd be limited to just a three-month stay in Caleb's Landing, if we weren't Americans anymore," Dave Young said. He chopped onions for the stuffing as his wife added flour to make the cookie dough.

"You and Mum love your house there, but you usually are only there in the summer." She hated the idea of having her parents live so far away, especially with the baby coming. She knew how hard it was for other families with parents in other parts of the world. It wasn't as if Argelès and Geneva were around the corner, but the two generations did manage to spend much time together. "You don't have to decide right away," Annie said.

"At least a car lease solved the immediate problem of not being able to get a car loan from the bank," Dave said.

Annie put down the rolling pin that she was using to roll out the cookie dough, which soon would be in the shape of trees, bells, stars and teddy bears, "Janet?" she called.

Janet came into the kitchen. She'd been staying with the Perrets since the police found *The Waiting*. Annie had insisted and Roger didn't argue. They knew that there was no one else that Janet could be with.

The police were more than ever convinced that Rod had killed Simon. Either he was dead or hiding on the continent.

"Are you going to call your brother-in-law and say 'Happy Christmas'?" Annie asked Janet, handing her dishes to put on the dining room table.

"He's not speaking to me, as if I'm responsible for the shape *The Waiting* was in when they found it. No great loss, we were never close."

Annie considered it a good sign that Janet hadn't teared up. For the first couple of weeks in Argelès, immediately after the two women had come back from Scotland, Janet had spent most of her time in bed, sleeping or crying.

The Perrets suggested she go back to Argelès with them. The next two weeks she set up her easel around the village and painted canvas after canvas, barely sleeping.

Then she began talking and talking and talking. Over and over she said how she regretted that she and Rod had not had a traditional marriage. "I never told him I loved him."

"Did you?" Annie had asked.

"In a way, but we each gave what the other needed."

Annie suggested Janet might want to talk to a shrink.

"I can't," she'd replied. "Confidentiality."

"You didn't kill Rod."

"I kept information from the police. The hardest part of it all was watching him shot." At that point Janet had wailed.

Annie had gone to Janet and rocked her until she quieted. That was the last time Janet had cried, to Annie's knowledge.

After the first of the year, Janet would rent Annie's nest. Her own home in Ely was rented, although she'd wanted to sell it and move to Argelès. The community of artists was large and she needed to start over.

"Don't sell the house. Not for a year," Roger had cautioned.

Maud had turned into such a good manager that Janet felt she could keep the business going; Annie would still go to Ely quarterly and check it out with Janet, although the baby would skew the schedule.

Susan Young opened the auxiliary oven's door to check the cookies baking in the auxiliary oven. She was the only other person who knew the true story of what had happened and she coached Annie on how best to help Janet.

Janet came back into the kitchen. "I need napkins and forks," she said. Susan handed them to her.

It almost felt like a normal Christmas—at least normal if no one thought too much about the events of the past few months.

Annie touched her stomach. What had been normal before would never be the same again, and maybe, just maybe, that was okay.

ABOUT THE AUTHOR

D-L Nelson, like Annie Young-Perret, is a Third-Culture Kid, only she is only bilingual not multilingual, much to her regret. She lives in Geneva, Switzerland and southern France and is the author of nine other Five Star novels, including *Murder in Caleb's Landing, Murder in Argelès, Murder in Geneva, Murder in Paris* and *Murder on Insel Poel*. Visit her website http://donna lanenelson.com and her blog http://theexpatwriter.blogspot.ch/.